MW00335501

Lesser Mountains

Lesser Mountains

Andrew Geyer

LITERARY PRESS
LAMAR UNIVERSITY

Copyright © 2019 Andrew Geyer
All Rights Reserved
Manufactured in the United States of America

ISBN: 978-1-942956-64-8
Library of Congress Number: 2019935399

Cover painting by Eric Beverly,
based on an image by Kerry Beverly

Lamar University Literary Press
Beaumont, Texas

Acknowledgments

Grateful acknowledgment is made to the following journals and anthologies in which versions of these stories first appeared:

Agave, A Celebration of Tequila, "Pink Elephants"
Amarillo Bay, "Troubadours"
Concho River Review, "Café le Coq" and "Things Roman"
Dancing on Barbed Wire, "Symmetry"
descant, "Lament for a Larcenist"
Langdon Review of the Arts, "Mexico" and "Tragic Voices"
Literary Dogs & Their South Carolina Writers, "Adventures with
       Seamus Heaney and My Mother-in-Law"
Siren Songs from the Heart of Austin, "Words to Live By"
Texas 5X5, "Fingers" and "Mineral Spirits"
Texas Review, "Chicken"
Texas Soundtrack, "Jelvis"
Texas Told'em, Gambling Stories, "Tells"

Other fiction from Lamar University Literary Press includes:

Robert Bonazzi, *Awakened by Surprise*
Kevin K. Casey, *Four-Peace*
Jeffrey DeLotto, *A Caddo's Way*
Gerald Duff, *Memphis Mojo*
Britt Haraway, *Early Men*
Michael Howarth, *Fair Weather Ninjas*
Gretchen Johnson, *The Joy of Deception and Other Stories*
Moumin Quazi, *Migratory Words*
Harold Raley, *Lost River Anthology*
Jim Sanderson, *Trashy Behavior*
Jan Seale, *Appearances*
Melvin Sterne, *The Shoeshine Boy*

For information on these and other
Lamar University Literary Press books, go to
www.lamar.edu/literarypress

for Hadley Grace

Seek not to follow in the footsteps of the men of old; seek what they sought.
    —Basho

And if I have the gift of prophecy, and know all mysteries and all knowledge; and if I have all faith, so as to remove mountains, but do not have love, I am nothing.
    —1 Corinthians 13:2

CONTENTS

Fingers
in which Rooster Stiles becomes a legend
(1982)

When Rooster Stiles and Rex Marshall both showed up for the big spring roundup at the Jubak ranch, there was going to be blood. Even Beau Mulebach knew that, and he was eight years old. The only question was whether there would be a killing. "Better get ready, Rooster!" somebody sang out as the cloud of dust roaring up through the heat waves turned into a big black dually and matching horse trailer, both brand new and custom painted with bright orange and yellow flames shooting down the sides. "Here comes Rex!"

The news spread like a brushfire as the pace of cattle-working slowed to a crawl. The tough brush-poppers getting ready to ride into the thicket after outlaw cows the helicopter couldn't flush out, the older men working the headgate, the young cowboys working the sorting pens, the boys Beau's age rousting cattle though the chute, even the cows bawling for their separated calves and the calves bawling back at their mamas— everybody seemed to have an opinion as to whether Rooster would beat Rex half to death again, or Rex would keep his promise to pull the 30-30 from the gun rack in his pickup and send Rooster to that big rodeo in the sky.

Beau hung on every word. Rooster Stiles was his hero—a cowboy's cowboy like the old-timers who rode the open range of Southwest Texas, rounded up wild longhorns and mustangs, and made the first cattle drives to the railhead in Kansas. Rooster was the best rider, the surest roper, the toughest fighter in a bareknuckle scrape. But bushwhacking was another matter. Since there was bound to be blood between Rooster and Rex, Beau was determined to help Rooster any way he could.

He hooked his cattle prod over the top of the chute and left the other boys—all fool enough to think that Rex would finally find a way to whip Rooster even without the 30-30—to push the cows up to the head-gate without him. He slipped through a sorting pen full of cows milling after lost calves and into a pen where three men he didn't know were castrating the bull calves that the cows were milling around after. He saw two of the cowboys throw a big Red Brangus calf. The third cowboy dropped to his knees on the calf's shoulder and pulled a front leg back, the whole time chewing tobacco and talking about Rooster and Rex.

"I was there the first time the two of them tangled at that rodeo dance in Jordan," he said and spat. "And I watched Rooster beat Rex like a rented mule."

"Who started it?" another one asked, slipping a rope around the calf's hind legs.

"You tell me. This was back when Rex and May Belle went together. Rex come in from drinking tequila with a couple of us in the parking lot and seen Rooster and May Belle slow-dancing like they was glued together. Rex walked up to the two of them and called May Belle a filthy—" The calf bucked and shimmied, throwing the tobacco-chewing cowboy into the fence and starting a wild scramble that ended with the cowboy back on the calf's front shoulder where he spat tobacco juice and went on like nothing had happened. "Then Rex stuck a hand into Rooster's face and asked how many of them fingers he could smell May Belle on."

"How many did Rooster say?" The cowboy who wasn't holding the calf or the rope took out a knife and reached the business end toward the calf's private parts.

"He didn't. Right after that, Rex spat on May Belle. Then Rooster busted Rex's face wide open and knocked out two of his teeth. That was just for starters. I never seen nobody move so fast or hit so hard—like a head-on collision at road speed, bodies flying around and blood everywhere. Rex is gonna need that 30-30 and then some if he aims to tangle with Rooster again."

"I don't know about that." The rope-holding cowboy yanked the calf's hind legs farther back. "Old Rooster has gotten a little long in the tooth for bareknuckle brawling. Rex'll take him this time. Hide and watch."

"Hide and watch my ass." Tobacco juice slapped the fencepost next to the calf's head. "Today's pay says Rooster whips Rex again. If Rex don't put a bullet in him."

"You're on."

"I'd like a piece of that myself," the cowboy with the knife said. "My whole $125 says Rex whips Rooster. But if gunplay starts, the bet's off." He cut off the bottom of the calf's scrotum. Then he squeezed the testicles out and started scraping the knife back and forth against the cords that connected the testicles to the calf—a sight that sent Beau scurrying out of the calf pen. He'd heard all he needed to anyway, and he wanted to find Rooster before Rex did.

Lean and wiry, his skin creased and sun-leathered, Rooster stood next to his big bay horse in the shade of an old mesquite. The other brush-poppers stood with their horses in a loose circle around Rooster, tightening cinches and adjusting stirrups. Beau could hear them talking as he walked up through the swath of dark red Indian blanket flowers that stretched between the pens and the lone mesquite. But just as he got close enough to make out what was being said, they all went quiet.

"Whoa there, little feller!" one of them called out. "This ain't no place for babies. Not today. You need to head back up to the pens where it's safe."

"I ain't no baby, and you ain't my daddy."

"How do you know I ain't your daddy?" The brush-popper uncoiled the rope on his saddle horn, tossed a loop across a mesquite limb, and stepped toward Beau. "I've got half a mind to string you up by your feet."

Beau kept coming on. Rope or no rope, the smells of horses and leather, and the sight of Rooster standing there cool as you please despite his looming showdown with Rex, drew the eight-year-old into the shade like nectar draws a bee. "My daddy's Mike Mulebach," he said. "He's over there working the headgate with Mr. Jubak. And if you go stringing me up by my feet, I reckon he's gonna have something to say about it."

"Looks like he called your bluff, Jeff," Rooster said in a gravelly voice that drew a laugh from the men around him.

"Who says I'm bluffing?"

"I do." Rooster stepped out from among the horses and grinned at Beau. "You think you're tough, little man?"

"Tougher than him." Beau cocked his chin at the brush-popper with the rope in his hand.

"We got us a gamecock, boys!" Rooster's grin covered half his face. He raised his fists and took a couple of slow sidle-steps toward Beau. "Let's see what you got."

Beau grinned back at Rooster and raised his fists, jabbing with his left at Rooster's midsection and looking for an opening.

"Mike teaching you to box?" Rooster asked, weaving and circling.

"Just shadowboxing. But when the real thing comes, I'll be ready."

"You know I work cattle for your daddy a couple of times a year, the same as I do for Mr. Jubak."

"Spring and fall both," Beau said. "I've watched you from the truck and from the top of the fence. This is the first time my daddy ever let me work the pens. I never seen nobody ride or rope like you do."

"Cowboying ain't just about riding and roping, boy. Out in the brush, you got prickly pear up to your knees and mesquite thorns above

15

your head. You gotta drive 'em through all that till you can get 'em roped, and then you gotta lead 'em out. You sure you got it in you?"

"Yep." Beau popped a jab into Rooster's belly and was surprised to feel it give a little under his fist. "When I grow up, I'm gonna be good as you."

"Oof. Maybe you will at that, young gamecock. If there's any cowboying left to be done in this country by then. What's your name?"

"Beau Mulebach."

"Well, it's an honor to make your acquaintance, Beau."

"Hey, Rooster!" somebody yelled from the pens. "Mr. Jubak wants to see you."

"On my way!" He vaulted up onto the big bay and rode off in the direction of the headgate.

The minute Rooster was out of earshot, the jawing started. The cowboy named Jeff, who had threatened to string Beau up by his feet, was doing most of the talking. "Maximally invasive," he said as he coiled the rope and slipped it back onto his saddle horn. "That's Rex's strategy."

"Say what?" A brush-popper standing next to a heavy-chested dun horse looked at Jeff like he was crazy.

"Maximally invasive. That's the way Rex put it to me. Said the way to deal with Rooster was to get him on the ground and hurt him bad enough so he couldn't get up. Wrestling, not boxing. That's the key. Rex is bigger and stronger, and Rooster ain't as young as he used to be. If Rex can get hold of Rooster, and get him down, he'll win this time for sure."

"Seems to me the best way to deal with Rooster is to leave him be."

"You can't blame Rex for holding a grudge," Jeff said. "Back when Rooster took May Belle away from him—then married her, despite the fact that Rooster was old enough to be her daddy—Rex and May Belle were engaged. Well, engaged to be engaged anyway. And don't forget that scar. The second time Rooster beat Rex bloody after that roping match in Uvalde, he left a scar on the corner of Rex's mouth where there used to be a lip—kind of a permanent sneer."

"You can't blame Rooster for goin' after May Belle neither," the brush-popper with the dun said. "If she was married to anybody but Rooster, I'd go after her myself. Anyways, I kinda like Rex's scar. Makes him look like Elvis Presley."

"He wishes," somebody else said, and all of them but Jeff laughed at that—even Beau, and he wasn't exactly sure who Elvis Presley was.

Just then Rooster came riding back up, hell for leather, and the laugh died. "Mr. Jubak says there's two crossbreed cows and a big Red

Brangus bull unaccounted for. That means three outlaws we gotta drag out of the brush. Time to hit the thicket, boys."

"Is that all he said?" Jeff asked.

"Is that just idle curiosity, Jeff? Or is there something you'd like to—"

"Howdy, Rex!" Jeff hollered and stepped away from Rooster.

Rex came pounding up on a sleek black horse that Beau couldn't help but admire, despite the way he felt about the man in the saddle. The black must have been seventeen hands high, solid muscle. The sheen of sweat on his coat was like riverwater flowing over the polished stones of the Frio. Rex waited until the last second to pull his mount up so that its chest bumped the left flank of Rooster's horse, spinning the bay around and sending it skittering and dancing until Rooster reined it in.

"Howdy, Jeff." Rex tipped the brim of his black Stetson in Jeff's direction and swung his horse around so that every man in the shade of the mesquite could see the 30-30 sticking out of his saddle scabbard. "Howdy, Rooster. How's May Belle? Still as luscious as I remember? Maybe I should smell your fingers this time."

"The only thing to do with a spoiled rich kid like you is beat him till his mouth quits moving. But I promised Bill Jubak there wouldn't be no trouble here today."

Rex's right hand slid down onto the butt of the 30-30. "Well I never promised Bill Jubak any such thing."

"I imagine that's why he wants to talk to you right now." Rooster pointed over at the cow pens, where Bill Jubak leaned over the top of the fence and waved his hat in their direction. Then he swung his horse around and leveled two fingers straight into Rex's face. "So either pull that rifle, or get your sorry ass to the pens."

Rex gripped the 30-30 so tight the knuckles on his trigger hand turned white as the jagged scar at the corner of his mouth. All sounds of cattle-working went silent. Even the wind had gone still so it seemed as though the Southwest Texas afternoon was holding its breath. Beau felt like his heart was about to explode in his chest. He stole a glance at the pens and saw men and boys in hats and boots climbing up onto the near fence, all waiting to see whether Rex would keep his promise to send Rooster to that big rodeo in the sky.

At long last, Rex eased his hand off the rifle. "This ain't over, Rooster," he spat through clenched teeth. "Not by a long shot."

"I reckon not."

Rex headed for the pens, and the brush-poppers hit the thicket

17

amid the crackle of broken branches and the scrape of thorns against leather. Beau walked back to the chute. His heart was still beating a mile a minute as he unhooked his cattle prod from the top rail and started rousting cows toward the headgate, and his head felt as thick as the mix of sweat and dust on his skin.

It wasn't until he was surrounded by boys jabbering questions about what had happened between Rooster and Rex that Beau came clear inside himself about the things he'd just seen and heard. He felt so proud of the way Rooster faced Rex down, and so privileged to have been there among the cowboys to see it, that he had to look down to make sure his boots were touching the ground. But he didn't let on.

"I'll tell the whole story," he said to the circle of boys, "blow by blow and word for word. But it'll cost all of you your apple pie this evening at the barbeque and the contents of your pockets right now." He had all five boys digging into their pockets for change when a pair of high schoolers he'd known since he was a baby shoved their way through.

"Hey, Bonehead," Cecil Jubak said, pressing the business end of his hotshot against Beau's left hip. "I've got a better idea. You tell us exactly what happened just now between Rooster and Rex, or I'll zap your ass into next week."

"Not unless you pay up."

There came a low hum, and it felt to Beau all of a sudden as if he'd just sat on a fire ant mound. It was like a hundred of them had swarmed up inside his jeans and gone to stinging him all at once. He tried to twist away, but found himself trapped against the chute.

"How's it feel to be a cow?" Cecil snickered, and the boys laughed in a way that made Beau feel ashamed and angry at the same time.

"At least I ain't a steer," he said, managing to slap the hotshot away with his cattle prod. He would've zapped Cecil back—even though Cecil outweighed him by a hundred pounds—if he'd had a hotshot to do it with. As a first-timer in the cow pens, Beau was stuck with a wooden cattle prod instead.

"We can make that happen," Joe Jasmine, the other high schooler, said. His daddy owned the ranch next to the Jubak place, and Beau couldn't remember a single time when he'd seen Cecil without Joe. "Easy. All it'll take is for us to burn your balls off. Zap him again, Cecil. Give him one between the legs this time."

"You do and I'll tell both your daddies," Beau looked Cecil in the eye and said. "Mr. Jubak is right over there at the headgate. And Mr. Jasmine is in the next pen over, vaccinating heifers. They'll both hear me

18

when I yell."

"Give him another one anyway," Joe said. "Burn his balls off."

"Not just yet," Cecil said. "We're going to give little Bonehead here a chance to save his family jewels. You've got until the count of three to start talking, or I'll fry your hairless testicles to a crisp. One, two—"

"First get that hotshot away from me. And stop calling me Bonehead. My name is Beau."

Cecil lowered the hotshot. "Now tell."

Beau didn't believe that the hotshot would really do what Cecil and Joe were saying it would, but his memory of the Red Brangus calf getting castrated gave him pause. Besides, the story was about to burst out of him anyway. "Alright. Rex tried to pick a fight with Rooster, but Rooster didn't bite. First Rex rammed his horse into Rooster's. Then Rex said some bad stuff about May Belle, and Rooster told Rex that he'd beat his mouth shut if he hadn't promised your daddy not to cause no trouble. That was when Rex acted like he was gonna pull his rifle. Rooster looked him square in the eye and dared him to do it, but Rex didn't have the nerve. Not even when Rooster pointed two fingers into his face like a pistol and called him a sorry ass."

"Too bad they didn't kill each other," Cecil said.

Joe heaved a sigh. "Yep. There'd be two less dumb shit-kickers in the world. Not to mention the possibility of collateral damage."

"You said it." Cecil looked down at Beau. "They might've taken at least one of these other shit-kickers with them."

"Who are you calling a shit-kicker?" Beau asked.

"I'm calling you a shit-kicker, Bonehead." Cecil poked one of Beau's boots with the hotshot. "And Rooster, and Rex, and every other one of these dumb boot-sporting sons of bitches that scratches out a living by tromping on cow pies."

"You're walking around these cow pens same as me."

"Am I? Look at my feet," Cecil said. "Go on."

Beau looked. Both Cecil and Joe were wearing leather sneakers instead of cowboy boots. And unlike Beau's boots, which were caked with the results of working the cow pens all morning and most of the afternoon, Cecil and Joe's shoes looked clean and new.

"How come you're not wearing boots?" Beau asked.

"Because we're not shit-kickers," Cecil said.

Joe nodded. "And the minute we graduate, we're getting the hell out of Southwest Texas and never looking back."

"But your daddies both own ranches. Ranches both their daddies

19

owned before them. How can you leave?"

"It's the only rational decision," Cecil said.

Beau wasn't sure what that meant exactly, but he guessed it must have something to do with not liking boots. "You don't have to wear boots to be a cowboy. Old Man Merriweather always wears moccasins on account of the bone spurs in his feet."

"It's not about boots," Joe said. "It's about the future. Even here in Southwest Texas, the cowboy business is not ten percent of what it used to be. And this is where the cowboy business was born. To make a living at ranching, you've got to be a big landowner like Rex's daddy. All the smaller operators are either broke, or barely hanging on."

"Or else," Cecil said, "they're building high fences and making their money stocking wildlife for hunters. But the smartest thing to do is improve the ranch, put in the high fences, then sell it to a corporation that can let their people come in and hunt. It's a win-win situation. The corporation gets a tax write-off, and you get to move the hell away."

"I don't wanna move away," Beau said. "I wanna be a cowboy like Rooster."

"Then you really are a bonehead," Cecil said. "Come on, Joe. Let's go get some barbeque."

The mention of barbeque made Beau's mouth water, despite the bullying from Cecil and Joe. In the big barbeque pit trailer he'd pulled into the backyard at the Jubak house, Old Man Merriweather had been slow-roasting brisket all afternoon. The old man had spent his whole life working cattle in the brush country, and Beau had heard stories about Merriweather's exploits as a cowboy. When all else had failed and outlaw cattle couldn't be moved or found or caught, Merriweather had been the man to call. Now that man was Rooster, and Old Man Merriweather was spending his twilight years barbequing for the big roundups in Southwest Texas.

Nobody smoked a brisket like the old man. As the cattle-working wound down, the men and boys drifted over into the shade of the mesquite trees in the Jubaks' backyard to eat barbeque, and the beans and potato salad Mrs. Jasmine had made. Mrs. Jubak's homemade apple pies would be brought out once the meat and fixings had been cleared away. The men mostly drank beer, and the boys drank cokes that came out of ice chests that sat next to the wooden picnic table where the food was laid out. Beau's coke was covered with ice chips and tiny beads of water, and it was about the coldest and best thing he ever drank in his life. The smell of roasted meat filled the air, reminding him of his empty belly and the seemingly endless stretch of time since he'd last tasted the old man's spicy redsauce. At long last Beau's mama, who had been at the house all day helping Mrs. Jubak and Mrs. Jasmine make and serve dinner and supper, brought him a paper plate covered with meat and beans and potato salad. She asked if he'd like to come inside where it was cool and eat with the other boys his age, but he said he wanted to stay outside with the cowboys.

Rooster sat at the center of the same bunch of brush-poppers from earlier—except for Jeff, who was sitting next to Rex—under a mesquite not far from the barbeque pit trailer. Jeff's place had been taken by Old Man Merriweather, who squatted like an Indian in his moccasins next to Rooster. Rex sat in the middle of a group of younger men under a mesquite tree next to the barbed wire fence that marked the edge of the yard. Beyond that, dark red Indian blanket flowers filled the stretch of open space that separated the backyard from the pens.

Bill Jubak, Big Joe Jasmine, and Mike Mulebach sat in wooden rocking chairs on the back porch. As Beau walked away from the table with his plate, his daddy waved him over to the porch—but Beau pretended not to see and headed for Rooster's mesquite instead. All the brush-poppers except Old Man Merriweather had paper plates full of meat and fixings on their laps. Most of them held cans of beer, but Rooster and Old Man Merriweather were drinking cokes.

When Beau came up, Rooster patted the grass next to him. "Howdy, Beau. That's a mighty big plate of food, even for a young gamecock like yourself. You better sit on down before your knees buckle."

The brush-poppers laughed, but Beau didn't feel angry or ashamed at the sound of it. He could tell the difference between Rooster's teasing and the bullying Cecil and Joe had given him in the cow pens. He was so proud that Rooster had invited him to sit, all he could do was smile down into his plate. That was when Beau noticed the funny smell coming from Rooster's coke, and he understood why his daddy wanted him to eat on the porch.

"We waited for your mama and the other ladies to go back inside the house before we brought the liquor out," Rooster said.

Beau felt his cheeks burn as he realized that Rooster must have noticed him sniffing the coke. But curiosity got the best of him. "Whatcha got in there?"

"Jack Daniel's Black Label. It's the best drink on earth besides black coffee," Rooster said.

"Truth be told, Jack Black goes right well with coffee," Old Man Merriweather said. "It'll peel your eyeballs wide open before daylight, and put a little extra zip in your giddy-up all morning long."

"Can I have a taste?"

"No indeed, young gamecock," Rooster grinned. "If you had any more zip in your giddy-up, we'd have to tie you to a mesquite."

The brush-poppers laughed again. Then the one with the heavy-chested dun horse leaned toward Beau. "You oughta listen to Rooster when he talks about tyin' things to trees. When we was bustin' brush earlier, me and a couple of the boys heard a crashin' in the thicket. When we got there to see, we caught sight of that ol' Red Brangus bull Mr. Jubak said was missin'. He was at the edge of a grassy *vega*, and he was big—I'm talkin' 2,500 pounds. Rooster had the bull lassoed, and the rope was tied off to his saddle horn. But Rooster's horse only weighs about nine hundred pounds soakin' wet, which made the tug o' war kinda uneven."

"What did Rooster do?" Beau asked, wide-eyed.

"I'd have a hard time believin' it if I hadn't been there to see it myself. Ol' Rooster hitched the rope around a fair-sized mesquite for leverage—it's all about angles—and that tree was bendin' like a bow and arrow when we rode up. But we dropped a couple more loops on the bull to even up the tug o' war, and we dragged him out."

"I always said Rooster had the makings of a cowboy in him," Old Man Merriweather said. Then he gave Rooster a sly half-smile. "Maybe it'll happen yet."

"Don't hold your breath," Rooster said.

"Next time, I'm gonna be there," Beau said. "If you'll let me ride with you, I mean."

"That's a call for your daddy to make. Anyhow, bringing in that bull today don't mean a hill of beans beside what this gentleman used to do." Rooster nodded at Old Man Merriweather. "I'll never forget the first time I busted brush. Merriweather and my daddy were working cattle on the Marshall spread, and they let me tag along after a stray down in the Frio River bottoms. She was a wily old outlaw, and would go horn-mad when cornered. There were dogs baying and chaos all around. I was the first one to catch up to her, after Merriweather. When I rode up, he'd been forced onto the back of the cow—it was the only safe place to be—and there he was, spinning and whirling on the back of that brindle beast. She was one-quarter bovine and one-quarter she-devil and the rest horns. Merriweather was bleeding and his horse was bleeding and the cow was goring anything that moved. But he hung tight in his seat until I dropped a loop on her. I'll never forget the sight if I live to be a hundred."

The old man shook his head at Beau. "Don't you listen, young mister. The back of that cow wasn't safe at all, so don't go jumping onto one—particularly not one with a rack of horns like hers. That she-devil nearly gutted my horse. I had to put him down that same afternoon. And she stuck one halfway through my leg." He patted his left thigh. "I'd show you the scar if the ladies weren't about to come back out."

"Did you kill the cow?" Beau asked.

"Wasn't my cow to kill. She belonged to Mr. Marshall—that's Rex's daddy—and she was an easy keeper. Dropped a healthy calf every winter for twenty years. He wasn't about to put her down for goring a hired hand."

"Tell the rest of it," Rooster said. "Tell young Beau here what you did do."

"When we got the cow back to the pens, I took a saw and cut off the piece of horn that she stuck into my leg. The next day I bored a hole through the business end and capped the open end with silver. Then I braided a lock of hair that I cut from my horse's tail after I put a bullet in him, and made a necklace."

"Do you still have the necklace?"

"Nope. I gave it to Rooster. If he hadn't come along when he did, the buzzards would've eaten me that afternoon and the coyotes would've gnawed my bones that evening."

"Can I see it some time?" Beau asked Rooster.

"How about now? It's kind of a good luck charm, I guess. I always wear it when I'm busting brush." Rooster reached inside his shirt and brought out the necklace. He pulled his hat off, took the cord from around his neck, and handed it to Beau.

Beau cupped it in his palms as if it were a living thing. The necklace felt smooth and warm from being against Rooster's chest, and Beau would have given anything he owned—anything in the world—to make it his. The horn was black, about the length of a grown man's fingers, but thicker at the back where the silver cap was mounted and tapering to a wicked point at the business end. The horsehair braid was blonde, almost white, the color of his mama's hair. But thicker and coarser, and he saw dark spots in it that he guessed must be blood.

"Was he a palomino?" Beau asked Old Man Merriweather. "The horse, I mean."

"He was. And like all fine horses, the best companion a man could have. It broke my heart to shoot him, but it was the only thing to do."

While Beau and the old man were talking, the women cleared the meat and fixings off the picnic table and brought out pie and ice cream.

The smells of fresh-baked apples and cinnamon and perfectly browned crust filled the backyard, and the cowboys who had been lounging in the shade and drinking beer and smoking now crowded around Mrs. Jubak's homemade pies and hand-churned vanilla ice cream. The boys Beau's age appeared from inside the house, and even Cecil and Joe joined the commotion around the table, all snatching paper plates and piling on the dessert.

Only Beau and Rooster and Old Man Merriweather stayed put. Still holding the necklace, Beau looked back and forth between the two men. He wanted more than ever to be like them, to do the things they did and have other cowboys tell stories about him. But what Cecil and Joe had said in the cow pens still nagged at his mind like the word problems he couldn't work in math class.

"Cecil Jubak and Joe Jasmine told me earlier that wanting to grow up and be a cowboy like you made me a bonehead," he blurted. "They said selling out and leaving Southwest Texas was the only rational decision unless your daddy was a big landowner like Rex's. Is that true?"

Rooster tipped his hat back and looked over at Cecil and Joe. "Maybe for them it is. But that don't make it true for you. The cowboy life ain't exactly a day at the beach," he said slowly. "Not even a Texas beach. But if you love it, there's no better way to live on this earth."

"Don't worry about what's rational," Old Man Merriweather said. "Follow your heart."

"And right now," Rooster said, "I've got my heart set on some of that apple pie and ice cream." He reached a hand toward Beau. "But I'm afraid I'm gonna need my good luck charm back, young gamecock, if I'm gonna keep busting brush."

Beau handed the necklace back and stood up. But as he turned to head for the table, he ran smack into Rex.

"Those two old men are full of shit," Rex said in a loud voice, even though he was only inches away from Beau. "And the time they're telling tales about is long gone. These days, real cowboys run ranches for money. And the way to run a business is with your head. If you go doing it with your heart, you'll wind up a broken-down hired hand smoking brisket on somebody else's ranch."

Almost too quickly for Beau to be able to follow the motion, Rooster slid between him and Rex. "Time to go find your daddy, young gamecock," Rooster looked at Beau and said. Then he turned to face Rex. "This spoiled rich kid has had one too many shots of tequila."

The jagged white scar at the corner of Rex's mouth seemed to glow.

"At least it ain't Jack Black. Old man." He looked down at Beau, who was rooted to the spot next to Rooster. "Two Fingers Tequila is a young man's drink, and one the ladies love. Especially ladies like May Belle. Remember that. And remember what I said about winding up a hired hand."

Rooster gently pushed Beau back into the ring of men and women and boys that was forming. "The difference between Rex and me is that I came here to work cattle. Rex came to show off his new roping horse and the dually and trailer his daddy bought him to pull it with." He narrowed his eyes at Rex. "And to run his foul mouth."

"Let's see if you're man enough to shut it for me."

"It'll be one of life's great pleasures." Rooster raised his fists and took a slow sidle-step toward Rex.

"Dammit, Rooster!" a voice barked from beside Beau, and suddenly Bill Jubak was in the circle with Rooster and Rex. "You gave me your solemn promise. So did you, Rex. By God, this stops right now."

Rooster slowly lowered his fists, but he didn't unclench them. "I did give you my word, Bill. But I've been pushed too far to back away from this."

"Fair enough," Mr. Jubak said. "But let's find a better way to settle it."

"How about a roping match?" Rex looked around the ring of faces. Then he fixed his eyes on Rooster. "Me and my new roping horse against this old man and his broken-down cow pony. With a thousand dollars as the stakes."

"You're on," Rooster said.

"Now hold up." Old Man Merriweather stepped into the open space and stood next to Mr. Jubak. "That ain't fair, and you know it. Rooster's horse is stove up from busting through the brush. He needs time for the thorns to work their way out and the wounds to heal. Rex's horse has hardly been rode."

"What do you think, Rooster?" Mr. Jubak asked.

Rooster shrugged. "Like his rider, a good brush horse is a brute for punishment and as game as they come. We're ready."

"We're not set up with a roping arena," Mr. Jubak said. "We'll have to make do with the pens."

"Fine by me," Rex said. "We'll go on straight time. No points."

"Agreed," Rooster said. "Rope tied to the saddle horn, and hands off the rope after you make the throw."

"Done," Rex said.

"Heard and witnessed," Mr. Jubak said. "Let's head to the pens."

"Not just yet." Rex pulled out his wallet, counted out ten hundred-dollar bills, and handed the thousand dollars to Mr. Jubak. "There's my wager. I'm not going anywhere until I see the color of Rooster's money."

"I didn't bring no thousand dollars to a roundup."

"No problem. I'll stake that thousand dollars, and you stake your horse."

"It's a bet," Rooster said.

"Heard and witnessed," Mr. Jubak said again, and everybody in the backyard cheered. Everybody that is, except Old Man Merriweather and Beau.

Beau didn't have a chance to talk to Rooster before the roping match. But he took in every detail of the setup, and he did his level best to keep an eye on Rex. It was decided that Bill Jubak would serve as time-keeper and judge. The three cowboys Beau watched castrate the Red Brangus calf were elected to throw and hold the calves for the match. To make sure the calves got a running head-start, Mr. Jubak measured out a starter box for the horses outside the corner sorting pen, three feet behind the gate. The cowboys would get the calves up and set them running. Once each calf cleared the corner gate, Rooster and Rex could start their runs. Beau stood next to Old Man Merriweather outside the cow pens and watched Rooster and Rex warm up their horses while the cowboys picked out two calves for the match. Rex's sleek black mount was smooth-gaited and powerful, exploding from a standing stop to a full gallop like water bursting through a dam. But it seemed to Beau like Rooster's bay had a hitch in his stride.

He looked up at Old Man Merriweather. "Is there something the matter with Rooster's horse?"

The old man's face was grim. "He's limping alright. Probably got a cactus thorn in a knee or a fetlock. This may be a bet Rooster lives to regret."

"But Rooster can't lose. He's the surest roper there ever was."

"So was I, once upon a time. And I've never seen the like of that horse Rex is mounted on." He shook his head. "Come on, young mister. It looks like they're about ready to start. Let's get us a prime spot."

They squeezed up onto the top fencerail next to the corner gate just as Rooster and Rex met Mr. Jubak at the starting box. The fence facing the action was lined with men and women and boys, and the sun was low and red over the thicket behind them as Mr. Jubak went over the rules for the match.

"Remember: time only, no points. Rope tied to the saddle horn, and hands off the rope after you make the throw. A cowboy whose horse clears the corner fencepost before the calf is out of the gate will be judged to have broken the barrier, and have ten seconds added onto his time. The tie-down has to go a full six seconds. If the calf struggles free of the pigging string, the roper is disqualified. The same is true if the roper fails to complete his run. Any questions?"

There were no questions, so Mr. Jubak tossed a coin to see who would go first. Rex called tails, and the coin came up tails. Rex chose to go second, which meant that Rooster had to lead off.

Before he mounted up, Rooster pulled his horse's head down and talked into the big bay's ear. Then he vaulted into the saddle and tipped his hat to the crowd on the fence. As Rooster backed his horse into the starting box, Beau felt as though his heart had stopped and the world with it. Finally, the cowboys in the sorting pen let the calf up and shooed it into a run. It was out the gate in a flash.

The big bay exploded into a gallop with Rooster swinging his loop in great circles—until the loop caught around the calf's neck, and Rooster pulled back on the reins and stepped off his horse as the bay ground to a halt in a cloud of dust. The calf hit the end of the rope as Rooster ran along it, his pigging string in his teeth. The calf kept its feet and Rooster flanked it quickly, tying the calf's legs in a blur of fast motion and then throwing his hands up over his head.

Some of the folks on the fence were clapping and some were cheering and others were quiet as the bay backed up, pulling the calf through the sand until the six seconds ticked off and Mr. Jubak announced Rooster's time: "Nine seconds!"

"Way to go, Rooster!" Beau shouted. Then he turned to Old Man Merriweather. "He'll win for sure."

"I don't know, young mister. He got a good jump, but not a great time. He overfed his loop when he left the box. We'll see what Rex does."

Rex backed the sleek black horse into the starting box and tipped his hat, and the cowboys in the sorting pen got the calf up and running. As the calf cleared the gate, Rex's horse pounded out of the starting box like nothing Beau had ever seen, hitting a full gallop on his second bounding stride. Rex swung his loop in a tight circle and kicked his horse up even faster—but the calf cut to the right just as Rex was about to toss the lasso, so Rex had to adjust his throw. The loop closed around the calf's neck, and the calf was yanked in a half-circle when it hit the end of the rope. It went down in a tangle. Rex went down too, clutching his roping hand against his chest. There was blood all over his shirt, and there looked to be something bad the matter.

"Don't look, young mister!" Old Man Merriweather said.

But he did look, just as Rex pulled his roping hand away from his chest, and Beau saw blood pouring down Rex's forearm and three of his fingers gone. As the black horse backed toward the cow pens, there was a stunned silence from everyone on the fence. A couple of boys Beau's age started bawling.

"Are you alright?" Old Man Merriweather asked Beau.

"What happened?"

"Looked to me like Rex tried to cheat. He kept his hand on the rope after he made the throw—tried to dally—and his fingers got caught in a freak loop. Three of them popped off: the pinky finger, the ring finger, and the middle finger."

"So Rooster won!" Beau whispered fiercely, but so quiet that only the old man could hear.

"Sure enough," Old Man Merriweather whispered back. "Rex never finished his run. Hell of a way to lose a thousand dollars. Now let's go see if we can help him."

Old Man Merriweather was the first to get to Rex, with Beau right on his heels. Rex's face had gone so white that Beau could hardly see the scar on the corner of his mouth, and there were dark red smears on his cheeks and neck. The old man pressed a clean handkerchief against the bloody nubs, and told Rex to keep direct pressure on them while a search was made for the missing fingers.

"If they're found quick enough," Old Man Merriweather said, "they can be reattached at the hospital."

Then a rush of people closed in, everybody talking all at once. It was hard for Beau to make out what was happening. He saw Mrs. Jubak and Mrs. Jasmine and his mama cluster around Rex, and heard them shoo the men and boys away—except for Cecil and Joe, who Mrs. Jubak sent up to the house for an ice chest; and Beau's daddy, who volunteered to drive Rex to the hospital.

"Not without my fingers," Rex said, his voice grimly determined. "I'll give a hundred dollars each to those that find them."

"Did you hear that, gentlemen?" Bill Jubak's shout stilled the confusion. "Rex has offered a bounty of a hundred dollars a finger. Let's get 'em found!"

Mr. Jubak told everyone to form a line an arm's length apart. They started at the pens and walked slowly across the dusty space where the roping had taken place, searching as they went. Beau's place in the line was between Old Man Merriweather and the brush-popper with the dun horse. The sun had fallen behind the thicket, and the light was starting to fail, and the dust had been churned by horses and calves and people. But two of the fingers were found on the first pass. Loudmouth Jeff picked up Rex's pinky finger, and the tobacco-chewing cowboy from the sorting pens snagged the ring finger. Mrs. Jubak wrapped both of them in a handkerchief and put them into the ice chest Cecil and Joe had brought. But the middle finger was still missing, and full dark was coming on fast.

28

"We're gonna need lights to make this next pass," Mr. Jubak said to the assembled searchers. "Any of you that's got a flashlight, fetch it. And a couple of you need to pull your trucks up to the corner fenceposts of the cow pens on this side. Shine your headlights into the search area."

"I don't know about the rest of these folks," the brush-popper with the dun horse said, "but I been here since daylight, and I got someplace else I need to be."

"It's been a long day, and we're all tired," Mr. Jubak said. "But Rex is still missing a finger. If we don't find it tonight, there's no point in finding it at all. And don't forget that hundred-dollar bounty. Now come on!"

The searchers scattered, some in the direction of the trucks and some to comb through the tall grass against the cow pen fence. But Beau was done with searching. He was tired, he was thirsty, and he wasn't sure he wanted to find that missing finger—hundred dollars or no, finding that thing would mean having to pick it up. So instead of looking, he slipped away through the dusk toward the Jubak house to locate an ice-cold coke and a seat in one of the rocking chairs. But as he climbed through the fence into the swath of Indian blankets that separated the pens from the house, he saw Rooster down on his hands and knees in front of him.

"Whatcha doing?" Beau asked.

"I ain't picking flowers," Rooster said, standing up. "Truth be told, I was looking for that finger. I don't believe they'll find it where they're searching."

"You think it's all the way over here?"

"Like as not. This ain't the first time I've seen fingers popped off at a roping match. Sometimes they'll fly thirty yards. Why don't you help me find it? It'd make me right proud if you did."

"You bet." Beau got down on his hands and knees, and started combing through the flowers along the fence. Not a minute later, he caught sight of the finger in a fire ant bed, completely covered with ants. The last thing he wanted to do was touch that ant-covered finger. But to make Rooster proud, he clenched his teeth and picked it up. It felt surprisingly cold and a little bit stiff. Strips of skin were caked into the dark red blood on the torn-off part. He brushed the ants off as best he could, getting a couple of burning stings on the thumb for his trouble. Then he carried the finger over to Rooster.

"Well done!" Rooster said, but he didn't take the finger from Beau. "I knew you could do it, but I'm still right proud of you for getting it done. And now I've got a proposition for you."

"What's that?"

"I heard Rex offer a hundred-dollar bounty for that thing a while ago. I'm prepared to give you the $125 I earned working cattle today, if you'll give that finger to me instead."

"I won't sell it," Beau said. "I didn't find it for the money. But I'd be willing to trade it."

"Trade it? What for?"

"For that cow horn necklace Old Man Merriweather made. Maybe if I've got that good luck charm, I can be as good as you someday."

"By God, I believe you may be better than me now."

Rooster took off the necklace and gave it to Beau, who handed the finger to Rooster. The necklace felt smooth in Beau's hand, and even warmer than before. When he hung the horsehair cord around his neck and put the horn inside his shirt, he could swear he felt the horn pulsing back against his heart.

Rooster tucked the finger into his shirt pocket. "Don't ever say anything to anybody about finding this finger, no matter what. I need your solemn promise."

"I promise," Beau said.

"You can roust outlaws out of the brush with me anytime, young gamecock. But right now, I need you to do me another favor."

"Anything."

"Do you see Bill Jubak over there?" Rooster pointed over at the dusty space around the cow pens where the search was still in progress. A line of men and boys walked slowly toward them, playing flashlights across the ground. In and around the pens there were other beams of light sweeping back and forth. In the bright white headlamps of his daddy's pickup, Beau saw Rex sitting on an ice chest next to where Mr. Jubak was directing the search. Rex was cradling his roping hand in his lap.

"I see him alright."

"Go tell Mr. Jubak that Rex can keep his thousand dollars. Tell him I said so, and make sure Rex hears you do it. Tell 'em I'm taking my horse and going home to see my wife."

"But you won the bet."

"Just go tell 'em," Rooster said. Then he patted his chest. "And remember your promise."

"I'll remember," Beau said.

But Rooster had already turned and was wading away through the sea of Indian blankets. As he faded into the gathering dark, Beau imagined a dark red flower of blood blooming in Rooster's pocket.

Flight

in which Joe Jasmine and Cecil Jubak have a change of heart
(1983)

I wade into the yowling, fur-covered swarm that converges on my boots as I approach the food pans. I stumble, manage to recover, stumble again. Then, resisting the urge to kick cats in all directions—as I've seen my father do, sending felines flying end-over-end like point-after-tries into the yard—I grab the door handle, swing the back door gently into the swirling black-and-white-and-orange mass, squeeze through the narrow space between the handle and jamb, and slip cat-free into the house.

The aroma of bacon and eggs and biscuits still saturates the inside air.

"Cat bait," my father called the breakfast smell, blackdark early, when we sat down to eat at 5:30 and the first plaintive meows began on the back porch. By the time my mother served steaming cups of black coffee, the caterwauling had reached a fever pitch. The old man winced, shook his head at the sound, met my eyes across the table. "Chum," he said, nodding down at the bright yellow platter between us piled high with breakfast food. He shook his head again, this time at me. "Are you and Cecil sure y'all want to do this cat-fishing thing?"

"Yes sir." I raised my coffee cautiously, blowing steam from its surface. "Cecil's bringing a casting net. Says he's been practicing. He's supposed to be here at 6:30, and I've got a bundle of towsacks already stacked on the carport."

"Fair enough. But I don't want your mother to've made all this extra food for nothing. And I won't put up with that plague of porch cats even one more day. Get it done with the casting net this morning, or I'll handle it myself with the shotgun this afternoon."

I gulped coffee, the searing liquid caught in the back of my throat and burned, and for an eternal moment—as I pictured my father blasting cats with a double-barrel twelve-gauge—it was all I could do not to spray a scalding mix of coffee and spit into the old man's face. The cats were feral, having wandered up onto the back porch over the course of the hardest winter to hit Southwest Texas in forty years. They ate up the dry food and scraps that were supposed to feed the dogs; they dug into the trash cans; and worse, they crawled up into warm truck engines on frigid

31

nights and got shredded by radiator fans in the early morning dark—with a sickening *whump-whump-whump*—damaging engine parts and upsetting my mother. And me. I understood that the cats needed to go. I just didn't have it in me to do it the old man's way.

But I knew better than to say so. Instead I choked down the last of my scrambled eggs, got up from the table, and headed outside to haul the dogs down to the hay barn and chain them.

Back in the dining room now, with the mantel clock over the corner fireplace showing 6:25, I have five minutes left before Cecil arrives with the net. Just enough time for a test run. The platter of leftover bacon and eggs and biscuits still sits on the table, but the rest of the breakfast mess has been cleared away. I make out, over the back-porch caterwauling, the soothing sound of dishes clinking together in the kitchen sink.

Then the dishwashing suddenly stops. "Joey?" my mother calls.

"Yes ma'am?"

"Have you figured out what you're going to tell Cecil about college?"

I slump against the door. It seems like the shotgun ultimatum ought to be enough for one morning. I'm still sweating from the effort of chaining up four big dogs that didn't want to be chained, and the t-shirt clings to my back where it presses against the wood. "Does it have to be today?"

"You promised me, son. If I fixed all that extra food this morning, you said you'd show Cecil those letters and tell him about your change in plans." She pauses, and I can almost see her standing there at the sink with a soapy sponge in one hand and a greasy plate in the other, worry lines creased into her forehead and around her eyes. Waiting for me to do the right thing. "We're into March now, Joey. It's time."

"It's past time," I say finally, knowing she's right but dreading what's coming. "I'll get it done."

I walk to my bedroom, fetch the two envelopes off my dresser, set them on the table next to the bait. Both are addressed to *Joseph Jasmine, Jr.* One has a Colorado Springs, Colorado, postmark. The other is from Austin. As I scoop a spoonful from the mound on the platter and wade back out into the yowling swarm to make my test run, the eggs and bacon and biscuits I ate earlier harden like cement in my guilt-heavy belly.

I sling the food into the nearest pan and feel my boots suddenly free of cat pressure when the entire throng converges on the decoy, as expected. I nod, walk to the edge of the porch, stare up into the sky. The stars are fading, the Southwest Texas hills backlit by the coming day. In the first red rays of the rising sun, the Indian paintbrushes that dot the pasture look like drops of blood floating on a pool of deep green coastal Bermuda, and the prickly pear in the fenceline is covered with crimson blooms. But I'm thinking about Cecil, and about the letters. The one from Colorado, dated a week ago, is an offer from the Air Force Academy to train me as a pilot—something Cecil and I have dreamed of since we were four years old, sitting in front of the TV in my living room and watching the first man walk on the moon. At thirteen in the big sycamore out front that served as our rocketship, we recited "High Flight," the sonnet all fourth-class cadets have to declaim from memory, and swore a blood oath to attend the Academy together to become fighter pilots and then astronauts. The other letter, dated February 15th, is a scholarship offer to study classical languages and cultures at the University of Texas. And despite my oath to soar with Cecil up the long, delirious, burning blue and touch the face of God, I yearn with my whole heart to go to Austin.

The *chunk* of a shovel biting into soft ground snaps my attention back down to earth. A little way up the fenceline, Moisés Mercado—a Mexican national who has worked every March through December for my father since before I was born—is digging up a fencepost that the bulls snapped in two yesterday. Once the broken-off piece is out of the ground, Moisés and I will set the new post together and retighten the strands of barbed wire.

"It's early to be out digging," I call, loud enough to cover the twenty yards between the porch and the broken post.

Moisés shakes his head and grins. "*¡En español!*"

"*No hay problema,*" I say, smiling back. This is a game the two of us have played since I turned ten and was put to work before school and after, on weekends, and through the grueling summers with their searing heat and blowing dust. "*Es pronto para estar fuera de excavación,*" I say again. During my eight years of working with Moisés, I've learned to speak Spanish like a native; and for the past two years, my Spanish teacher at Jordan High School has taught me formal grammar. The words come so easily, the way things do when you really love them. And that love has supplanted my boyhood desire to soar away into blue.

"I didn't come early for the digging," Moisés says. "I came for the show."

"*¿El espectáculo?*" I repeat. We're both speaking Spanish now. "I don't understand."

"The cat rodeo," Moisés says. "Your father told me about the towsacks, and about the net." The grin splits his sun-leathered face like the

33

post he's excavating. "I wouldn't miss it. Not for all the tequila in Jalisco."

I feel my own smile fade. It's obvious now what my father thinks about the chances of getting rid of the cats my way. And Moisés clearly shares the old man's opinion. More determined than ever that the twelve-gauge will stay in the gun cabinet, I turn my back on Moisés and head for the carport.

I pause to make a rough estimate of cat numbers as I skirt the porch. About three dozen, I guess. Clumped around the food pans, growling and hissing and tussling over scraps, the cats are impossible to really count. And Cecil is overdue. But the carport, which we plan to use as a staging area, is ready to go. I moved my mother's Suburban to the edge of the backyard last night, and left my own beat-up old ranch truck down at the hay barn. My father took off in the four-wheel drive a half-hour ago to check the cattle.

I cross the covered concrete slab, strap on my work gloves, and start counting out towsacks. The bundle sits next to the faded red roping dummy that the old man used to teach me to lasso cattle off a horse. I drape each brown burlap bag over the welded-pipe horns as I count, remembering the acrid smell of Grullo, my big gray roan, sweating underneath me in the summer sun and the mind-numbing repetition— heading, heeling, heading, heeling—with the dummy steer swinging around on its pivot each time I managed to drop my loop over the horns, and my father effortlessly catching the welded-pipe heels with every toss. As much as I love Grullo and the rest of the horses, I've always hated cattle—hulking, stupid, shit-smelling, walking hamburgers—even more. And the fall and spring roundups are the bane of my existence, the things I most look forward to leaving behind when this senior year is finally done. Despite the Spanish lessons, patching barbed wire fences isn't a whole lot better.

Two more months, and I'm gone.

Just as that thought flashes through my mind, I make out a low rumble from the direction of the highway. Cecil. Has to be. As I count out my twentieth towsack, the rumble becomes a roar. I look up to see Cecil's bright red truck shoot past the big sycamore that was our rocketship, and the site of our blood oath, and feel the breakfast harden again in my belly. But the time for talk about the future is later, after the cats have been caught and delivered, and Cecil has a little cash in his hands. In the meantime I square my shoulders, scoop up the towsacks, and walk out to meet the best friend I plan to betray.

"Is everything ready to go?" Cecil asks, hopping out of the truck almost before it stops moving. "What do the numbers look like?" The dustcloud of his passing sweeps across the two of us as he heads straight for the back porch.

No pause for a greeting, I think to myself. No apology for being late. But under the circumstances, I decide to let it pass. "Thirty-six, more or less."

Cecil stops abruptly, swinging around to face me. "What do you mean *more or less*?"

"I mean if you think you can do a better job of counting that cat swarm," I say, "have at it."

"Mmm . . ." He slits his eyes in the direction of the back porch and works his tongue around in his mouth as if taste-testing the possibilities. He calls it *savoring the angles*, and there is nobody better at it than Cecil. In the same way that I've always been book-smart, Cecil is business-smart. It seems like, no matter what the payoff, he can figure a way to get a taste of the pie. The money end of the cat operation was entirely his idea. "No," he says at last. "Like I told you before, Rooster Stiles says he'll only pay us for twenty. Five dollars a cat—adults only, no kittens—a hundred dollars max. We'll just count 'em as we catch 'em. Unless you think your pop might sweeten the pot with a little bonus money. Say a dollar a head?"

"Not a chance," I say, remembering the shotgun ultimatum but keeping it to myself. "The old man says he wants to hold on to a dozen or so anyway, to keep the rat numbers down and the rattlesnakes away from the house."

"Yep. That's what Rooster's paying us for. Says his barn's so full of rats they're fouling the hay. Says the horses won't eat it." He glances down at my boots. "Speaking of horses, what you got that shit-kicker regalia on for? This is a cat-fishing operation, not a rodeo."

I give one of Cecil's white leather sneakers a quarter-strength kick with a worn brown boot. "First pile of cat crap you step in will answer that," I say. "And speaking of cat-fishing, where's the net?"

"Almost forgot." He trots back to the truck and returns with an armload of white mesh. A rope is attached to a swivel threaded onto what looks like an open cone at the top end of the netting; on the bottom end, a heavy line weighted with sinkers has been sewn around the perimeter. "Feast your eyes," he says.

"Are you sure you know how to use that thing?"

"I practiced after school yesterday until it was too dark to see. Got me out of mucking stalls. Under the circumstances, Pop's all about me making as much extra money as I can."

"What circumstances?" I ask, my gut a conglomerate rock of guilt and suspicion. Cecil's mother and mine get together for coffee and gossip at least three days a week. But surely she wouldn't have said anything about the letters yet. "Is there something I should know?"

"No time right now. Later maybe. I told Rooster we'd deliver the cats at eight, and it's pushing seven."

"An hour?" I eye the net doubtfully. "We're only going to get one chance at this. Don't you think you'd better take a warm-up throw?"

"Don't need one." Cecil slides his right hand through a loop at the end of the top-rope. "This is the hand line," he says. He coils the rope around his right forearm, then firmly grasps the weighted line around the bottom of the net with his left hand. "This is the lead line. I toss and spread the net with my left hand. I guide and set the net with my right. See?" He makes a mock throw, keeping hold of the net. "You just bunch those cats up tight. I'll cast this thing over 'em sure as sunup."

"We'll need to anchor the net down once the cats are underneath it. Give me a minute." I put the towsacks down on the back porch next to the trash cans, then I take a dozen white bricks from the big stack left over from building the house and set them next to the sacks. "Now come on," I say. "Slow and easy."

Cecil sidles up next to me, and the two of us survey the cat situation. It looks as though someone has spread a blanket of black and white and orange fur outside the back door. Cats of all colors cover the porch, basking in the light of the sun that has cleared the low hills now and is warming the cement.

"Gravy," he says, licking his lips. Then he raises the net, partially spreading the bottom with this left hand. "You ready to make some easy money?"

"As soon as the scraps hit the pans," I say, "those cats will be all over them. Don't wait for me to get clear. Go ahead and cast the net. I'll be out of the way by the time it gets there. Okay?"

"Okay." Cecil juts his chin in the direction of the fenceline. "But what the hell is he doing?"

On the far side of the pasture fence, Moisés leans on his shovel and stares at Cecil and me. The grin still splits his face like the post he's supposed to be digging out.

"*Está mirando el espectáculo,*" I say.

"Say what?"

"Watching the show," I snap, this time in English. Although Cecil has taken the same two years of Spanish as me, he's gotten through mostly by copying my homework and crib-noting the tests. "Let's go."

I ease back around to the carport and slip into the house, hoping to avoid my mother. Through the kitchen and into the dining room, I see no sign of her. But the letters have been pulled from their envelopes and left lying open on the table next to the breakfast scraps. A reminder, I realize. And a threat. If I don't tell Cecil about my decision to break our blood oath, she'll do it herself. Slowly, as I stare down at the open letters— my letters, my future, my choice—I feel the rock in my belly melt in a frustration-fueled fire that fills my whole body like the scalding coffee I choked on at the old man's shotgun ultimatum. I'm furious at my father, at my mother, at my best friend, even at the cats—so absolutely livid at being trapped in the middle of all their needs and expectations that my fingers shake as I snatch up the cat bait and let the letters lie.

I swing open the back door, toss the entire plate of bacon and eggs and biscuits into the nearest pan, and feel my hemmed-in world grind down into slow motion. Feral cats swarm the food pan. The casting net swirls out of Cecil's hands and spreads like a sail. I plant a boot and take flight, leaping over the cats, ducking under the net, swinging my body around in midair, and landing hard on my hands and knees in the grass between two piles of cat crap.

The casting net settles gently over the tight-packed black-and-white-and-orange mass engaged in its feeding frenzy. And for a long moment, all is still. I glance away at the fenceline and see, instead of a grin, a mix of shock and amazement on Moisés's face. I glance over at Cecil, and the look on his face is the same. Even the cats seem awestruck, crouching silently under the nylon mesh.

In the next instant, fueled by the anger that still bubbles inside me, I swing into action. I run to the trash cans, grab an armload of rough white bricks, and set each one just inside the weighted line at the perimeter of the net. I make another trip, and another. Moisés and Cecil never move. But in a matter of seconds all twelve bricks are in place, and the cats— which suddenly begin flopping and floundering and fighting the nylon mesh—are securely held.

"I did it!" Cecil crows, slipping the hand line from around his wrist. "Didn't I tell you I'd do it? Gravy. Didn't I say so?"

I have to grind my teeth together to keep from saying something I know I'll regret.

"Now all we have to do is stuff the cats into towsacks." Cecil fetches the sacks I counted out and shakes the first one open. "Twenty of them anyway. I'll hold the bags, you stuff the cats. Then we'll deliver them to Rooster and collect our pay."

"That's a bad idea," I hear. In Spanish. From the fenceline. And despite the liquid heat of the wrath threatening to spill out of me, I look over to see Moisés shaking his head in the direction of the porch. "A very bad idea. Don't do it."

"What the hell is his problem?" Cecil asks, shaking the towsack.

Instead of answering, I reach under the net, grab a cat by the scruff of the neck, and haul it out. The cat, a black-and-white-and-orange calico with a two-inch stump for a tail—the rest having been hacked off by an engine fan—arches its back, spreads its legs wide, and bares its claws as I swing it toward the open sack. The back claws catch the burlap, allowing the animal to spin in a whirlwind of fangs and talons. And with a spitting snarl, the calico shreds my arms that are bare above my work gloves, then shoots across the yard leaving a bloody trail of bites and scratches from my wrists to my armpits.

"I told you that was a bad idea," I hear in Spanish from the fenceline. "I wouldn't try it again."

"What did he say?" Cecil asks, glancing from the blood on my arms to the cats floundering under the net.

"He said it's your turn to try cat-stuffing," I say through clenched teeth.

"He did not. And anyway, what the hell would a wetback know about stuffing cats into towsacks?"

"Moisés is not a wetback," I hiss. "Now gimme that bag."

"Then gimme those gloves."

We trade out, and I shake open the towsack while Cecil reaches under the net, grabs a cat by the scruff of the neck, and hauls it out. This time the cat is a coal-black tom with its tail intact. But the result is the same—a blur of claws and fangs and blood in fast motion—the only difference being that it's Cecil left staring down at his shredded arms while the cat shoots across the yard.

"So much for what Moses knows," Cecil says. "Oh, excuse me: *Moisés*. And unless you figure that son of a bitch parted the Rio Grande and walked across the dry riverbed, he's a wetback alright."

I feel my wrath bubbling toward rage. But the pain in my arms perfectly balances the white heat that fills the rest of me, and with a supreme effort of will, I manage to ignore Cecil. "What would you do?" I ask Moisés in Spanish.

"Put the cats into those metal trash cans instead of into the towsacks," Moisés says. "They can't dig their claws in that way. They'll go right in."

"Goddamnit!" Cecil throws the work gloves at me. "Stop talking gobbledygook with that wetback and grab another cat. We've got a deadline to meet."

My first punch, a looping roundhouse, glances off the side of Cecil's head. But the second, an uppercut, catches him square on the jaw. He goes down, and I leap on top of him, and we roll over and over across the porch. He scrambles on top, and I feel a solid punch connect with my left cheek. And another. Then I feel him wrap both hands around my throat and squeeze. Until finally, I manage to roll on top again and pin his arms against his sides.

"I'm not going to the Air Force Academy!" I yell into Cecil's fight-reddened face. "I'm not training to be a pilot! I'm going to the University of Texas to study Latin instead!"

He blinks, bug-eyed. "You mean you actually got into the Academy?"

"Hell, yes. Didn't you?"

"Sons of bitches turned me down. I got the rejection letter last Saturday, and I've been trying to figure out how to tell you ever since."

It's my turn to blink, bug-eyed. "I got the acceptance letter last Saturday. And I've been trying . . . Damn. I'm sorry I hit you, Cecil."

"Yeah, yeah. Now get the hell off me. I'm laying in cat shit, and you're bleeding on my shirt."

"I always figured we'd both get accepted." I get to my feet and help Cecil up. "I've spent the last week eating my heart out because of our blood oath."

"Truth be told, I don't much care. I don't really want to go to college at all. What I'd like to do is go into business for myself."

"You mean take over your old man's ranch?"

"Hell, no. I'm out of here. There's no future in middle-of-nowhere Southwest Texas." Cecil looks me square in the eye. "Are you serious about going to Austin?"

"I've never been more serious about anything in my life."

"Then I'm sorry I choked you."

"So we're both sorry," I say. "What now?"

He slits his eyes and works his tongue around in his mouth. "I've got a business proposition for you," he says slowly. "Hear me out. There's a construction boom going on in Austin right now. Apartments, condos, you name it and they're building it. I was thinking about moving up there and starting my own subcontracting company. My uncle L.B. has got some connections. There'll be work for us both."

"You mean we'd be partners?"

"Not exactly. I was offering you a job. But we could rent an apartment together," he says. "Be roommates."

"Even with the scholarship they're offering, I can't afford to live in the dorms."

"Then I'd like to propose a new oath," Cecil says. "Instead of flight school, we go to Austin together. We get the hell out of Southwest Texas the day after graduation, and we never look back." He holds out his right forearm that is still oozing blood. "What do you say?"

I extend my own still-bleeding forearm and press it against Cecil's. "Done," I say. Then I shake his hand.

"Now we've got some cats to deliver," he says. "Does your buddy down at the fenceline have a better idea than the towsacks?"

"Moisés says we should stuff the cats into the metal trash cans instead. Says they can't use their claws that way."

Cecil looks ruefully at the shredded skin on his arms. "Sounds good to me."

An hour later, we're sliding the last of four trash cans into the bed of Cecil's truck. Except for the rotten meat smell from the trash bags we had to pull out of the cans to make room for the cats, it was almost fun.

"Better late than never," Cecil says. "Let's go get paid."

"You go ahead. All that's left is to turn the cats loose in Rooster's barn. And I've got work to do here." I nod at Moisés, who has gone back to digging.

"What about the money?"

"You can have my half. You've got a business to start in Austin, and I'm counting on you for a job."

As Cecil roars away in a cloud of dust, I walk to the back porch and gather up the casting net, sending the remaining cats scattering in all directions. Then I grab a shovel from the tool shed and head down to help patch the fence. The sun is climbing higher in the sky, the heat already starting to build. But I find myself smiling.

"*Dos meses más*," I say, savoring the words as Moisés and I lift out the broken post together. Two more months.

Café le Coq

in which May Belle Stiles, mourning Rooster, dreams of France
(1997)

The word of the month for December at the Jordan Independent School District was *self-control*.

The floodlit sign where the word of the month was posted stood out in front of the cafetorium where May Belle Stiles had been slaving five days a week for the past thirteen years, with the exception of summers, since her husband Horace Burnett Stiles—who everyone had called Rooster—moved on to that big rodeo in the sky and left May Belle alone with a house, a hundred and eighty acres, the orneriest roping horse that ever shat oats, and forty-seven dollars in their bank account. She had to take out a loan against the land to put Rooster six feet under, and to help pay off the mother lode of debt she hadn't finished uncovering until months after burying her heart with the only man she would ever love.

As May Belle pulled into the parking lot, she was thinking about Rooster. The mascot for Jordan was the Cowboys, and there was a cowboy on the sign riding a bucking bronco, something Rooster would've loved. But beneath the flying black hooves and the back-flung white hat, the end-of-term announcements loomed like an ill-omened moon:

EARLY RELEASE: DECEMBER 21

WORD OF THE MONTH: SELF-CONTROL

The word for November had been *honor*, something every cowboy May Belle ever knew was consumed by. And Rooster had been a cowboy's cowboy: a horse breaker, cowhand, and competition roper by trade; a bare-knuckled scrapper by disposition; the best dancer she'd ever seen. He'd been the most honorable man in Southwest Texas, an honest-to-God living legend, but utterly lacking in *self-control*.

The early release announcement was almost too painful to bear. Rooster had certainly been released too early. She would give anything for one last waltz.

After unlocking the cafetorium and turning on the lights, May Belle walked across the multipurpose floorspace in front of the stage and into the kitchen. The time clock on the wall next to the manager's office read 6 a.m. On a typical day in the Jordan School Cafetorium, the lights came on at 5:45 when the cafetorium manager, Genevieve Sumps, arrived to get things started. The head cook, Lydia Rodriguez, and the assistant cook,

41

May Belle, came in at 6:00 to finish setting up for breakfast together while Genevieve—who, despite state anti-nepotism laws, was the niece of school superintendent Arthur Sumps—headed to her office. Sonya Gutierrez came in at 8:00 to help on the serving line.

But today was not a typical day, and as she punched in, May Belle sighed at that. It was the twenty-first of December, the last day of school before Christmas break. Every December, as the Christmas holidays approached, the children went crazy. And the early release day that marked the end of the term was the worst. The same thing happened every May as the end of the school year approached, but she had her impending European escape to bear her up under the burden of bad kids.

When she finished expelling her breathy sigh—a heady mix of Crest toothpaste and an unfiltered Camel cigarette—May Belle slipped on a fresh hairnet and a crisp white apron, and paused a moment to check her look in the polished stainless steel refrigerator door. She liked what she saw. Her strawberry blonde hair was still free of gray, even though she would turn forty-two the day after Christmas; and with the exception of tiny crow's feet at the corners of her striking honey-colored eyes, she had no wrinkles either. As her dear departed Rooster would've been the first to attest, May Belle's lack of visible aging was not a result of clean living. She believed in savoring life's sweetness like an ice cream cone on an August afternoon. But unlike Rooster, who swilled the ice cream of life until his heart exploded, May Belle knew when to put the cone down and walk away. She allowed herself two unfiltered Camels per day, one just before she left the house for the cafetorium and one just after she got home. The first Camel was accompanied by a cup of scalding black coffee, the second by a glass of Jack Black over ice. Rooster, who'd gone completely gray in his early thirties, smoked two packs a day and mixed the Jack Black with the black coffee.

Three words defined May Belle: *self-control, solitude,* and *travel.*

The only one of those words Rooster ever had any use for was *travel,* and with the exception of their honeymoon, his definition was limited to roping matches, rodeos, and country dancehalls in Southwest Texas. Aside from the inevitable fistfight at the end, there was nothing more boring than a roping match—a bunch of supposedly grown men swilling liquor while taking turns tossing lariats around the necks, or horns and heels, of calves and steers after betting on which cowboy could do it fastest. But May Belle loved the rodeos. Instead of just a fistfight, they were followed by a dance. And no one had two-stepped like Rooster. That grace on the dancefloor was the reason May Belle fell in love with him. Well, that and the fact that he didn't want kids.

Rooster literally swept her off her feet at a rodeo dance one night, spinning and dipping her under the colored lights, their bodies pressed so tightly together she could feel the play of every muscle in his wiry roper's body. Until her boyfriend, Rex, came back from drinking tequila in the parking lot, that is, and saw May Belle and Rooster two-stepping. Rex staggered across the dance floor straight at them, stuck a hand into Rooster's face, and asked how many fingers he could smell May Belle on. Then Rex yelled the most awful insult at her that a man could hurl at a woman's honor—a word so despicable she had not repeated it to this day—and spat into her hair. Before he turned to face Rex, Rooster paused for what seemed to May Belle an eternal moment and looked deep into her eyes.

"My lady," he said, "save me the waltz. Honor calls."

Then Rooster proceeded to beat Rex, bare-knuckled, to a bloody pulp. May Belle and Rooster eloped to Corpus Christi a month later. They spent two nights drinking and dancing at every country bar in town and two days lying in the Mustang Island sun; and even though it was only a Texas beach, and her bathing suit was ruined by the tar balls that washed up from all those oil rigs in the Gulf, that weekend with Rooster was the best of May Belle's life. She made a solemn promise to herself, as she looked out across the wide water, that she and Rooster would travel together again. But next time, they would leave the state of Texas for parts abroad.

Self-control. That was what May Belle was thinking about as she set up the serving line and the eating area all by herself. She pulled the bucket and scoop off the top of the ice machine. Then she took a deep breath and transported herself mentally to the Cote D'Azur—at Cannes, on the Plage de la Croisette, where the sand was luscious and the water was a perfect turquoise she could lose herself in every day for the rest of her life. Instead of scooping and hauling ice to the serving line, May Belle envisioned herself carrying sand that had been washed up by the Mediterranean Sea and warmed by the French sun. Once the ice bins were full, she nestled containers of orange juice and apple juice and milk in among the cubes like the crenellations on a sandcastle wall. She put away the bucket and scoop, and shifted her mental picture from the beach to the shopfront side of the Boulevard de la Croisette, where it was May Belle's dream to open a little café close enough to the beach to see the turquoise water all day, and at night to smell the scent of freedom that wafted in on the sea breeze. Instead of fold-out tables and plastic chairs in the cafetorium, she saw herself setting up round marble-topped tables and stylish wrought iron chairs for the breakfast service at her sidewalk café. She would call it the Café le Coq, after her beloved Rooster, and there would be a red neon gamecock over the front door big enough to be visible a mile out at sea. In ten years, when she reached the magic early retirement number of seventy-five—a combination of her calendar age and her years in service—May Belle planned to walk away from the cafetorium with her head held high, sell everything she owned, and make her dream come true.

Trash bags, dishwasher, kitchen prep. She knocked out the first two and started on the third. It was now 6:45 a.m. There was still no sign of Genevieve or Lydia, and May Belle was starting to get nervous. She set sausage links to sizzling on one half of the flat-top griddle and got scrambled eggs crackling on the other half. She put rolls in the oven and set out boxes of cereal. Then she scooped the sausage and eggs into containers and carried them to the serving line.

Solitude. That was what May Belle was thinking about at 7:25 a.m. when she looked out the front windows and saw the children gathering. Except for summers, when she abandoned sweltering Jordan for greener pastures abroad, May Belle preferred being alone. But today she found herself fervently wishing for the presence of the other lunch ladies who she usually couldn't stand. The only thing they ever talked about was the bad behavior of the schoolchildren, in particular a little hellion they called Boxer for reasons not entirely clear to May Belle. Her job description did not include serving food. On a typical day, Lydia would be heading to the serving line right now, and Genevieve would be walking to the front to take the names of the kids who poured through the door, while May Belle retreated into the peace and quiet of the dishroom and started washing pots and pans. The children would shove their way along the counter to Lydia, who would serve them breakfast—between answering back their complaints and calling them down for their misbehaviors—while May Belle washed dishes, taking her time and enjoying the absence of contact with kids. Children, particularly the unruly and ill-mannered variety, had always given her fits.

She was feeling downright agitated right now. Seeing and hearing the crowd of children out front, rowdy in their impatience to be fed, May Belle felt her heart pounding and her cheeks starting to burn as her blood pressure rose. In her mind's eye, she saw herself dragged from her café on the Cote D'Azur and dumped at the Alamo, where the Mexican Army was getting ready to storm the walls.

Just as she felt the onset of a full-blown panic attack, she saw Genevieve wade through the crowd and slip in the front door. "Thank God!" May Belle said. "I was about to dial 9-1-1. Is Lydia out there, too?"

"Lydia won't be coming in today," Genevieve said, her jowls bouncing as she came to a halt next to the scrambled eggs. "She's setting up a Christmas brunch for Superintendent Sumps and the school board.

Didn't I tell you?" She cut her beady eyes away so they almost disappeared into her fat chipmunk cheeks. "I'm sure I did."

Smelling a rat, May Belle refused to be distracted by the notification issue. "If Lydia isn't going to come in, then who is going to take her place on the serving line?"

"You are."

"Me? You know what kind of fits those kids give me. Your Uncle Arthur promised me, when I took this job, that I would never have to work the serving line."

"Superintendent Sumps felt sorry for you, because you were about to lose everything you had to the bank. I would never have hired you under that condition. But I've done my best to honor it since I took over. On a typical day in this cafetorium, you scarcely lay eyes on a child. But today is not a typical day." Genevieve turned and gaped at the kids out front who were now banging on the door. "And we don't have time for this. Sonya will be in at 8 a.m. She can take over the serving line after that. But you are going to have to hold yourself together for this breakfast rush."

Travel. That was what May Belle was thinking of as Genevieve hustled to the front, unlocked the door, and started taking the names of the children who pushed their way in. Rooster had always promised May Belle that when he finally hit it big at a roping match, he would take her to France—to Paris and then on to the Cote D'Azur. At the end of the seven years it had taken her to pay off the bank loan after Rooster died and left her destitute, travel became May Belle's sole remaining passion. During the school year, she scrimped and saved every cent so she could spend two weeks out of every summer in Europe with her only true friends. They called themselves the Merry Widows, and they met each year in a foreign land to let their hair down. The thought of travel was the only thing that carried May Belle through difficult days at the cafetorium. She stared into dirty dishwater and remembered lying topless on the Plage de Tahiti at St. Tropez. She saw foodstains on her apron and dreamed of the day she would open the Café le Coq with its marble-topped tables, its view of the beach at Cannes, and its red neon gamecock visible a mile out at sea.

May Belle took the deepest breath of her life, slipped on a pair of clear plastic gloves, and started spooning food onto plates and handing them to the children who jostled for position along the serving line, snatching each breakfast-laden plate while complaining about the quality and/or quantity of its contents. She glared across the serving line at the ungrateful brats she'd worked so hard to feed. Seeing them scowl back at her and hearing them badmouth the food she'd made, May Belle felt, instead of the old familiar nervousness, a heady mix of anxiety and anger start to rise—a feeling so powerful it frightened her. Rather than the scowling faces of children, she tried to envision the sly smile of the Mona Lisa in the Louvre. But she felt that strange, unsettling mix of agitation and aggression burn hotter.

"One at a time!" May Belle growled at the greedy graspers across the serving line. "Calm down right now, or no one else gets breakfast!"

To her complete surprise, the children did calm down. The scowls faded from their faces. They looked as shocked as May Belle felt. During the moment of silence, she glanced at the clock. It read 7:50. She was beginning to think she might actually make it through to 8 a.m., when Sonya would take over on the serving line while May Belle slipped away into the dishroom and resumed her kid-free typical-day routine. The hot burst of wrath gave way to cool relief, and she turned her attention back to eggs and sausage.

But just then, she heard someone grumble a string of obscenities. These were not just run-of-the-mill cusswords, but the kind of God's-name-in-vain-taking that put cowboys onto the devil's pitchfork. She felt that potent blend of anxiety and anger burn bright again. And she looked up to see a fat kid with skinny legs and a buzz cut waddling along the serving line. At least a foot taller and half again as broad as the other children, he was shoving them aside in his haste to reach May Belle. A half-smile twisted one corner of his mouth, but the smile was a taunt.

"Who do you think you are?" she asked, incredulous.

"They call me Boxer, and I want my goddamn breakfast." He stretched the half-smile into a yellow-toothed sneer and launched a new string of obscenities, even louder than the last. Then he started punching the air like a maniac in miniature. "Who the hell are you?"

"I'm the person who is not going to feed your filthy mouth any of my good food!" May Belle snapped.

"Then you are a filthy —!" Boxer yelled, scooping a handful of eggs off the plate of the kid next to him and flinging it at May Belle.

It was the same awful name that Rex had called at her all those years ago—the worst insult a man can hurl at a woman's honor—and the gooey egg mess hung like a glob of spit in her hair. Feeling the fiery wrath that had been building explode into rage, she slammed down the spoon and whipped off her gloves. Then she reached across the serving line, grabbed Boxer by the shirt, and slapped his face with every ounce of the righteous fury that was in her, sending drops of blood flying onto her apron.

But in her mind's eye, instead of the apron, the blood from his dirty little mouth stained the marble-topped tables of the Café le Coq.

46

Synesthesia, Sisyphus, and Unrequited Love
in which Arthur Sumps, at long last, reaches out to May Belle
(1997)

I. Synesthesia

With a name like Arthur Vanhouten Sumps, I've had to push harder. Do more.

Add a nervous facial tic, an accompanying stammer, and the curse of seeing colored character-revealing auras around all the people I meet, and life becomes an uphill struggle on the best of days. And this particular Friday is not shaping up to be the best of days.

I close the file in front of me and steal a glance across my desk at the woman entering my office. Her name is May Belle Stiles. She is forty-two years old, and since I hired her thirteen years ago—a day I will remember as long as I continue to breathe—she has worked in the cafetorium of the Jordan Independent School District without a single incident. Until yesterday. All this information is in the personnel file on my desk, along with a report detailing the altercation that took place between May Belle and one of the students in the breakfast line. Based on the contents of the file, my duty as superintendent is clear: May Belle must be fired, the sheriff must be called, charges must be brought. But there is so much that May Belle's personnel file does not reveal about her: the lovely auburn hair, the striking honey-colored eyes, the pink aura surrounding her angelic form like a halo.

Not everyone experiences synesthesia in the same way I do. Instead of seeing auras, some people can taste colors. Others can see sounds. The condition runs in families. Along with my middle name, synesthesia was my mother's legacy to me. I have spent my whole life reading the energy projected by the public I spend so much time in contact with, and a thousand life lessons have taught me that the colors people radiate from inside themselves reflect their true natures much more accurately than their words. Or the contents of their files. May Belle's pink aura denotes gentleness, sensitivity, a heightened concern for the welfare of others—a combination as lovely and rare as the Nightblooming Cereus flower that graces the Southwest Texas desert for a single midsummer's night each year and then fades at the coming of day. Orange, yellow, and green are also positive auras; and therefore also uncommon, but not so rare as pink. They surround people with a basic goodwill toward others. Brown, gray, and black are the most negative auras. Those who project these darker colors range from pessimistic in their outlooks to purposely harmful in their actions. Tragically, the world of humankind is mostly a world of brown, gray, and black.

I gesture toward the chair in front of the desk, wishing I'd had a second glass of Chablis with the cold-cut sandwich I lunched on at home. Alone. The same as always. "Please sit down, May Belle," I say gently.

"Thank you, Dr. Sumps."

"I assume you know why I've asked you here?"

"To fire me, I guess, for slapping that boy in the breakfast line yesterday."

"That would seem to be the course of action duty requires. Among other things." I feel the tic in my left cheek start to leap and stop, leap and stop, as May Belle meets my eyes. And feeling my face burn with the old familiar shame—May Belle is a beautiful single woman, and I am a lonely Sisyphus pushing my boulder over and over up the same hill—I breathe deep, count to three, and manage to continue without stammering. "But I'd very much like to hear your side of the story first."

"Is there a point in that?" May Belle politely shifts her eyes away from the lunatic gyrations of my left cheek, down onto the file on the desk and the little stack of papers beside it. "No disrespect intended, Dr. Sumps. I appreciate you doing this in person, rather than having Genevieve do the dirty work. But if you brought me in here just to fire me, let's get it over with."

"As I said before, terminating your employment would seem to be the course of action indicated by the contents of your file. But in my experience, a personnel file is merely a black-and-white summary of a person's life. I like to consider the whole color spectrum."

"What do you mean?"

"Please, indulge me," I say, wondering whether getting fired from the only job she's ever held, and arrested on top of that, will turn May Belle's pink aura dark. How many times have I seen the boulder of misfortune roll over those blessed with positive auras and grind them down into the darker and more negative colors?

"Alright. As you know, I normally don't have much contact with the children in the cafetorium. My duties focus on the back of the house: set-up, clean-up, support. But yesterday, because of that Christmas brunch you ate with the school board—no offense meant—we were shorthanded. Genevieve made me serve breakfast, something I'd never done. To make a long story short, this boy that everybody calls Boxer, and that has been terrorizing the lunch ladies for years, came through the food line and acted in a way that provoked me."

"Provoked you how?"

"He insulted the food and then called me a filthy —! Pardon my French."

May Belle's cheeks burn a bright reddish-pink, the color of a perfectly decanted glass of Bandol rosé. I find myself remembering the day thirteen years ago when she walked into my office, newly widowed, looking fresh and lovely but so sad in a black cotton dress, smelling faintly of herbs and orange blossoms—I think of her every time I open a bottle of Domaine de Terrebrune—and my disappointment is almost too much to bear. An insult, even as foul an insult as the one leveled at May Belle, is no justification for slapping a ten-year-old boy in the face.

"And then you hit him?" I ask, feeling sick.

"Well, not exactly. Then he smacked me upside the head with a handful of scrambled eggs. That was when I reached across the serving line, grabbed him by the shirt, and . . . well, you know the rest."

"So he didn't just curse you, he physically assaulted you? Before you yourself struck him?"

"Yes sir."

"That's, um, not in the file! You're, ah, absolutely certain that his, um . . ." I feel my tongue and lips start to trip over each other as a surge of hope shoots through me, but I force myself to keep speaking through the stammer. "His, ah, his egg-throwing, um, happened before you, ah, laid hands on him?"

"Yes sir."

"And you're sure that Genevieve, ah, forced you to, um, serve food?"

"Absolutely."

"Did, ah, anyone besides yourself and the, um, young man in question, ah, see what happened?"

"Genevieve saw the whole thing. So did the other kids in the breakfast line, but I don't know any of their names."

"How many, um, times did you, ah, slap him?"

"Just once that I remember. I'd give anything if I could take it back."

I lean across the desk and look into May Belle's face, full-on. I see tears in the corners of her eyes welling into the delicate lines time has etched there. I see the flush of heartfelt remorse on her cheeks. I see her pink aura undimmed. She is telling the truth—at least, the truth as she sees it.

I take a deep breath and focus my entire being on enunciating every crucial syllable. "I am not going to fire you," I say at last, clearly. Firmly. "At least, not yet. Before I take any action at all, I'll make a couple of phone calls and add a little more information to this file. If things go the way I suspect they will, I'm going to need you to make some photocopies when I'm done. Then I want you to go home and take the copies with you. And don't say a word about this to anyone until I get there."

II. Sisyphus

I take my time walking up the hill to the cafetorium. The crisp December air helps me center myself as I rehearse my strategy for dealing with my niece, Genevieve, one of the slyest rats who ever skulked or backstabbed. Since getting her Administrative Certificate online, she has been politicking for a principal's position with an eye toward putting me out to pasture. And I am virtually certain that she keeps my personal secretary in her pay as a spy. More concerning by far though, with regard to the matter at hand, are Genevieve's thinly disguised loathing for May Belle and her repeated efforts to get May Belle fired—an outcome my niece must consider inevitable given the contents of the incident report she filed.

The gut-wrenching truth is that she may well be right.

But if I have learned anything in more than two decades as an administrator in rural Texas schools, it is that with careful preparation and the right connections, almost anything is possible when it comes to gaming the system. Of course, it never hurts to have leverage—and a little luck. To that end, I carry May Belle's personnel file in one hand and my cell phone in my jacket pocket. When I reach the cafetorium, a big yellow-brick building that serves as both a cafeteria and an auditorium, I slip up the front steps and quietly let myself in. Fluorescent lights gleam in the gloom deep inside. I pad softly across the linoleum and barge into Genevieve's office without knocking.

Genevieve's jowls bounce as she bolts from her chair and extends a hand across her desk in my direction. "Oh, Uncle Arthur!" she huffs. "Hello. You startled me."

I do not shake hands. Instead, I seat myself in the chair opposite the desk and open May Belle's personnel file. "That was my intention," I say.

"Oh? Well. What brings you over? I was just writing up a job ad for a new lunch lady to replace May Belle Stiles."

"What a coincidence." I stare hard into my niece's ratlike face, noticing the way her dark gray aura contrasts with her pale skin and bleached hair. "May Belle Stiles is precisely the subject I came over here to speak with you about."

"Well, good riddance is what I say. That woman was a thorn in my side from the moment I took over the cafetorium. Her refusal to serve food vastly complicated the schedules of all the other lunch ladies."

"Let's leave talk of scheduling for later, shall we?" As I pull Genevieve's incident report from the open file on my lap, I feel the tic in my left cheek start to leap and stop, leap and stop. But I do not blush. Instead, just like in the rehearsals on my walk over, I breathe deep. I count to three. I continue slowly and evenly. "Right now, we need to revisit what happened yesterday morning in the breakfast line. Specifically, I'd like to address the discrepancies between your written account and the testimony of the other people I've spoken with."

Genevieve studies me, slit-eyed. "If you're talking about May Belle Stiles, that woman would say or do anything to keep her job. In addition to her refusal to serve food to the schoolchildren, she comes to work every morning reeking of cigarettes. And I have it on good authority that she drinks liquor, and picks up cowboys at rodeo dances, during her time off."

"May Belle is just one of the people with whom I spoke this morning. I also had conversations with Bobby Lindell and Bobby's mother, Sarah. You might be surprised at what they had to say. I certainly was."

My niece's façade of righteous indignation would be perfectly convincing to anyone who knew her less well. "Based on the contents of my incident report," she shrills, "I expected you to call the county sheriff instead of those redneck Lindells!"

"That's a call I may yet make, depending on what happens here in this office, over the course of the next few minutes. Specifically, it depends on your answer to my next question."

"What question is that?"

"I'd like to know why you decided to falsify this incident report."

Genevieve's beady eyes bore into my facial tic, which continues to twitch uncontrollably. The look on her face is a mixture of shock and disgust. "In all honesty," she says, "I can't believe you're going to take the word of that trailer trash over the written testimony of a family member."

"*Honesty* is, um, not a term I would, ah, use at this moment, um, if I were you." I feel the words start to stick in my mouth, despite my careful rehearsals; but I press on, a feeling not unlike pushing a heavy stone uphill. If I let the boulder roll down now, it will crush May Belle. Partly to intimidate Genevieve, but mostly to give myself time to breathe, I thrust the incident reports—both Genevieve's and the one I personally typed up after speaking with May Belle and the Lindells—across the desk into my niece's face. I inhale deeply, exhale slowly. I count to three. "*Written testimony* is the term that applies here. In the interest of family ties, I'm going to give you one last chance to change that written testimony before I call the sheriff."

Instead of answering, Genevieve snatches the reports from my hand and tears them both to bits. As the tiny pieces of paper settle onto her desk, she fixes her glare again onto my left cheek that continues its lunatic twitching. She jerks her own left cheek in imitation of my disorder, and then she smiles a smile of pure hate.

"What are you going to do now?" she asks.

"It may interest you to know that I personally typed up that second report, and had May Belle make photocopies, instead of using my personal secretary."

The smile fades from Genevieve's face, but the malice remains.

I pause. Not to breathe, but to savor the moment. "Let me tell you what it says. Bobby Lindell admits that he struck May Belle Stiles with a handful of food before she so much as touched him. In the eyes of the law, she was defending herself. Bobby's mother, Sarah, says that he has been violent with her also. She says that, until yesterday, Bobby was too much for her to handle and that she was afraid of her own son. She says that she'd like to shake the hand of the woman who put the fear of God into Bobby. And May Belle says you forced her to serve food on the breakfast line, in direct violation of her job description and despite my explicit instructions not to do so."

"What happens to me if I revise my report to reflect the information that you have just brought to light?" Genevieve asks through clenched teeth.

"Nothing. Provided, of course, that you go before the school board and explain in graphic detail the misunderstanding that has occurred."

Pure malevolence seems to radiate from her whole body, and the dark gray aura that has surrounded Genevieve since she was a child turns jet black. "And if I refuse?"

"Then I'll go before the school board myself and show them proof that you deliberately lied." I pull the cell phone from my jacket pocket. "A call to the sheriff's office will be a necessary part of the paper trail."

III. Unrequited Love

By the time I pull up in front of May Belle's ranch-style house, the sun is setting. I spent the entire drive from my office to my home, and from my home to hers, preparing for this moment—drilling myself to forget about the heartrending crush I've had on May Belle since that blazing August afternoon thirteen years ago when I hired her, willing myself not to think about all the times that I dropped by the cafetorium just to catch a glimpse of her, rehearsing the things that I will say. A part of me has always wondered whether the Sisyphus in the Greek myth gave up all hope, and his long and lonely trips uphill were filled only with the agony and resignation of eternal labor; or whether there came a moment, just as the boulder reached the top of the slope and hung suspended between the momentum he had imparted and gravity's relentless grip, when his pounding heart paused also—brimful with the possibility that this time, finally, the boulder would remain and he could walk away unburdened toward a place of rest and wine and companionship.

I climb the front steps and knock on May Belle's screen door. I carry her personnel file in one hand, and in the other a bottle of Paso Robles Sisyphus Red that I took from the rack in my dining room. It is my favorite wine. Its aroma is bold and spicy; its flavor a mix of blueberry, blackcurrant, smoke, and pepper. Its label depicts a man pushing a giant stone up a steep and rocky hill. The Sisyphus on the wine label is nude, tanned, heavily muscled—nothing at all like the pale, scrawny shadow I see when I look in the mirror. But like me, he is alone.

May Belle appears in a flannel shirt and cut-offs. She is barefoot despite the chill in the air, and all the windows in her house appear to be open. "Well, am I fired?" she asks through the screen.

"Not exactly. Aren't you going to invite me in?"

"It depends on what you mean by *not exactly*."

Despite all my careful preparations, things have already gone off-script. Completely at a loss, I hold up the bottle of Sisyphus Red. "I brought you a present," I manage to say without stammering.

"What for?"

"As an apology for all the hurt my niece has caused you."

"Apology accepted," May Belle says, swinging open the screen door. "Come in."

She leads me through the living room and the kitchen and onto the back porch where the sun has just dipped behind what looks like a combination stable and hay barn, and the western sky has turned the exact same shade of pink as the glow that surrounds May Belle's body. A black wrought iron table and two chairs are the only furnishings on the porch. May Belle takes one of the chairs. I take the other. An ashtray and a glass of what looks to be liquor on ice sit on May Belle's side of the table. I set the bottle of wine and the personnel file down in front of me.

"Might I interest you in a glass of wine?" I ask, feeling every bit as awkward as I sound. I am carrying a wine key in the pocket of my sport jacket, next to my pounding heart. But I brought no wine glasses, and May Belle did not stop to fetch any as we passed through the kitchen. Once again, things have gone off-script.

"I'm drinking Jack Black on ice. Would you like a shot of that instead? It'll warm your heartstrings."

My heartstrings have been on fire for more than a decade, but I cannot find it in myself to say so. Feeling the tic in my cheek start to betray me, I sit staring at May Belle. "More, um, than you could possibly, ah, know," I blurt at last.

May Belle leaves me on the porch with only the western sky and the bottle of Paso Robles Sisyphus Red for company. I take a deep breath and let it out slowly, hearing a delicate clinking in the kitchen. I count to three. By the time she returns with a glass of ice and a fifth of Jack Daniels Black Label, I'm feeling better. May Belle fills my glass to the rim, then she drops a couple of ice cubes into her own glass and pours it brimful of whiskey.

"So," she says, "am I fired or not?"

I take a slow sip, feeling the liquor burn my nose and throat in a not-unpleasant way. "There may be a way out of this mess." I tap May Belle's file, back on-script. "But first, we'll have to get to know each other better. As I told you earlier, there is so much of life that can't be fitted into a personnel file. That's what I'm interested in."

May Belle reaches into her shirt pocket, pulls out a cigarette, lights up. "You have me at a disadvantage, Dr. Sumps. Before I say anything else about my life, you're going to have to tell me some things about your own. Isn't that how it works? I show you mine, and you show me yours?" The tip of her cigarette glows bright red in the dusk as she draws in smoke, then blows a cloud in the direction of the sunset.

My face burns with a heat that has nothing to do with the whiskey. "Please call me Arthur. I'm only Dr. Sumps at work."

"Alright, Arthur. Is that the only thing in your file?"

"No." I take a long, gulping pull from my whiskey glass. "My full name is Arthur Vanhouten Sumps. Vanhouten was my mother's family name. And in the grand Southern tradition—my mother's family being very grandly Southern—it became my middle name. I was born on August 29, 1958. I have never been married. I earned a BA in English from Stephen F. Austin University, an MA in Comparative Literature from Texas A&M University, and a PhD in Educational Administration from Texas Tech. I've been employed as an administrator in rural Southwest Texas school districts for a total of twenty-five years. I spent four years as the elementary school principal over in Carlotta, and two years as their middle school principal. Then I served six years as the high school principal here in Jordan. I've spent the past thirteen years as Superintendent of Jordan Schools. One of the first things I did after moving into the superintendent's office, and I think the best thing, was to hire you."

"That's it?"

"The entire contents of my file."

"Then I'll add some more to mine. The only man I will ever truly love was my husband, Horace Burnett Stiles, who everyone called Rooster. He was the best dancer that ever lived, and he made my life an adventure until the day he died. I don't much like living in Jordan, and I don't like my job at the cafetorium at all. But I need the money because I love to travel. I scrimp and save the whole year so I can spend two weeks out of every summer on the French Riviera with the only real friends I have. In ten years when I can retire with full benefits—if I'm not fired, that is—I'll sell everything I own and open a restaurant on the Boulevard de la Croisette just off the beach at Cannes. I'll call it the Café le Coq, after Rooster."

May Belle crushes out her cigarette, and the scents of tobacco smoke and whiskey waft through the air where the words *the only man I will ever truly love* still echo like a dirge. I stare into the ashtray, willing my broken heart to stop beating so I won't have to draw even one more breath in the absence of all hope. Finally, I look up at May Belle, who is gazing away west—pining for Rooster, probably—then I glance at the Sisyphus on the wine label, posing golden and gorgeous as a Greek god. Although I never met May Belle's husband, I feel a sinking certainty that even the wine-label Sisyphus could never measure up to Rooster, and I know now that the kind of romance I've dreamed so long of having with May Belle is beyond my power. But does that mean I have to be completely alone?

"I am not going to fire you," I say at last. "You can't go back to your old job at the cafetorium, though. I'd like you to become my personal secretary instead."

"I thought you already had a personal secretary."

"She will be taking over your position at the cafetorium. What do you say?"

May Belle studies my face in the sunset-tinged twilight. "I'm tempted. But to be perfectly honest, I have questions about your intentions."

"Fair enough. But if you want to hear answers, it will cost you one of those cigarettes. Bargain?"

"Bargain." May Belle lights two cigarettes, hands one to me.

I take a cautious drag off the unfiltered Camel. "Go ahead."

"This is just about a job, right? You're not expecting any kind of fringe benefits?"

I feel my left cheek explode into motion as my tongue and lips go numb for an eternal heart-hammering moment. "The truth is, um, that it's not, ah, just about a job," I manage to stammer. Then—maybe because of the whiskey, maybe the fact that I really have nothing left to lose—instead of desperation at the thought of struggling on alone, I feel myself enter a place of calm. It is a steep and broken-hearted place, but not completely unhopeful. And for the first time in my life, instead of trying to shove the boulder a little farther up the slope single-handed, I reach out. "For me, living has always been a lot like pushing a heavy stone up a giant hill. What I really need is someone I can trust to help when I get stuck."

"What about Genevieve and the school board?"

"Genevieve will cooperate. As for the school board, you and I will have to go before them together. But this is not the first time that Bobby Lindell, the boy you had the altercation with, has been violent. And his mother wants to testify on your behalf."

"What will they do?"

"The school board? I'll have to put an official reprimand in your file. Other than that, they'll do what I tell them. Or I'll leave them with no superintendent."

"You'd quit for me?"

"In a heartbeat."

May Belle lights up the evening with a wry smile. "Then I'll take the job."

"Thank you," I say. She is still smiling as I rise unburdened, still aglow as I set the wine key on the table next to the bottle of Paso Robles Sisyphus Red and take my leave of her . . . for the present moment only. "I look forward to seeing you Monday morning. In the meantime, I hope you'll try the wine."

Chicken

*in which Paulina Marshall embraces her destiny
and Beau Mulebach makes out in the back of a bus*
(1999)

It must've been the red Mustang convertible.

Paulina Marshall walked up to the rent-a-car counter; requested a compact from the spearmint-smelling, gum-smacking counter girl; and after filling out the paperwork, walked outside the terminal to wait for the Escort she'd ordered, feeling the same as always—no-nonsense, plain, timid in the way of small animals that rely more on their sense of smell or hearing than on their sense of sight.

But instead of a plain little no-nonsense gas-miser, the carhop screeched up in a sleek red Mustang convertible, and reeking of what Paulina knew to be marijuana smoke—despite the fact that she'd never taken a hit of the stuff in her life—he silenced Paulina's objections with the news that they were all out of Escorts, so they were renting her the Mustang for the same price.

"But," she said, "but it's—"

"Your lucky day," he said in a bass voice with a beautiful lilting accent she'd never heard before. "*Carpe diem.*"

"But I can't . . ." He was the darkest-skinned man she had ever seen, she realized, staring up into his face, his skin so deep black it looked almost blue—like the Southwest desert sky on a crescent moonlit night. His eyes looked like the dark side of the moon.

"*Carpe diem*, Paulina."

The next thing she knew, she was circling away from the terminal toward long-term parking, struggling with the stick shift and clutch, and wondering whether it was the marijuana smoke swirling thickly around the plush leather interior or the engine throbbing in her blood that was making her feel lightheaded, or whether it might not be the carhop's final words.

Carpe diem. It was as though he'd read her mind.

She seized her luggage from the back of her own vehicle—a buckskin-and-tan Suburban that her father bought her mother, and that Paulina had inherited after her mother disappeared—and put the ragtop down on the Mustang before she wound her way out of the airport, leaving the big gas-guzzling beast to wait in long-term parking until she returned the rental car.

On an impulse, she pointed the Mustang south on I-27—instead of north like she'd planned—feeling the wind blow through her hair thick with the scent of dusty cotton fields and the first edge of July heat. Although the last wisps of marijuana smoke had vanished in the rush of clear West Texas air, Paulina felt her head-in-the-sand worldview swirling skyward like the dust devils she could see kicking up in the flat distance. For the first time since her mother disappeared from her life like a heat mirage, Paulina had the feeling she could finally make something happen. Maybe the only thing she'd been lacking, she told herself, was a stroke of luck—a little something to put the *car* in *carpe diem*.

She got the hang of the clutch and stick as she accelerated through traffic toward the heart of Lubbock nightlife. She whipped off the freeway onto 19th Street and cruised Buddy Holly Boulevard, riding past all the bars she'd never once, in the nine years she'd lived here, stepped inside. She'd driven by them late at night, looking through plate glass windows at pairs of faces that gleamed in the barlights and pretending she was neon-lit, accompanied.

She'd done a lot of pretending since her mother disappeared.

She'd pretended for the past six years that she was working on her dissertation. She got through her coursework in three years and passed the PhD qualifying exam in 19th Century American Literature with distinction on her first attempt. Then her mother went missing, and all semblance of forward progress stopped. It wasn't until six months after her father filed the missing person report that Paulina actually started her dissertation on the life and works of Ambrose Bierce. She'd spent the next five and a half years haunting the English Department at Texas Tech University, writing and rewriting Chapter 1.

She'd pretended to be a working academic. She taught the same composition courses, got paid the same pittance of a stipend, lived in the same rent-a-hovel on West 32nd Street. But she published nothing. Submitted nothing. Wrote nothing new. Only revised and revised and revised that first dissertation chapter, coming up with theory after theory for Ambrose Bierce's mysterious disappearance in revolutionary Mexico. Until finally she'd been given the boot by her dissertation director, banished with a single sentence scrawled in red ink across the bottom of her latest revision: SIX YEARS FOR ONE CHAPTER IS QUITE ENOUGH.

She'd pretended, while she was driving herself to the airport to pick up her rent-a-car, that she was flying away. Flying someplace where green mountains towered around a clear blue lake that she'd climbed to, and where she was meeting a man who was interested in her not because she was a smart girl or because she was a nice girl, but because she made the climb.

Paulina circled back to 19th Street and headed toward the freeway, bound, in the flat brown world of the here and now, for Ardmore, Oklahoma. She had a job interview for a full-time Instructor of English position at Murray State College in Tishomingo, and the thought of facing a group of strange, possibly hostile, men—men who would determine the direction her life would take—left her feeling terrified, but without options. The man she'd talked to on the phone, Dr. Pirkle, the Dean of Academic Affairs, told her that there were no decent hotels in Tishomingo and recommended that she stay the night in Ardmore instead. Her interview was scheduled for 9 a.m., so he suggested that she drive the thirty miles or so from Ardmore to Tishomingo in the early morning and check out the town and the campus before she met with the recruitment committee. Then he asked if she had any questions.

"Are there any mountains in Tishomingo?" she asked.

"No," he said. "But there are limestone hills. And a lake."

"Then I'll see you at 9 a.m."

It would be only the third time she'd left the state of Texas, and the first time she'd done so alone. Her father had made her promise to take the freeway all the way. "Just to be safe," he'd said. They sat on either end of a telephone line—Paulina in her rent-a-hovel in Lubbock, her father in the sprawling ranch house outside Jordan where she and her brother, Rex, grew up—while he mapped out her route: I-27 North from Lubbock to I-40 in Amarillo, I-40 East from Amarillo to I-35 in Oklahoma City, I-35 South from Oklahoma City to Ardmore. "Promise me, Paulina, that you'll go exactly this way." His voice, hard and wiry as the mesquite and prickly pear on the eighty-thousand acre ranch that her great-grandfather founded and that had been in the Marshall family for three generations, wrestled the promise from her. But as the I-27 overpass loomed ahead of her, she heard again the lilting accent of the carhop: "*Carpe diem, Paulina.*" And instead of getting on the freeway, she kept heading east on 19th Street, determined to make her way across West Texas by back roads even if it killed her. Compared to the prospect of public humiliation at the hands of the recruitment committee, the idea of death on a lonely highway didn't seem half bad.

As she picked up her atlas from the floorboard on the passenger side of the car, she caught sight of what looked like a hand-rolled cigarette

59

sticking out from under the seat. A joint, she realized suddenly, that the carhop must have left for her. Instead of throwing it away, as every fiber of her life up until now was screaming at her to do—in a voice that sounded very much like her father's—she pressed the cigarette lighter button in. When it popped out, cherry red, she slid the joint into her mouth and lit up, drawing in the heavy sweet-tasting smoke warily at first and then deeper, coughing and exhaling in turns over her shoulder into the West Texas breeze.

She took East 62/114 out of Lubbock, choking down half the joint and putting the rest in her ashtray for later. The road unfolded ahead of her like a strange dream. She felt like a different person, her senses heightened in a way she'd never experienced. Flat, wide-open fields spread out around her, broken only by occasional pumpjacks and ranch-style houses with salt cedar windbreaks. It was the same kind of scenery she'd driven through her whole life, but she felt as though she was seeing it for the first time. It struck her that the lines of trees around the houses weren't windbreaks, but walls—walls of juniper and salt cedar shutting out the cotton fields, letting the people inside pretend that the dusty and unforgiving plains weren't there. The sky stretched between the flat horizons, blue up high, hazy-white at the edges, bright and hard and without mercy.

She headed for the spot where the plains met the sky, slowing down for the towns, stopping at the very occasional traffic lights that even more occasionally happened to be red. Idalou. Lorenzo. Dusty, windblown collections of houses lightly sprinkled with convenience stores, Dairy Queens, cotton gins.

In Ralls, she struck East 82/114 and kept on eastward to Crosbyton, where she dipped down off the Caprock into a shallow valley surrounded by red rock mesas with the White River in the bottom flanked by mesquite and scrub brush. After climbing back up into flatlands, she drove through cultivated fields.

At Dickens, she pointed the Mustang down into a deep red rock canyon with a rodeo arena off to her left. She was so taken with the sight of the arena set against its backdrop of red rock walls that she pulled over into a rest stop to take it in. She parked the car in the shade, killed the engine, and stepped out to stretch her legs, walking far enough out onto the highway so that she could make out the sign across the road: DICKENS RODEO ARENA. It was perfect. Timeless in the way of mountains or monuments or great literature. The midmorning sun ignited the red canyon walls so they glowed like lava from an active volcano, and the arena there in the middle of it all seemed magical—a piece of the bigger, bolder Wild West carried forward undiminished into the present moment.

"Impressive, isn't it?" she heard someone call out behind her.

She turned back toward the Mustang and saw a man standing next to it. He was tall. Older, but not yet elderly. Quite good-looking, at least from a distance. He was dressed in an old-fashioned Western suit and boots, and his hat looked to be a white felt Stetson. It was the exact same hat her father wore on all non-work occasions; and although such occasions had been few indeed, the sight of the Stetson was familiar enough to put Paulina at ease.

"Magical!" she called back. Then she started toward the car, wondering why anybody who could afford that Stetson would be out here in the middle of nowhere on foot. She figured he must've walked across from the arena. "I wish I'd brought my camera," she said, once she was close enough not to have to yell. "I'd love to have a photograph to remember this by."

"*Photograph*," he said. "A picture painted by the sun without instruction in art."

"Why, that's Ambrose Bierce!" she said. "It's from *The Devil's Dictionary.*"

"You mean *The Cynic's Word Book*?" he asked. Then he shot her a sardonic half-smile. "The name's Gwinnett."

"I'm Paulina," she said. She was close enough to make out his features now—he was indeed good-looking, in a craggy sort of way—and she had a funny feeling that she'd looked into those sharp gray eyes before. "You look very familiar, Mr. Gwinnett. And you seem to know a lot about Ambrose Bierce."

"A lot of people have my face," he said. "And I'm continually surprised that, in as enlightened an age as the present moment, people aren't more familiar with the works of Mr. Bierce."

Paulina laughed at that. "No, I really think we've met," she said, trying to place him, but still feeling a little fuzzy from the joint. "I don't suppose you've spent any time in Jordan, Texas?"

"I passed through there once, I believe, on my way to the border." He said this with another sardonic half-smile. "And speaking of passing through, I don't suppose that I might prevail upon such an educated and eloquent young lady as yourself for a ride to the Narrows? Due to circumstances beyond my control, I find myself temporarily unhorsed."

"The Narrows?"

"An interesting geological formation just east of here."

"Do you have a ranch there?"

"Let's just say I have an interest there," he said and smiled again, this time showing even white teeth and weathered creases around his eyes that seemed to be piercing through her. "We could continue our discussion of Bierce. What do you say?"

"*Carpe diem*," she said.

"*Quam minimum credula postero*," he answered as they climbed into the car.

"Excuse me?"

"Trust as little as possible in tomorrow," he said. "It's the rest of your quote. 'Seize the day, and trust as little as possible in tomorrow.' It's from Horace, a poet and critic Mr. Bierce knew quite well."

They spent an awkward moment figuring out how to move his seat back so that his knees weren't against his chin. "Sorry," she said. "I never learned much Latin, and I can't seem to figure out this seat."

"*Learning*," he said. "The kind of ignorance distinguishing the studious."

"More *Devil's Dictionary*," she said. They got the seat moved back, finally, and got on the road, heading back up into rolling pastureland along past mesquite and scrub brush and occasional cross-fences. "You're very familiar with Bierce's dictionary and his reading tastes. Do you know any of his other works?"

"All of them," he said. "But I like the definitions best. I think they come closest to capturing my personality."

"Are you a cynic then, Mr. Gwinnett?"

"Of the very worst sort," he said and half-smiled again. "Let me prove it to you." They were passing the headquarters of the Pitchfork Ranch. Red horsefences divided dirt-floored corrals from pastures of deep green coastal Bermuda. He pointed at the red PITCHFORK RANCH sign and grinned. "I've worked up some new entries for *The Devil's Dictionary*, or *The Cynic's Wordbook*, whichever you prefer. Updated entries, I suppose I should say. Would you like to hear them?"

"It seems appropriate," she said, laughing at the sign. "Shoot."

"The first one is *hipatitis*."

"That sounds interesting. What's the definition?"

"'Terminal coolness,'" he said. "The next one is *karmageddon*."

"Hmm. Definition?"

"'Bad, bad vibes.' What do you think?"

"Well . . . it's not like the original."

"It's a new century. It's time for a new form."

"I like the old form better."

"I think I like the old form better myself," he said. "But sometimes you have to try something new. You seem to be pretty familiar with the works of Bierce yourself. What's your favorite?"

"This may seem weird," she said. "But my favorite work by Ambrose Bierce is a letter. The next-to-last letter he wrote his niece, Lora, just before he crossed the border into Mexico and disappeared. I've read it so many times I know it by heart: 'Goodbye. If you hear of my being stood up against a Mexican stone wall and shot to rags please know that I think that a pretty good way to depart this life. It beats old age, disease, or falling down the cellar stars. To be a gringo in Mexico—ah, that is euthanasia.'"

"That's your favorite?" he asked. "Not to say, of course, that it's not witty and well-written. It's Bierce, after all. But why that particular piece of cornpone?"

She looked over at him, trying to see if he was teasing her. But he was looking away at the Pitchfork Ranch that kept passing and passing on both sides of the car. "Because at that point in his life, he'd lost just about everything he ever loved," she said. "His sons. His wife. He was crossing into Mexico to join Pancho Villa. A lot of people think that his trip was a form of suicide—that he was running toward death. But I don't think so. I think it was something else. I think he was running away from pain."

"You must be quite the critic, to have gotten all that from just one little letter."

"Not exactly. I got a letter like that once myself."

"From an uncle?"

"From my mother." Paulina looked back over at the man in the passenger seat. He had turned to face her now, and all trace of sardonic wit had left his eyes. "I've never talked about that letter with anyone," she said. "But I have this crazy idea, maybe as a result of having just smoked marijuana for the first time in my life, that I'd like to talk about it with you."

"Is that a marijuana cigarette sticking out of your ashtray?"

"What's left of one."

"Ah, cannabis. It's a vice I've wanted for a very long time to cultivate, but I've never gotten the chance."

She laughed out loud at that. Then she pressed the button on the cigarette lighter, and the two of them proceeded to smoke the rest of the joint the carhop had left. They passed it back and forth, more and more awkwardly as the remnants got smaller and hotter and harder to hold.

Finally, Paulina tossed the last bit of coal over her shoulder and looked her passenger in the now-bloodshot gray eyes. "If I tell you about the letter from my mother, will you swear to never tell a soul?"

"You have my word as a gentleman."

"My mother loved my father very much. But my father is an alcoholic, and what he values above anything else in this world is the chunk of ranchland on the Frio River that my family has owned for three generations. When I was growing up, he treated everything on that ranch as his personal property: the horses and cattle, my mother, my brother Rex and me. I guess he still does. My father doesn't like to be told *no*. And when he drinks liquor, he gets violent. He used to hit Mother. He'd yell things—things about my mother's life before they met, awful things. Then he'd hit her. It always happened, no matter how my mother responded to the awful things he said. If she denied them, he'd call her a liar and hit her. If she agreed, he'd call her a whore and hit her harder."

"But she wouldn't keep quiet?"

Paulina shook her head. "Sometimes I would pray for God to seal her lips. But He never would. And she always had to say something. Finally, I asked her about it. She said that God gave everyone in this life a mountain to climb. 'Some people's mountains are lesser and some are greater,' Mother said, 'because of those to whom much has been given, much will be expected also.' Then Mother hugged me close and said, 'And I have been given so very much.'"

"And you asked God to put the burden on you," came the voice beside her, softly. "You asked God to give you the greater mountains to climb, instead of hurting your mother."

"No," Paulina said. "I prayed for lesser mountains." She looked away at the headquarters of the 6666 Ranch passing by in the bright midday sun. She looked at the maroon horsefences and barns. She looked at the herds of horses, at the maroon 6666 supply house. "When I went off to college, finally, I guess I sort of pretended it never happened. I never had the guts to confront my father. And my mother and I never talked about it again. Then my mother disappeared, and it was too late."

"You said you had a brother. Why didn't he do anything?"

"My brother is a carbon copy of my father, only younger. They look alike. They think alike. The only difference between the two of them is that Rex is missing a finger. He lost it in a drunken roping match."

They took 82/83/114 into Guthrie, past a couple of gas stations— one with a RESTROOM OUT OF ORDER sign posted in the window—and some closed-up businesses and not much else. They crossed the Wichita River, which was dry, and then lost Highway 83 on the other side of the dry riverbed where it split off for Abilene.

"You said something about a letter," he said at last.

They were on 82/114, not far out of Guthrie, surrounded by pastureland of grama grass and cedar. The plains were rolling now, punctuated by windmills, pumpjacks, distant mesas.

"About six months after my father filed the missing person report on my mother, I got a postcard from Guatemala. The postcard had a picture on it of a place called Panajachel. It's in the Guatemalan Highlands, on Lake Atitlan. The card read: 'The mountains here are tall and beautiful. I've burned through to the center of myself, breathing the high air. The lake is blue and quiet. I've learned to be silent sitting by its side. Although it has cost me everything I ever loved, I have finally found peace. Please don't tell your father.'"

"Have you heard from her again?"

"Not a word. The picture on the postcard was beautiful. Green mountains around a lake that was incredibly blue. But there was no return address. Why didn't she give me a return address? For God's sake, I'm her daughter."

"At least she didn't use the word *euthanasia*," he said.

The mesquite, which had been cleared for miles and miles, was suddenly back again, mixed among the cedars. The mesas got closer and higher as they drove in silence into cultivated fields alternating with pastureland. The crossfences were much more frequent now, and the land looked richer.

"That wasn't funny," Paulina said at last.

"It wasn't meant to be," he said. "Sometimes people get to a point in their lives where it is no longer possible for them to keep on the way they've been going. When that happens, they make a clean break." They were passing through Benjamin, a prosperous-looking little town surrounded by rich fields and lush pastures, but there was no one on the streets and nobody on the lawns outside the houses. "For some people it happens between one breath and the next. For others, it takes years. Some people pick up stakes and make a new beginning. The best others can manage is an ending. But the thing they all have in common is that the idea of laying eyes on anything from the lives they've left behind is too painful to bear."

They rode in silence for a while, climbing up into a part of the country that looked very much like the land outside of Dickens. Red rock canyons dotted with mesquite and scrub brush passed by on both sides of the car. "Thank you," she said at last.

"For what?"

"Perspective."

"Speaking of perspective, there's a rest stop up around this next bend in the road," he said. "Would you mind stopping there? I'd like to show you something."

"If you'll answer one question."

"It seems appropriate," he said, half-smiling at her. "Shoot."

She pulled into the rest stop, killed the engine, and looked him straight in the face. "Are you Ambrose Bierce?"

"Ambrose Bierce died drunk in Mexico," he said matter-of-factly, "on the wrong end of a firing squad. Or the right end, depending on your perspective."

"Then are you the ghost of Bierce?" she asked quickly. "I know how that must sound. But Gwinnett was his middle name. I'm doing my dissertation on Bierce. I've read just about everything he ever wrote, including his letters. And you know more about Bierce than I do."

"*Ghost*," he said. "The outward and visible sign of an inward fear."

"Stop quoting *The Devil's Dictionary*! You promised me an answer."

"This place is called The Narrows," he said, sweeping an arm at the red rock canyon country around the car. "The ridge we're on separates the drainage basins of the Wichita River, whose waters flow into the Mississippi, and the Brazos River, which winds through Texas into the Gulf of Mexico. It's a perfect place to make a clean break. You look to me like a person who's had enough of being afraid. But the only person who can answer that question is you."

With that, he climbed out of the car and walked across the freshly cut grass past the facilities to a wooden footbridge that spanned a barbed wire fence. The last she saw of him was his Stetson disappearing into a red rock canyon as he walked away from the road.

She sat for a long moment, considering. Then she fired up the Mustang and continued on alone. She had grown more comfortable with the car, and as she pulled out of the rest stop, she pushed the Mustang hard, driving at what her father would've called insane speeds, passing the 100-mile-per-hour mark for the first time in her life. She zoomed by beat-up old farm and ranch trucks and flirted with the male drivers—something else she had never done in her life.

"Nothing ever happens to me!" she yelled into the onrushing air as she flashed through Vera. The wheat fields, mesquites, and grain silos whizzed by her in a blur and it seemed as though she was watching the empty chapters of her life zooming by instead of the empty plains outside the car. Paulina remembered both of the times she'd been outside of Texas. The first time was when she snuck off to the Cadillac Bar in Nuevo Laredo with two of her friends from high school, Wanda and Tammy Holigman. After paying too much for silver because she was too timid to haggle, Paulina had been made the designated driver because she refused to drink even one of the famous Ramos Gin Fizzes—unlike Wanda and Tammy, who got smashed and flirted with every man in the bar. The second time was when she traveled with the youth group from her church to Carlsbad Caverns in New Mexico.

She sped across the long asphalt line of 82/183/277/283 past miles and more miles of rolling fields, mostly wheat, mixed with mesquite and scrub pastureland. She kept thinking about the trip to Carlsbad. It was something she'd built up in her mind for months as the experience of a lifetime. But what she'd gotten, after a ten-hour busride, was a walk down a ramp into a hole in the ground, spotlights on rocks, and a burger meal at the cafeteria in the bottom followed by an elevator ride back to the bus—where she sat alone in her bench seat and listened to Wanda Holigman and her cowboy boyfriend, Beau Mulebach, making out in the dark all the way back to Jordan.

She sped along 82/277 through more rolling pastureland with mesquite and some scrub, but not thick like the brush country she'd grown up in. No prickly pear, no cactus at all. No thorns except on the mesquites. Mankins. A few fields in among the pastureland. Holliday. Mixed fields with pastureland. And she was starting to run low on fuel and patience. She'd been nothing, in her life up to now, if not patient. She'd spent day after day waiting for something—for someone—to happen. She was not the kind of woman, she realized as she headed through Seymour, to initiate change on a personal level—the kind of woman who'd meet a strange man, for example, and head to a hotel for an afternoon of sex. Maybe the ghost of Ambrose Bierce would be the harbinger of change.

She stopped in Wichita Falls for gas, and as she stood there at the pump, a guy with a salesman's look—short blonde hair and a flashy suit—complimented her on the Mustang.

"Sweet ride," he said. "How does it handle?"

"Like a dream," Paulina said.

"I own a 97 model myself," he said, making eye contact. "I'd love to do a side-by-side comparison."

"Mine's just a rental," she apologized, looking down at her shoes. "I've only driven it from Lubbock to here." His eyes, she had noticed in that brief moment of contact, were gray.

"Where are you headed?"

"Ardmore, Oklahoma."

"I'm headed to Denton myself. But maybe we could draft each other awhile. See how the 97 model holds up on the open road, at least until we hit I-35."

"Why not?"

She followed him out of Wichita Falls, through rolling pastureland where the trees were bigger than the ones she'd passed farther west. She recognized pecans, oaks, and elms as they slowed down into Henrietta. She passed him in the rolling pastureland outside town, whizzing past hardwoods in the creekbottoms that alternated with rich grasslands. His Mustang was black, so highly polished it blazed back the sun. It wasn't a convertible. But he had the windows down, and they kept making eye contact as they passed each other back and forth at more than 100 mph without looking at the road—a game of chicken the likes of which Paulina had never played in her life. She caught flashes of her face in the rearview mirror: windblown, sunburned, wild-eyed. Nothing at all like her usual hair-pulled-back, eyes-on-shoes self. Her father would hardly have recognized her.

She hardly recognized herself.

Sometimes Paulina was leading, sometimes following the daredevil with his close-cropped hair who leaned out the window and flashed her back-facing grins, the speedometer dipping below 100 only in the towns—Nocona, St. Jo, Muenster with its German restaurants, Lindsay—and then winding back up into triple digits again as they sped back into cultivated fields. The game of chicken reminded her suddenly of her first kiss, with a friend of her brother's named Jeff, when she was six years old and he was eleven. They were watching the bicentennial together at the ranch house. There was a banner that read: 1776–1976, and beyond it the tall ships were sailing into Boston Harbor. In the living room, on the shag carpet, her mother served the kids a fried chicken picnic in front of the TV. Rex headed to the kitchen to get another coke, and all of a sudden, between one bite of drumstick and the next, Jeff leaned across and stuck his tongue into her mouth. She realized, driving alongside the black Mustang with the wind howling through her hair, that she didn't know the salesman's name—but that she would very much like to feel his tongue, tasting of fried chicken, in her mouth.

Then they were zooming into Gainesville, and the I-35 overpass loomed ahead of them. She remembered that he was headed south toward Denton, and her path led north to Ardmore on I-35. And she felt herself, once again, acting without thinking. She pulled up next to him at the last light before the freeway, met his gray eyes, and said: "I'll be at the Motel 6 in Ardmore. If you decide to make a detour, dinner's on me."

She burned out through the light that was still red, dodging a tow truck pulling what looked like a broken-down Suburban, and squealed underneath the overpass in a cloud of smoke.

On the way north on I-35, it was dry. The grass on both sides of the freeway was almost white, and the Red River was nearly empty of water when she drove across it. She passed the WELCOME TO OKLAHOMA sign—it looked like a gravemarker—with a sinking feeling. The salesman's black Mustang had yet to appear in her rearview mirror. Ahead, she saw smoke. There were fires in the distance on the Oklahoma side of the Red. Her mouth felt as dry as the grass on the roadside, and she kept thinking about the Cadillac Bar in Nuevo Laredo. She remembered her mouth, dusty-dry after the walk from the Greyhound Bus Station where they left the car, across the bridge and past the silver vendors to the Cadillac Bar. She remembered sitting at the long bar, looking down at her single Ramos Gin Fizz—the sleek glass was frothy, ice cold, a liquid chalkiness within, served with the stainless steel shaker and a strainer, a bit extra ready to pour—and sipping bottled water while her friends downed drink after drink and flirted with every man in sight. If she had it to do over again, she would drink gin.

As she pulled into Ardmore, she thought again about her first kiss. And even though the rearview mirror was still clear of black Mustangs and blonde daredevils, she picked up a bucket of Church's chicken before she stopped into the Motel 6.

The pool was full of rednecks and children. The guy at the front desk, who smelled like an ashtray and looked to have seen better days, didn't know how to tell her to get to her room. The room, #204, was apparently located on the south side of the motel, as was the office. So it seemed to Paulina that it should've been directly over their heads. All she should have to do, it seemed to her, was walk out of the office and up the stairs, and she said so.

But the middle-aged male desk clerk tipped back his battered camouflage cap and looked at her as if she were insane. "No, it's on the south side," he said.

"This is the south side," Paulina said.

"Right," he said. He flipped the motel map—laminated, with one floor diagrammed on each side—back and forth. He couldn't seem to get the two sides to match up.

Then Paulina heard the bell on the door jingle, and her heart leaped up into her throat—but instead of a blonde, stylishly dressed young salesman, two more middle-aged guys in camouflage t-shirts and pants walked in. One of them wore a cap colored like the Confederate flag, and both of them sported scraggly salt-and-pepper beards. The one in the Confederate cap elbowed her out of the way, bellied up to the counter, and after a brief explanation from the desk clerk about what the holdup was, took over map duty.

Confederate Cap sided with the desk clerk. "It's on the south side," he muttered around a wad of tobacco. "Around by the chicken place."

"Church's," she said. "That's on the west side."

"Right," he said.

"Right," echoed the desk clerk and the other camouflage-clad redneck, together. The three of them stared at Paulina, their faces hostile, as if she were the stupidest and most annoying creature on earth. For a moment, she could've sworn she saw her father's face there among them—it was the same look he used to turn on her mother after a couple of Southern Comforts on ice—and she felt an overwhelming urge to lower her head, mumble something conciliatory, and back out the door.

"Listen!" she heard herself say, all of a sudden, in a voice she'd never heard come out of her mouth in her life. "The sun sets in the west. If you face the setting sun, which even a blind man could probably see out that window there, north will be to your right. South, which happens to be the side of the building on which my room is located, will be to your left. That's a fact I've known since I was five years old. And it's something you great white hunters might want to memorize, if you're capable."

She walked out of the office with her key in her hand, feeling as though something that had been dammed up her whole life had finally broken loose inside her, and saw that her room was indeed directly over her head. She smiled a sardonic half-smile as she walked to the red Mustang convertible and took her suitcase from the trunk. The ghost of Ambrose Bierce would've been proud.

She carried her suitcase and her bucket of chicken upstairs, put the suitcase on her bed, and then stood on the balcony eating chicken with her fingers and looking west into the setting sun. While she was tearing the last bit of flesh off the drumstick in her hand, she caught sight of a black Mustang pulling into the hotel lot. She held her breath as it rolled slowly up to the office. Then the salesman from Wichita Falls leaned out the window, looked up, and made eye contact with her.

She looked deep into those gray eyes and felt herself breathe, thinking that they were having a life moment—one of those instants outside of time that mark a change in direction—when she realized that her mouth was full of chicken. Instead of feeling horrified, she laughed out loud.

She stood on the balcony laughing around her mouthful of chicken and wondering whether her salesman was going to come upstairs. The sun was setting behind him, bronze and beautiful but also hard, as though the drought was reaching up into the sky and even the sun could feel it. There were no clouds, just smoke from the Oklahoma fires. And in the distance she could see a line of hills. Lesser mountains, she realized, as she waited to see whether the Mustang door would swing open, and whether he, too, would make the climb.

Tells

in which Corlis Holybee is sorely tempted

(2000)

Climbing up and down stairs was the least of his worries. Being a mailman sometimes put Corlis Holybee into delicate situations. Throughout the day, he intruded into the space of many creatures such as dogs, cats, and people. He'd always heard that dogs were the postman's biggest adversaries, but he soon found out that people were the true menace. Some folks treated Corlis like their government-issued whipping boy, hurling obscenities at him for not delivering their expected checks. Others called the post office to tell on Corlis for such untrue acts as him stomping through their flowers or driving on their lawns with his mail truck. Still others called in to report having witnessed him sitting in his mail truck doing nothing for thirty wasted taxpayer-subsidized minutes—something Corlis liked to call *eating lunch*.

Being the seat—and by far the most populous town—of a brush-country county in Southwest Texas, Jordan was the station through which the mail for the smaller towns in the county, Carlotta and Pleasantville, was processed. Jordan had a large and bustling post office and an assortment of delivery routes. All the routes had various pluses and minuses. Some were in-town, which involved a combination of driving and walking. Some were rural, which involved driving only. Despite the fact that the in-town routes forced Corlis to intrude into the space of the greatest number of people, which meant being subjected to the greatest amount of unearned harassment and unfounded complaints, it was the in-town routes Corlis liked best. Truth be told, the delicate situations he sometimes found himself in as a result were about the only interesting things that ever happened in Jordan.

The Sugar Britches route would certainly fit into the interesting category.

On one of the in-town routes where Corlis carried mail lived a woman named Selma Berry. Some of the mailmen called her *Sugar Britches*. She weighed between three hundred and four hundred pounds, and had a hard time getting around—so much so that she had to use a heavy-duty scooter just to leave the house.

Selma lived on South Prospect Street, on the western edge of

71

Jordan next door to May Belle Stiles, a widow woman of indeterminate age who was every bit as lithe and lovely as Selma Berry was large and plain. But unfortunately for Corlis, with the exception of occasional tourist brochures from the south of France, May Belle didn't get much mail. Selma, on the other hand, received as much correspondence as most of the businesses in town. Corlis would never forget the first time he'd been assigned the Sugar Britches route. It was his first day soloing as a postal carrier, and he'd been taking special care with every detail.

The first thing that had struck him funny, as he sorted the mail, was that the only items in one of the delivery bundles were flyers and letters from gambling casinos. There were a dozen of them, six flyers and six letters, all from casinos in Shreveport. He rubber-banded together flyers from the Eldorado Resort Casino, the Gold Strike, Hollywood, Lucky Jacks, Sam's Town, and the Silver Star, all of which promised discount rooms, player's club perks, and even free food and entertainment if Selma Berry would just grace their particular establishment with her presence. Not that Corlis would ever open anyone's mail. These flyers were printed on both sides, and as he packed them into her delivery bundle with a half-dozen letters from the same casinos, it would've been impossible for him not to notice what they said.

The second thing that had struck Corlis funny was the mailbox itself. As he walked up the concrete ramp onto the front porch, he caught sight of what looked like a miniature slot machine on the wall next to the front door. The box was nickel-plated, with the house number—777—in shiny red letters where the spinning wheels would've been on a real one-armed bandit, and with a nickel-plated handle that Corlis had to pull to open. When he pulled the handle, the mailbox made a ringing sound as though he'd just hit a payout.

The ringing had scarcely ceased when Corlis heard a woman's voice call out, "Could you bring my mail in to me?"

Which brought Corlis to the third thing that had struck him funny, although he guessed *bizarre* might be a better word for it. Being, he liked to think, a helpful person—and having taken note of the wheelchair ramp that led up onto the porch—Corlis was happy to oblige. Besides, he was curious to see in the flesh the owner of the slot-machine mailbox and the recipient of all those casino lures. He opened the screen door and stepped, mail in hand, into the smell of stale cigarettes and fried bacon. Once his eyes adjusted to the dim interior light, he noticed a profoundly obese woman, dressed in nothing but an overflowing and quite revealing black nightgown, lying on a sagging couch.

"Come closer, darling," the woman said, "and allow me to show the depth of my gratitude."

Stunned as much by the idea of all that gratitude as by the sight of all that exposed flesh, Corlis froze. The only sounds in the room were the labored breathing of the woman he assumed was Selma Berry and the creaking of the couch as she reached a bloated hand in his direction.

"No thank you, ma'am," Corlis stammered finally, his polite Church of Christ upbringing coming to his rescue. Then his practical armor crewman training took over. He fired the mail in her direction and advanced to the rear, stumbling out the door and down the wheelchair ramp into the blinding Southwest Texas summer sun.

He staggered to the last two houses on the block—May Belle Stiles at 779 and Camellia Stroman at 781—and then collapsed into the driver's seat of his mail truck. Despite a couple of wrong turns and a good bit of backtracking, he somehow managed to make it through the rest of his route. The only other time Corlis could remember his brain feeling this scrambled was after his tank had taken an artillery hit during Operation Desert Shield. He would never forget the *spang* of hot metal ricocheting off the armor of his M1A1, or the bleary deaf-and-dazzled sight of the desert afterwards with all those oil wells on fire in the gathering darkness.

When Corlis finally pulled his mail truck back into its spot behind the post office, the postmaster was waiting for him in the parking lot. "Corlis," the postmaster said, "is there anything you'd like to share with me?"

"Well, I—"

"Because there's a lady over on South Prospect Street who called in and said you tried to force yourself on her."

"Oh my God."

The postmaster was lean and grizzled-looking, the twice-decorated veteran of an infantry unit in the Vietnam War, and his grip felt firm and steady on Corlis's elbow as the older man led Corlis to the back door. When they stepped through into the sorting area, he saw that all the other mailmen were waiting for him with huge grins on their faces.

"Bring my mail in to me," someone said in a wheezy falsetto.

Corlis felt his jaw drop.

"Come closer, darling," the postmaster said with a slow smile, "and allow me to show the depth of my gratitude."

"But," Corlis stammered, then stopped. "How—"

"We've all had a brush with Sugar Britches's gratitude," the postmaster said, and his smile turned into a belly laugh that spread to every mailman in the sorting area.

As the laughter died down, they led him around the corner into the postmaster's office where there was beer on ice. Then they all sat around and drank cold beer and told their own Sugar Britches stories. Apparently, Selma Berry and her revealing nightwear had been a rite of postal passage for the past five years.

"Now that you've lost your Berry cherry," they said, "you'll be okay."

When the beer was gone, and the crowd had dwindled down to just Corlis and the postmaster, the older man gave Corlis that slow smile again. "We've got a running Texas hold'em tourney here in the sorting room on Sunday nights. Hundred dollar buy-in. Winner gets to choose his mail route for the week. Loser gets Sugar Britches. You interested?"

"Yes sir," Corlis said. "You bet."

The following week, Corlis was once again assigned the Sugar Britches route. And he was a hundred dollars poorer for the privilege. He spent his driving time Monday morning trying to figure out how he'd managed to lose his buy-in so quickly—it had taken less than an hour—but his walking time was wholly devoted to coming up with a plan to avoid another glimpse of naked gratitude. Finally, as he approached 777 South Prospect Street, he slunk stealthily along the hedge that lined the front sidewalk. He crept up the ramp and crossed the porch on tiptoes. Instead of pulling the handle on the slot machine mailbox, he slipped the rubber band holding Selma Berry's delivery bundle over the handle. Then he turned and ran.

This strategy got him through the rest of the week. But the following Monday found Corlis right back on the same route, down another hundred dollars. And just like the week before, he was mystified by the speed at which he'd lost. It seemed like all he ever managed to win was blinds, and it was a quick slide from short-stacked to pot-committed to done for the night.

He'd even managed to earn a nickname: *Short Stack*.

There was one interesting thing, though, that he had discovered as a result of his second hundred-dollar debacle. This Monday, just like last Monday, the delivery bundle for 777 South Prospect Street contained—in addition to all the usual enticements from Shreveport casinos—a check from PartyPoker.com. After rubber-banding the check in with Selma Berry's mail, making good his escape once he'd slipped the bundle onto the handle of her slot machine mailbox, and finishing the rest of his route, Corlis logged onto PartyPoker.com and checked out the site. Although he was too cautious to play online with real money, he spent a couple of hours on their free poker trainer. The next night he logged on again, and subsequently spent every evening that week sharpening his Texas hold'em skills. Then on Sunday night he walked into the sorting area with two hundred dollars in his pocket and some swagger in his step—with the result being that he managed to lose his buy-in and his rebuy in half the time it had taken him to lose just the buy-in in the past two weeks.

Corlis also managed to earn himself a new nickname: *Dead Money*.

Seeing another payout check from PartyPoker.com in Selma Berry's Monday delivery bundle, Corlis resolved to double his practice time before the upcoming tourney. There wasn't much of anything else for Corlis to do in Jordan anyway. He lived with his mother, an early-onset Alzheimer's victim who spent most of her time watching reruns of crime dramas on cable TV. Truth be told, the Alzheimer's was almost a blessing for his mother, who hadn't done much of anything except go to church and watch crime drama reruns in the three months since Corlis's father died. Because she could never remember whodunit, no matter how many times she had seen a particular episode, she was never bored. Corlis, on the other hand, spent the majority of the time he wasn't actively caring for his mother surfing the web. This had become much more enjoyable since he'd gotten his job at the post office. He'd traded his old desktop computer for a state-of-the-art laptop with his first paycheck from the USPS, and purchased wireless networking hardware and software with his second. The wireless network had proved a particular blessing because it allowed him to sit out on the front porch while he practiced his poker game.

He had just gone all in on a set of queens in a poker-trainer game of Texas hold'em when he caught sight of Sugar Britches at the Cowboy Mart across the street. There was a handicapped van that went around to the houses of the homebound and drove them to run their errands in town. Corlis's mother sometimes took the van to church. As he watched Selma—in an olive drab dress that looked like an Army tent—roll out the front door of the Cowboy Mart with a fistful of Lotto tickets and a carton of smokes, Corlis hit a fourth queen on the river. If he'd been playing for real money, he could've retired at twenty-nine. What he did instead was wait until the handicapped van drove off in the direction of the high school, and then log off and trot across the street to the Cowboy Mart to ask about Selma Berry's gambling habits.

The cashier, a tattooed, pierced, and unwed mother of three named Rosemary—who Corlis had graduated from high school with eleven years before, and who was still surprisingly attractive despite the rough patches she'd been through—was only too happy to fill Corlis in on the Lotto strategy of "Miss Selma." Apparently, the *Sugar Britches* nickname had not spread beyond the post office.

"Miss Selma," Rosemary said, "comes in every Tuesday and Friday, and buys a hundred tickets for the next night's drawing. Half her numbers are pre-selected on the pick 6, and half of them are quick picks." Here Rosemary paused, looked across the beef jerky and the pre-paid phone cards on the counter, and met Corlis's eyes.

Despite his determination to get the low-down on Selma Berry's betting secrets, he felt his heart skip a beat. Rosemary had captivating blue eyes, the color of a robin's eggs. And although he'd never had the guts to do anything about it, he'd been captivated by those robin's-egg eyes more than once.

"So she does everything the same way, every time?" he asked, looking down at the beef jerky and trying to focus back in on gambling.

"Well, not quite everything," Rosemary said. "Usually, Miss Selma pays for her numbers with winnings from the previous drawing. But she has hit a few of the bigger payouts, ones she had to go to Austin to collect on. Every time she does, Miss Selma takes the Lotto money and heads to Shreveport to play poker."

This brought Corlis's eyes up off the beef jerky. "What does she say about playing poker?" he asked eagerly, gripping the counter with both hands as he connected the Shreveport lures, the Lotto tickets, and the payout checks from PartyPoker.com.

"Not much of anything about poker," Rosemary said. "But she always says the same thing when she hits a big payout."

"What's that?" Corlis asked, his grip on the counter white-knuckled now.

"'You have to bet big to win big, darling.'"

It was a revelation. Sunday night, after practicing five hours a day on the PartyPoker.com poker trainer for the remainder of the week, Corlis put five hundred dollars in his pocket and headed for the post office—and managed to go through the whole five hundred in about the same time it had taken him to go through a hundred in week one. It seemed like every time he went all-in, he went down on a runner; every time he bluffed, everybody at the table called or raised.

Corlis also managed to earn a nickname that, for the first time, brought unfriendly snickers from the other mailmen: *Rebuy*.

But the postmaster said he felt so bad about Corlis losing all that money—even though the postmaster had taken the vast majority of it himself—he offered to send somebody else on the Sugar Britches route.

"No sir," Corlis said, thinking about the payout check she got every

Monday. "I guess I'll take what I got coming."

The next morning Corlis was at work early, sorting mail. Just like every other Monday morning, Selma had a check from PartyPoker.com. He slipped the check into his pocket, then rubberbanded together the usual flyers from every Shreveport casino, and went about his route the same as always. But this time, after he crept up the ramp and tiptoed across the porch, Corlis pulled the handle on that one-armed bandit.

Almost before the ringing stopped, he heard a woman's voice call out from inside, "Could you bring my mail in to me?"

"Happy to oblige, ma'am." He opened the screen door and stepped inside, smelling again the mix of stale cigarettes and fried bacon.

Huge, pale white, naked beneath what looked to be that same sheer black nightgown as before, Sugar Britches stretched a hand in Corlis's direction. "Come closer, darling," she said, "and allow me to show the depth of my gratitude."

"I didn't come in for the gratitude," he said. "And I'm not here just to bring in your mail. I'm here to ask you a question."

The couch groaned in protest as she levered herself into a sitting position and narrowed her eyes at Corlis. "All right, fire away."

He pulled the PartyPoker.com check from his pocket and slipped it into her outstretched hand. "How do you win?" he asked.

"No, I don't think so, darling." She set the check down on the end table next to the couch, then pulled a cigarette from a pack next to the check, lit up, and blew smoke in his direction. "I don't see a percentage in answering that. Of course, if you'd come a little closer, we might be able to work something out."

"I can't come any closer." Corlis tried not to think about what all that flesh was doing underneath the negligee every time she made a move. "Anyways, not for that."

"What else have you got to offer?" she asked, blowing smoke.

"If you'll answer that one question for me, I'll answer as many for you as you like."

"Done! Come back tonight after you finish your route."

Corlis went through the rest of his route feeling almost as scrambled as he had the first time he'd laid eyes on Sugar Britches. He parked the mail truck and headed home, fed his mother, got her in front of a *Law and Order* marathon on TBS, and then drove back across town to 777 South Prospect.

It felt strange pulling up in front of the house instead of creeping along the hedge. It felt even stranger knocking on the screen door instead of pulling the handle on the slot machine.

"Come in, darling," he heard from inside before he'd even finished knocking. "And bring your question with you."

Corlis walked inside, smelling again stale cigarettes and fried bacon, and wondering whether he'd be having another encounter with that black nightgown. Sure enough, once his eyes adjusted to the dim interior light, he saw Sugar Britches and her see-through nightie. This time, though, there was a card table in front of the couch she was reclining on, and a chair on the far side of the table.

"Have a seat. Make yourself at home."

"Thank you, ma'am," Corlis said, sitting down in the chair and looking at everything in the room except the vast expanse of woman across the table. He admired the expensive laptop computer on the table in front of him. He noticed the deck of cards with the GOLD STRIKE logo next to the laptop. He studied the photos on the wall of Selma Berry, younger and thinner, standing in front of legendary casinos he'd heard of but never seen: Horseshoe, Golden Nugget, Four Queens, Circus Circus, Flamingo, MGM. "So," he said, still not looking at her. "How do you win?"

"No, darling," she said and laughed a little. He heard her light a cigarette, inhale, and blow smoke. "You first. But before we begin, please fetch me a coke from the fridge. Feel free to get one for yourself."

"Yes ma'am." He fetched two cokes, opened both cans, and reached one across the table. "What do you want to know?"

"Do you have a girlfriend?"

"No."

"Have you ever had a girlfriend?"

"In high school."

Selma laughed again. "If you want to get details, you're going to have to give details yourself."

Corlis took a long sip of coke. "All right. My girlfriend's name was Tammy Holigman. She had red hair and freckles and pale skin, and she wasn't just some dumb high school crush. I wanted to marry her."

"That's better. So what kinds of things did you and Tammy Holigman like to do?"

"Tammy's favorite thing was for us to slip off to the Cadillac Bar in Nuevo Laredo with her sister Wanda, and Wanda's boyfriend Beau. Beau and Wanda are married now, but I don't see them much anymore. Tammy and I got engaged right after graduation. I enlisted in the Army, and she went off to college at Howard Payne up in Brownwood. Even though the only thing I ever wanted to do was fly helicopters, I picked an armor MOS so I could be stationed in Texas when I finished training. But when I shipped out to Kuwait for Operation Desert Shield, Tammy said we'd better put the engagement on hold. By the time I got back, she was married to somebody else."

"I'm genuinely sorry to hear that," Selma said. "Have you had any other girlfriends since?"

"I've been with other women, but I wouldn't call them *girlfriends*."

"What does that mean?"

"A dinner here, a couple of movies there. They were always a letdown. It's been a long time since I met anyone I was even interested in dating. Except for Rosemary."

"Rosemary?" she asked.

"You know her. She's a cashier at the Cowboy Mart."

"I do indeed, darling. What a lovely young lady! And always so sweet. But what was it like with those other girls?"

"About like you and the mailmen, I expect," Corlis said. "That is, if any of them ever allow you to show the depth of your gratitude."

"Let me tell you something about those mailmen." She took a deep drag and blew smoke all over Corlis. "They may laugh at me and call me names, but you'd be surprised at how many of them ring the bell on my slot machine when they're out on their routes."

"The postmaster?" Corlis asked.

"Yes."

"Did you teach him how to win?"

"Yes."

"Will you teach me?"

"That depends, darling, on the level of detail with which you answer the rest of my questions."

"Then let me save you some trouble. I grew up in Jordan. I've spent my whole life, minus an eight-year stint in the Army, here. My dad owned the Cowboy Mart back when it just sold gas and groceries. I used to work there when I was growing up. I enlisted when he was forced to sell."

"Forced to? Why?"

"Because he refused to gamble. My father was a devout Church of Christ member, not one of those 'Do as I say, not as I do' types. So he refused to sell Lotto tickets. That meant he lost a lot of his trade to the station down the street. It was run by another Church of Christ member who not only sold Lotto tickets, but also sold beer on Sunday mornings in violation of the blue law."

"You don't go to church anymore, do you?"

"No."

"Neither do I," she said. "What does your father do now?"

"Not much of anything. He's dead. That's why I got out of the Army. I had to come back here and take care of my mother."

"What's the matter with your mother?"

"Alzheimer's."

"I'm sorry. What did you do in the Army?"

"Liberated a monarchy from a dictatorship, for one thing, riding across the desert in an M1A1 pumping DU ordnance into Iraqi tanks. I spent the rest of my time at Fort Bliss, making trips back and forth across West Texas to watch my father die. But it was the Army that helped me land the post office job. That and the Gulf War. All of the mailmen are veterans."

"What's it like to ride in a tank?"

"Okay, I guess. I assisted in target detection and identification. I operated the main gun controls and firing controls. In other words, I identified bogeys and blew them to kingdom come."

"How did you feel about that?"

"It beat the hell out of changing my mother's diaper. Now it's your turn."

"Fair enough. But before we start, tell me about the tourneys at the post office."

Detail after humiliating detail, including the nicknames, Corlis filled her in on his miserable performance on Sunday nights—culminating in his five-hundred-dollar loss the night before.

"I can tell you this right now. You need to stop playing cards and start playing poker. The smarter you play, darling, the luckier you'll be."

"So how do I do that?"

"How much money did you bring?"

"None. I didn't figure I needed any."

"It's probably better that way." She took a chip rack from beneath the table and gave each of them a thousand dollars. Then she picked up the GOLD STRIKE deck and started dealing Texas hold'em. In less than fifteen minutes, she had all his chips. But she didn't say anything for a long time.

"So?" Corlis finally said.

"So you have a tell, darling. No, that's not exactly accurate. You have a lot of tells. I always know when you have a hand, and when you don't."

"How do I fix it?"

She pulled another cigarette from her pack, lit up, and blew smoke all over Corlis.

"Stop doing that," he said, "or I'm out of here."

"Tell me the truth. Do you want to become a gambler? Or do you just want your money back?"

"My money, and my self-respect."

"That's good," she said and blew smoke all over Corlis again. "You're not a gambler by nature."

"What does that mean?"

"That means I knew you wouldn't go anywhere if I blew smoke all over you again, darling. You'll have to go against your nature to win."

"Excuse me?"

"Whatever you'd usually do, do the opposite. I mean that quite literally. If you'd normally check, go all in. If you'd normally muck, bet. If you'd normally go all in, just check or call. If you'd usually sit and stare across the street pretending to look at your computer, get up and go talk to that girl."

"That's it? That's all I have to do?"

"No. Come back next Monday and let me know how you do this Sunday night."

Monday morning Corlis was at work early, sorting mail. Just like every other Monday, Selma Berry had a check from PartyPoker.com. He bundled the check in with the usual mailings from Shreveport. When he got to 777 South Prospect, he walked boldly across the front porch and pulled the handle on that one-armed bandit.

"Come in, darling. And tell me all about it."

He opened the screen door and walked inside. Once his eyes adjusted to the dim interior light, he caught sight of Selma sitting on the couch and leaning over her laptop computer. But instead of a see-through black negligee, she had on the olive drab dress she always wore to the Cowboy Mart.

"So?" she asked.

"So I won."

"And?"

"And here's your mail." Corlis stepped in close and handed over the delivery bundle.

"Thank you."

"No, thank you," he said. "I mean that. I've got my money back, and most of my self-respect, because of you. But I've retired from Texas hold'em."

"Hmm . . . So what will you do now?"

"Deliver mail. And spend more time across the street at the Cowboy Mart."

"Not a bad idea, darling. I rather like her."

"So do I."

Love Songs

in which Rosemary Stroman is lost and Rosemary Holybee found
(2000)

Music is a type of storytelling, and so is my life. Sometimes I tell the story out loud, and sometimes it only plays in my head. But the songs and the things that have happened to me are joined so tightly together, it's impossible to separate one from the other. It has been this way since the story of the real me—of Rosemary Stroman who was, and Rosemary Holybee who is now—began.

I have no memories of my mother. My earliest recollections are of my father listening to songs that made him cry. I remember him sitting on the futon in the living room and drinking Wild Turkey 101. Scratchy vinyl albums by Patsy Cline, Tammy Wynette, or George Jones blared on his old stereo. He tried to sing along, but got too drunk to keep up with the words. Tears rolled down his face as his big pipe-welder's fists, hardened by work in the Southwest Texas oil patch, cut back and forth through the air out of synch with the beat. At the time I thought it was funny. As I got older, I realized that his heart was breaking. The country and western musicians he listened to every night when he was drinking sang love songs. He thought of my mother when he heard those songs. He always said that my mother was the one he loved more than any other woman—that when she ran off with another man, she took my father's soul and left him with only me.

Then came the night that he pulled me down onto the futon with those big out-of-synch fists I used to think were so funny and said, "You look just like her." Patsy Cline was singing "I Fall to Pieces" on the stereo, the smell of whiskey filled the whole world, and he mashed his lips against mine in a way that no father should ever do to a daughter. He proceeded to do to me all of the things he used to do to my mother.

I guess the title for part one in the story of the real me should be: "Rosemary Stroman Falls to Pieces, Thirteen Years Old." It wasn't always Patsy who sang. But the fists and the whiskey and the rest of it, they were always the same. And the heart that was breaking was mine.

When my father died in the first big fire, I saved those old albums. Afterward, in the second part of my story, I still listened to the love songs sometimes. They were all about life gone wrong, about heartbreak, in the

83

same way my story was back then. And I did the same things with other men that my father used to make me do. It wasn't that I loved those men more than any other man, or that I felt like my soul was gone. But the heartbreak and the music were all tangled up together, and the story kept repeating like the deepest scratched places on my father's vinyl records, playing the same line over and over. On and on. Until the day Corlis Holybee walked into the Cowboy Mart and looked deep into my eyes— instead of talking to the nipple rings that showed through my t-shirt, like all the other men who stepped up to the cash register—and everything changed. But that is part three in the story of the real me, and it comes much later, after I melted my father's old albums in the second big fire.

The songs I listened to most often during part two—after my father burned alive on the futon in our living room, and before Corlis stared into my eyes at the Cowboy Mart—turned angry. I went from country and western to heavy metal: Mudvayne, Godsmack, Pantera. If I could make the present moment burn hot enough, I could reduce the past to ashes for a little while. I tried to make every ragged breath like the grand finale at a fireworks show when the world disappears in a rolling burst of heat and light and sound, and the sky is a conflagration.

According to my high school chemistry teacher, the Greek philosopher Heraclitus regarded the soul as a mixture of fire and water, with fire being the nobler and water the baser part. He believed the goal of the soul was to purge its water and become pure flame. Mr. Bynum told me that one afternoon in the storeroom behind the lab. He'd invited me to meet him after school, saying he wanted to show me the violent reaction raw sodium has when placed in water—"Like fireworks," he said, "on the Fourth of July"—but we both knew what he really wanted to make explode.

So I dropped a hit of acid at lunch, skipped my afternoon classes, and climbed in the window Mr. Bynum opened for me. He led me into the storeroom and told me about Heraclitus while he set up the experiment on a metal table in the middle of shelf upon shelf of chemicals and lab equipment. Next he undressed me, and leaned me over the table to stare point-blank into the petri dish he'd filled with water. He dropped in a chip of sodium, with a tiny piece of tissue paper on top to restrict its movement, while at the same time turning off the lights. Then he shoved himself into me. The sodium sizzled and smoked, and a flame bloomed in the dark, arcing across the surface of the water until it died with a sharp pop.

"Heraclitus," Mr. Bynum said when he was finished, "considered fire to be the most fundamental of the four elements. He believed that fire gave birth to earth, air, and water. All things were an interchange for fire, and fire for all things, just like goods for gold and gold for goods." Then he gave me twenty dollars.

I got dressed and crawled back out the window. Later that evening, I used the money to get my nipples pierced.

Mr. Bynum wasn't the only teacher at Jordan High School of whom I had carnal knowledge. But he was the one who taught me the most about how seemingly abstract ideas can impact real life. For example, in addition to being fascinated with gold and with fire, alchemists believed that the processes which affect metals and other substances could also affect the human body. The universal solvent they sought—which had the power to dissolve every other substance—would also be invaluable for its medicinal qualities.

"If you learned the secret of purifying gold, for instance," Mr. Bynum told me on another afternoon in the storeroom as we were undressing, "you could use the technique to purify your soul." He went on to say that in alchemic tradition metals like sodium and gold were incubated by fire in the womb of the earth, and alchemists only accelerated their development. There in the dark with Mr. Bynum, an idea blossomed in my mind like the sodium flame that arced across the surface of the water: I would purify my soul with a mixture of arcane chemicals and fire.

The heavy metal band Mudvayne has a song called "Solve et Coagula" that I played for Mr. Bynum once. It is not a love song. But then again, love had not much to do with my life then. I had separated the act of love from the feeling of love. Mr. Bynum said that in Latin *Solve et Coagula*, an alchemical term, means "to separate and bring together"—to disassemble a substance so that you can reassemble something pure. The Mudvayne song is about destroying yourself and your world so that both can be reborn. When I think back on that time, I hear electric guitars and screams while flames bloom in the night.

I call part two in the story of the real me: "Rosemary Stroman Destroys Herself in Hopes of Recreating Something Pure, Seventeen Years Old." Although it began at seventeen, this part of the story lasted a dozen years. I see it now only in flashes. Like an upturned face at a fireworks show, I flicker and fade with each new blast. Drugs. Piercings and tattoos. Jail. Three children incubated by fire and accelerated in the earth of my womb: Blaise, Cole, Ash. Three sons by different fathers.

Camellia Stroman, my father's mother, took the boys when I got sentenced to a year for intent to distribute meth. When I got out, she wouldn't let me near them—despite the fact that I was practically clean and had my cashier job at the Cowboy Mart.

When I asked why she wouldn't let me see my children, Camellia said that she was going to save them. From me. Then she ticked off a list of my transgressions: the drugs, the arrests, the jail time, and seven step-fathers for the boys in eight years. She used the word *stepfathers* even though I never married any of those men.

"If you managed to keep track of all that," I said, "then how could you not have known what my father—your son—was doing to me? Why didn't you save me from him the way you're trying to save my sons from me?"

My father's mother—I won't call her *grandmother*—stood on the front porch of her house in Jordan. I was on the bottom step looking up at her. The afternoon sun reflected off the French doors that Camellia stood in front of. Despite the sunlight blazing off the glass and the broad barricade of her body, I saw the curtains move in the windows as my boys peeped through at me. I hadn't seen their faces in more than a year.

"You're crazy!" Camellia said, loud so the boys could hear. "Or else you're high on meth again. Either way, I've got a court order. Get off my property, or I'll call the police." Then, in a voice that was more hiss than whisper, "What you really are is a whore, the same as your mother. You look just like her."

The sun blazed down so strong it felt like I was bathed in fire. I looked up at my father's mother—at the big fists clenched on her broad hips, at the hard lips, at the beady brown eyes burning into me—and I saw my father. I remembered coming home that final night and finding him passed out on the futon. It was cold outside, but our old space heater warmed the tiny living room. I took his bottle of Wild Turkey 101 and emptied what was left onto the futon and the carpet around the couch. I slid the heater over until the red-hot element kissed the fabric. Then I took my father's favorite albums and walked back out into the cold. The cleansing flames lit up the night sky behind me, and I would've burned the whole world if I could.

When Camellia walked back inside to follow through on her threat to call the police, I turned away from her house, and my boys, and staggered through the afternoon heat back to the trailer I was renting. I went straight to the kitchen, laid a couple of towels next to the stovetop, set a pot of water on the big butane unit next to the towels, and turned the flame up as high as it would go. Then I put one of my father's old Patsy Cline records on the stereo, swallowed my whole stash of Xanax, and lay down on the couch.

The next thing I clearly remember is Corlis at the Cowboy Mart, standing at the counter and staring into my eyes. I have only hazy recollections of that second fire: tumbling down the front steps of the blazing trailer, glancing back just in time to see the roof collapse on the neighbor who must've pulled me up off the couch and shoved me out the front door. I'd never met the man, despite the fact that I lived next door to him for a month, and only found out later that his name was Frank Davis. I have no idea why Frank Davis sacrificed himself to save me. I certainly wouldn't have done the same for him.

As was the case when I burned my father alive, the investigators ruled the trailer blaze an accident. "An inadvertent kitchen fire that quickly spread to involve the entire structure," they said. "A total loss."

I know none of that is true, even for Frank.

For me, it was the eureka moment I'd been searching for since I was thirteen years old. As I lay at the base of the steps, surprised to be breathing but still facing the flaming shell my life had become, I realized that it's not possible for one person to save another—despite what I'd said to my father's mother, and what she'd said to me. What Frank, and later Corlis, did was make it possible for me to save myself. I often wonder which of them had the harder part to play.

The day after Corlis walked into the Cowboy Mart and looked at me in a way that gave me hope that life might actually be livable, he was back again. And once again, as he stood at the counter and spoke in awkward fits and starts, his gaze never once strayed to my breasts. It didn't matter that all he talked about was the Lotto and a nice lady named Selma Berry that we both knew and the price of the beef jerky he eventually bought. The important thing was that he'd come to the Cowboy Mart just to speak to me.

It wasn't all that long a walk, I guess. Corlis lived across the street with his mother, who has Alzheimer's and who he's taken care of since his father died. For a week after that second visit, the whole time he wasn't delivering the mail—Corlis is proud of his job as a postal carrier—he sat on the front porch in his uniform pretending to work on his laptop. But in reality, he was watching me. Every time I glanced through the big plate glass window, lit blue-and-yellow by the neon PLAY LOTTERY sign shaped like the state of Texas, his eyes met mine for a long moment before he looked back down at the computer screen.

Finally, instead of looking back down, he flipped the laptop shut and walked across the street. "I've been trying to work up the nerve to ask you out on a date," he said, his fingers fiddling nervously with the cigarette lighters next to the register. "How about dinner?"

"How about tonight?" I asked.

That evening at the Chuckwagon Barbeque we sat in a booth across from each other, and I listened as Corlis punctuated the uncomfortable silence with stories about the crazy things that sometimes happened on this delivery routes. He wore a dark green button-down shirt and a black silk tie. Racks of ribs slathered with spicy sauce sat steaming on the red-and-white checkered tablecloth. After a long string of pop country songs I didn't recognize, Willie Nelson started singing "Always on My Mind" on the corner jukebox. Suddenly, Corlis stopped telling me about his job and leaned across the table.

"Did you know that your eyes are the color of a robin's eggs?" he asked.

He seemed to be waiting for an answer. But I hesitated, not quite sure whether he was serious, or whether this was just the part of the date where the man tries to get inside the woman's pants. Corlis's face, framed by his military-style haircut, was very close to mine. His eyes, the same deep green color as his shirt, were open so wide I could see the entire iris of each—as if he were inviting me to stare straight through into his soul and weigh the things I found there.

"That's honestly something I've never heard in my life," I said at last.

"Well, it's true," he said slowly, holding my gaze. "I didn't bring you here because I wanted a one-night stand. I want to get to know you. The real you, I mean, not just the one that works at the Cowboy Mart."

"I'd like that, too."

Corlis nodded, leaned back, glanced away at the jukebox. "It was me that played the Willie Nelson song." He took a gulp of sweet iced tea. "I've been waiting for it to come on so I could tell you that about your eyes, and about wanting to get to know you. The only thing that's really been on my mind for the past week is you."

I didn't tell him that this was my first real dinner date. And I didn't tell him that I wanted to get to know the real me as much as he did. I had some things to figure out before I could tell my story out loud. But looking across the table at Corlis—and listening to him talk, in between bites of ribs, about how his father used to own the Cowboy Mart—I had the feeling, for the first time in my life, that anything was possible.

I guess "Always on My Mind" is a love song. But it isn't like the ones my father listened to. Instead of heartbreak, it's about missed opportunities and the chance to set things right. When Corlis took me back to the apartment I rented after the second big fire, he asked whether I'd mind if he didn't kiss me goodnight. "It's not that I don't want to," he said. "I promise. I just think we should wait."

On our second date, Corlis gave me a robin feather. "Because of your eyes," he said. The feather was gray, edged with white. As he drove me up to Garner State Park, I brushed it back and forth across my finger-tips and marveled at its softness and lightness. We swam in the Frio River, rented a paddle boat, then walked over to the concession building for jukebox dancing. Of course, Corlis played "Always on My Mind." That day he told me about his time in the Army, about what it was like to fight in a tank in the First Gulf War, about how the shells he fired turned into flame when they penetrated another tank's armor and burned the enemy crew alive, and about how that made him feel. When he dropped me off, he asked if he could kiss me. His lips were as soft and light as the robin feather.

On our third date, we picked up fried chicken and went to Corlis's house. He introduced me to his mother, Darlene, and we visited for a while as best we could with someone whose brain was wasting away like my soul had been before Corlis looked into my eyes. After he put his mother to bed, he and I went out onto the front porch and ate our chicken, and I told him the story of my life. In fits and starts, the same way Corlis had spoken to me that first day at the Cowboy Mart, I told him about my father and about the first big fire. I explained as best I could about what happened at Jordan High School, and about my life after that. I talked about the second big fire and the reasons behind it. By the time I finished, the blue-and-yellow neon PLAY LOTTERY sign had long since gone dark in the Cowboy Mart window, and the only light in the neighborhood came from the streetlamps. In the faint greenish glow, I searched Corlis's face for some kind of reaction to all the awful things I'd done.

"I am so sorry," he said finally. There was no judgment in his eyes and no pity either. Just love. It was the first time I'd seen that emotion in a man's eyes. Anyway, the first time I'd seen it directed at me. "Do you remember how I told you on our first date that the only thing on my mind for the past week was you?" he asked softly. "It's still true."

I spent the rest of that night in Corlis's bedroom. He fed me bacon and eggs at first light. When we stepped outside, dawn was breaking, the clouds sun-streaked feathers in the Southwest Texas sky. Then he walked me across the street to work.

Three weeks later, we were standing in front of the Justice of the

Peace at the historic courthouse in downtown Jordan. Corlis had on the same green button-down and black silk tie that he wore to the Chuck-wagon. I wore the dress he bought me, robin's egg blue, the color of my eyes. The courthouse in Jordan looks like a castle with a red-tile roof. And as I stood there next to Corlis, I felt like a happy ending might actually be possible if I could just find a fairytale that fits the story of the real me.

For now, I'll call part three in my story: "Rosemary Holybee, Always on Corlis's Mind, Twenty-Nine Years Old." I don't know how long this part will last. I've never been around a relationship that worked, much less been in one. And even though he hasn't said so, I worry that Corlis has doubts of his own—the least of which is helping raise other men's kids.

But the boys are with us every other weekend now. Corlis's military record and his job at the post office helped me win the visitation case against my father's mother. Corlis's mother, Darlene, with her advanced Alzheimer's, doesn't know who the boys are most of the time. Sometimes I feel the same way. But they all love Corlis's postal carrier uniform, and they want to drive the mail truck. I guess that's a start.

We are all a work in progress. So far part three in the story of the real me is a love song, one I've never heard before but have been waiting my whole life to sing. Corlis and I, and the boys, are writing the words as we go.

Mexico
in which Beau returns Rooster's gift
(2000)

The rising sun smeared the sky bloodred, stained the coming thunderheads into mounds of raw meat roiling up off the Gulf. The south wind whooshed through the catclaw and mesquite thicket Beau Mulebach was making slow progress through, the horse limping along behind him as the first heavy drops of rain started to fall.

"Easy there, old man," Beau said as the horse spooked, jerking back against the reins in his hand. "It's just a hurricane is all." He turned, stroked Mexico's neck, rubbed the bony outcrop of withers beneath the saddlehorn.

The horse nudged Beau, pressing him back toward the left stirrup, and he couldn't help but smile despite the nature of their errand and the big weather coming on. Pushing thirty years old now, snaggle-toothed and arthritis-bent, Mexico was once as game a brush-popper as there'd ever been and the best roping horse in Southwest Texas—as devil-may-care as the man who'd spent his life in the saddle Beau strapped on before day-break: Rooster Stiles, for Beau's money the greatest all-around cowboy who ever lived.

"One last ride?" He scratched the base of the bay's mane. "I don't know about that." In the bloody half-light he took in Mexico's swollen knees, his legs gnarled like the storm-bent mesquites the two of them stood among, his wasted muscles. Beau had led the horse all the way from the old Jubak stables—Mulebach stables now, although that was still hard to wrap his head around—to the thicket they stood in now, a distance of almost a mile. Saddled and bridled, yes. But only as a gesture of respect on this final trip into the brush. "We'd best walk this last bit."

He felt Mexico nudge him again, urging him to mount. As if the horse knew about the pistol in the saddlebag, knew the reason the two of them were here. And against his better judgment, Beau snugged his hat down tight and swung up into Rooster Stiles's saddle, feeling Mexico stagger forward, the branches crackling and popping as thorns snagged Beau's shirt and jeans and the wind snatched at his hat. He'd dreamed of sitting in this saddle since he was eight years old, watching Rooster beat Rex Marshall in the thousand-dollar roping match that had cost Rex a finger and become a legend in Southwest Texas. But this wasn't the way Beau had envisioned his first time on the hurricane deck of Rooster's big bay stallion—a stumbling, one-way ride to a mercy killing.

The rain was coming down harder now, stinging his face like the catclaw branches. But it was welcome. A drought-breaking rain, despite the flooding and tornadoes that were predicted to come with it, a rain to refill empty lakes and get the Frio River—that had run completely dry—flowing again. The best the old horse could manage was a lopsided half-lope that joggled Beau in the saddle as they burst out of the thicket into a patch of fire-blackened prickly pear grazed almost to the ground by his hungry cattle. He'd seared the spines off the nopales with a pear-burner the week before because the grass was gone, the brindle crossbred cows that usually ran at the sight of a man afoot following close behind him through the August heat, descending on the cactus leaves the minute the flames scorched them bare of thorns. He knew that the rain would send green shoots of native grama and bluestem grass sprouting again, provide planting moisture for pastures of coastal Bermuda, make possible a new start for this brushcountry land that was newly his. And in the spring he'd buy the beginnings of a herd of registered Black Angus that would vault this nineteenth-century holdover of a cattleranch into the modern era.

But first, he told himself, he had to make an ending.

It had been coming for six months now, that ending, since the day he and Cecil Jubak sat down with the banker and signed the papers to make the old Jubak ranch Beau's. To celebrate, he'd walked out of the Jordan State Bank and paid May Belle Stiles a thousand dollars—that should've been spent on fixing fences and building pens, clearing brush and seeding pastures—for Rooster's horse and saddle. As he worked to modernize the Jubak place he'd bought when Cecil's father died, and integrate it with the Mulebach ranch he'd inherited when his own father passed, Beau watched the equine arthritis worsen despite the pampering he gave the horse: Mexico's stride shortening more every day, his back hollowing, his knees twisting so bad he could barely bend them. The last thing Beau had wanted to do at five o'clock this morning was crawl out of his and Wanda's bed in the old Jubak house that they were still settling into and lead Mexico into the brush to put a bullet in his brain. But Beau couldn't bear to see the horse suffer even one more day, and cleaning up after the hurricane that was blowing in would have to occupy his full attention—or the future he was birthing for the ranch and for his family would die stillborn.

It was as if the horse had known all along where they were headed.

Mexico staggered through a thicket of huisache and guajillo into the once-grassy, now barren, vega where Beau had spent the last three mornings digging a grave broad enough to hold a horse and deep enough so the starving coyotes couldn't dig up the body. It was in this very spot that Rooster Stiles had died of a heart attack almost twenty years ago, in the saddle Beau sat in now, riding after outlaw cattle at the Jubaks' fall round-up. He brought the horse up next to the mound of dirt he'd left at the edge of the pit and dismounted, draping the saddlebag over his shoulder as he led Mexico down the gentle slope to join Rooster at that big rodeo in the sky.

"Well done, old man," Beau said, stroking the horse's neck that felt warm after their ride despite the rain that was slashing sideways in sheets now and the wind that was howling. "I should've known all along you had it in you."

He opened the saddlebag and pulled out the cow horn necklace that Rooster had given him at his first roundup, and that Rooster's mentor, Old Man Merriweather, had given Rooster at his. The horn was black, about the length of a grown man's fingers, with a silver cap at the base and a wicked point at the business end. Old Man Merriweather had sawed it off the outlaw cow that gutted his horse in an epic brush-battle that had become as much the stuff of legend as Rooster's thousand-dollar roping match. The horsehair braid that served as a chain had been cut from the dead horse's tail after the mercy killing. It had once been blonde, almost white; but Beau had taken black hair from Mexico's mane and extended the length of the braid so it would stretch around the horse's neck. And he put it there now, reaching up and tying it carefully. Beau had worn that good luck charm to every roping match and rodeo, every round-up and cattleworking he'd been a part of since the day he'd gotten it from Rooster, and he was loathe to let it go. But the time had come to return it.

"Before I do this," Beau said, looking deep into the horse's soft brown eyes, "I need you to know why. It's better for a greatheart like you to go out clean than to waste away so stove up he can't even move. I couldn't let May Belle send you off to the kill auction in Stephenville, then on that awful trailer ride to the Beltex slaughterhouses in Juarez. Don't get me wrong. It ain't May Belle's fault that she had to part ways with you. She couldn't keep you up anymore. I thought I might be able to pamper you, make you game as a green-broke colt for a little while. But turning back time is beyond my power. This thing I'm about to do, it's the right thing to do."

He reached into the saddlebag, and grasping the pistol, leaned his face against the horse's face, breathing into Mexico's nose with his nose and scratching the horse's whiskery chin. As he felt Mexico relax, Beau stroked the horse's broad forehead, counting the distance of four fingers down the midline. Then he eased the pistol up out of the saddlebag and into the kill spot, closed his eyes, and squeezed the trigger.

The explosion left Beau deaf and smelling burnt gunpowder, and when he opened his eyes after the longest moment of his life, the ringing in his ears was still so fierce he could hardly hear the storm. The horse lay peaceful and still as though he was sleeping. The cow horn necklace rested against his chest, the silver shining back the red half-light, and all of a sudden Beau found himself remembering Rooster's funeral. He saw again the sea of hatband-creased foreheads bowed in prayer and Rooster lying there in that casket looking so small, the same way Mexico looked lying here in a homemade grave slowly filling with rain.

And it seemed to Beau, as he put the pistol back into the saddlebag and picked up the shovel, that instead of up off the Gulf, the hurricane had come howling straight out of the Book of Revelation. He felt the wind take his hat as he started shoveling, not knowing whether the wetness on his face was tears or blood, or whether he was making an ending or a beginning.

Words to Live By

in which Joe learns a lesson about loyalty

(2000)

I. Big Picture

5:39 a.m. Wife, thirty-two years old. Son, six months. Both mine. Elizabeth and Jacob. Spooned together in the bed I've just left, they are probably asleep again after my frenzied departure. House, three-bedroom, one bath. The bank's. 3616 South 2nd Street. Built in 1983, 132 thousand dollar note at 6¼ percent cosigned by my father, monthly payment more than half my take-home pay from job #1.

Job #1. Mine. Full-time faculty at Austin Community College, a 5/5 load at $32,532 plus a coffee cup, a living wage only when supplemented by job #2.

Job #2. Mine also. Part-time waitperson at Aqua Vitae Café, $2.01 per hour plus tips, sufficient to cover my student loan payment and a mostly beans and rice diet for Elizabeth and myself. Jacob, nursing still, has no idea.

5:39 a.m. Father, fifty-nine years old. Mother, fifty-six. Both mine and mine alone. Big Joe and Edna. They are probably sitting elbows-down at the kitchen table in the ranch house where I grew up, finishing their second cups of coffee as they wait for enough daylight so the old man can check the cattle—which he believes to be the most loyal animals on earth—and questioning the wisdom of cosigning the oversized mortgage of their overeducated and underpaid only son.

II. Day-to-Day

5:39 a.m. Self. Thirty-five years old. Hunched bleary-eyed over the steering wheel, I find myself losing sight of the big picture, getting bogged down in the day-to-day. I am blowing through stop signs and red lights like a hurricane up off the Gulf of Mexico, calling in late to job #2 for the second time this morning, predawn. As I speed past the police substation at Oltorf and South First Street, I remember the recurring dream in which I am a lobster about to be tossed into a pot of boiling water, and I whisper a prayer: "Please God no please God—"

"Aqua Vitae Café!" someone shouts into my ear. "Home of the twenty-four hour pterodactyl. Glow-in-the-dark latenite land. Birthplace of the Mother's Day Lobster Brunch. This is Bruno! How may I help you?"

"Bruno, it's Joe again," I say into the cell phone that Elizabeth's father is paying for. "I'm running—"

"You mean Joe Teacher Joe, or Joe the Lead Singer of the Pixels Joe? You don't sound much like Joe Manager Joe, and anyway—"

"It's Joe Teacher Joe!" Seeing the police substation unmanned and the parking lot empty, I run the red light at Oltorf and South First with the cell phone in one hand and my Austin Community College coffee cup in the other, steering the car with one knee. "Bruno. Listen. Take a message. Tell Manager Joe I'm running a little later than—"

"Joe Manager Joe's right here! Hold on, Joe Teacher Joe."

"No, Bruno!"

"Half past five was ten minutes ago," Manager Joe snarls into my ear. "Be here by quarter till six, or don't come at all."

"I'll be there, I swear! Just don't fire me when I walk in the door. And don't hang up! Put Bruno back on."

"Hey, Joe Teacher Joe."

"Hey, Bruno. Listen. I'll pay you ten bucks to start my brunch set-up for me. Ten bucks, Bruno, to cut and stock desserts. What do you say?"

"Sold, Joe Teacher Joe! What do I do?"

"Just give the phone back to Manager Joe."

"The next words out of your mouth better be: *I'm pulling into the alley right now.*"

"Even better. Bruno's agreed to start my set-up for me. If you'll just walk him through cutting and stocking desserts, and agree not to fire me, I'll work this shift off the clock."

"Slave labor? Hmm . . . Words to live by. You've got a chronic time-management problem, Teacher Joe. But I like the way you talk."

I hang a right on Johanna, hearing the tires squeal as I fishtail once and line out. Then I whip into the alley behind Aqua Vitae Café, skid to a stop inches from the back fence, and—apron in one hand and briefcase in the other—hurdle the back gate, one-hop the patio steps, and duck in the side door.

III. Food Mud, Screaming Music, Latenite, Aqua Vitae Café

5:42 a.m. The only thing I can smell is the dishroom—two sinks full of food-caked pots and pans behind a partition of shelves stacked with bustubs that have been full of the ashtray-and-egg remains of too many breakfasts for too many hours. The music—some kind of weird keening scream—invades my ears in the same way the dishroom invades my nostrils. I stride up the narrow throughway that runs the length of the back of the house at Aqua Vitae Café, past the kitchen on my right and on my left coffeemakers and coffee cups and tea urns on stainless steel counters that should all be sparkling clean in the bright shift-change light but are instead dull with food slime.

The food stink and the keening scream prod my sleep-starved brain like dirty fingers as I try to tally up shift-change duties that the latenite waitpeople have left undone. Farther up on the right, I see Manager Joe's waist-length black braid whipping back and forth as he harries the much larger Bruno like a cow dog driving a herd bull. "More cutting, Bruno! Less grazing!" I hear Manager Joe bark. "The next bite of apple torte comes out of your check."

"I'm unofficially here!" I shout at Manager Joe, once I'm past his line of sight.

"Congratulations. Finish shift change by six, or it's officially your ass!"

5:43 a.m. Considering the circumstances, the state of latenite-to-brunch shift-change affairs in the front of the house looks almost rosy. The breakfast counter is empty except for two latenite waitpeople, Gothic in black leather and multiple silver studs poked through various body parts. The waitgoths—a guy with blond dreadlocks and a junk habit named Jeremy and a girl named Chay with blue Chinese characters tattooed on her face and arms—are doing their checkouts and smoking hand-rolled cigarettes. Out on the waitfloor, beneath the trademark Aqua Vitae Café pterodactyl dangling from the ceiling on invisible wires, all four seated tables have their orders already. If I can get the Quote of the Day done, get creamers out on the tables, get coffee and tea brewed in seventeen minutes, and get the waitgoths to knock out the rest of their closing duties while I'm getting it done, I'll get to keep job #2 another day.

Through the window in the wall above the breakfast bar, I see Manager Joe still giving Bruno hell. But the keening scream is so loud I can hardly hear him. "Those back counters are still filthy," I shout in Chay's direction as I step up to the bar. "Whose closing sidework would that be?"

"Actually, that would be opening sidework," Chay shouts back at me and half-grins. Then she stabs a half-smoked butt in my direction. "Yours, for coming in fifty-eight minutes late."

"No way."

"Way!" Manager Joe snarls through the breakfast bar window, his hearing apparently more acute than mine. "Wipe down the back counters,

Teacher Joe. And get it done by 6 a.m., or get the hell out!"

Chay's half-grin widens so that it wrinkles the Chinese characters on her face.

I stow my briefcase in the hoststand cabinet, pull out the magic marker bag, haul down the special board for the Quote of the Day, then squeeze into the narrow wedge of breakfast counter not already occupied by latenite waitgoths, their piles of tickets, their stacks of crumpled money, and the ash-coated remains of their breakfast food. I pull a red magic marker from the bag, grip it tightly, and—visualizing the business end as a tongue depressor mashing down on Manager Joe's offending member—I write across the top of the special board: QUOTE OF THE DAY. I pull out a green marker, and—visualizing the business end as an otoscope poking through Manager Joe's overly acute eardrums—I write across the bottom of the special board: WIN A TWO-EGG BREAKFAST! Then I pull out a black marker, stare into the vast expanse of blank white space between the red and green letters, and grope for a Latin phrase that captures my feelings about Manager Joe but does not contain the word *colonoscopy*.

"I think you should write: *Accept humiliation as a surprise*," Chay says, flicking ash onto the special board. This phrase from the *Tao Te Ching* is the quote Chay has tattooed in blue Chinese characters across her forehead. The quotes on her arms are from *The Art of War*. "Words to live by. Wouldn't you say so, Teacher Joe?"

"I think you should write something for Mother's Day," Jeremy says.

"Mother's Day and humiliation go together like lobster and eggs," Chay says. "Just ask Teacher Joe." She jabs her cigarette into my face like a smoking gun. "Besides, Teacher Joe owes me one. I'd be home by now, if I hadn't picked up those four tables for his tardy ass. And he'd be fired."

"You're right, Chay," I say. "I do owe you. And this particular Mother's Day has already been humiliating enough to surprise even me."

Manager Joe's snarling face reappears in the breakfast bar window. "I'm headed back to check the lobster tank," he says. "If you want to avoid any more surprises, you'd best get your ass in gear."

I look at Manager Joe's black braid swinging from side to side as he stalks off into the back of the house. I look down at the blank white space on the special board. Then I write, in letters the color of Manager Joe's hair: *VESCERE BRACIS MEIS.*

IV. Eat My Shorts

5:46 a.m. "That doesn't look like *Accept humiliation as a surprise*

98

to me," I hear Chay say over my shoulder. "What does it mean?"

"'Eat my shorts.'"

"Eat mine, you ungrateful son of a bitch."

"No, Chay. That's what the sign says. *Vescere bracis meis*. Eat my shorts."

"Bullshit."

"I swear to God."

"Don't swear to God," Jeremy says. "It's bad karma."

"Hey, maybe that Latin crap is good for something after all," Chay says. "*Vescere bracis meis*, Jeremy."

"*Vescere bracis meis* yourself, Chay."

"Darling!" Chay says. "Your place or mine?" She locks her mouth on Jeremy's and blows smoke out his nose.

5:47 a.m. I hang the Quote of the Day sign over the hoststand; dump, clean, and rinse the coffee pots and tea urns; put fresh coffee and tea on to brew.

5:53 a.m. I fill the creamers from the milk cow—a stainless steel milk dispenser with a valve-stem for a teat—and place fresh creamer set-ups onto all twenty-four tables on the waitfloor. Then I make a rapid-fire round beneath the dangling pterodactyl, pulling old creamers and dirty ashtrays off into a bustub and wiping all twenty unseated tables with a rag soaked in bleachwater strong enough to sterilize the floor of a barn.

5:58 a.m. I wipe the food slime off the back counters with a rag soaked in that same bleachwater, then toss the rag into a slime-filmed bleachwater bucket for the second brunch waitperson to dump.

"Time!" I yell down the throughway in Manager Joe's direction.

6:00 a.m. The weird keening scream is suddenly cut off. Everyone in the restaurant pauses. Blinks. Looks around. Then the moment of silence that marks the official transition from latenite to brunch gives way to *The Emperor Concerto*'s opening chord, and we all start moving again in E-flat major.

"Shift change!" I say, clearing the ash-coated breakfast remains from in front of Chay and Jeremy, who are still locked tight at the lips. "No more smoking. And take the lip-lock outside."

I find Bruno in the dishroom, working hard to catch up. "Hey, Joe Teacher Joe!" he says, without looking up from the twin pot-and-pan-filled sinks he would've emptied already with his bulging, tattoo-covered arms, if doing my desserts hadn't put him behind. "What's the Quote of the Day?"

"*Vescere bracis meis.*"

"Cool! What does it mean?"

"'Thank you very much,'" I say, "in Latin." Then I step into the dishroom and slip a ten-dollar bill into his apron pocket.

"Way cool! *Vescere bracis meis*, Joe Teacher Joe!"

"*Vescere bracis meis*, Bruno," I say. "And don't forget to thank Manager Joe when he cuts you loose."

I carry the clean pots and pans back to the prep room, thinking of Chay's sly half-grin. It's a stupid expression—about on a level with cows chewing their cuds—and probably the most obnoxious form a smile can take. But at least she's smiling. I stand in the prep room, trying to remember the last time I smiled.

Then I catch sight of the lobster tank. There are at least a dozen lobsters hunched around the aerator, their claws wired closed, crawling all over each other in a blood-colored pile. Instead of a smile, I find myself remembering my recurring lobster nightmare—the pots and pans in my hands like cold metal claws as I fight for room to breathe, waiting on a one-way trip to the lobster pot.

It's all I can do not to duck back out the side door and run for my life.

V. Room to Breathe

6:02 a.m. Wife, red-haired, pale-skinned, lovely. Hopeful in the face of our house-poverty, she is probably still sleeping peacefully as the first rays of sun steal through the blinds. Her middle name is Faith but ought to be *foolhardy*. Son, pale-skinned like his mother, all his other features mine. His middle name is Joseph, after his grandfather and me, but ought to be *Mastercard*.

6:02 a.m. Father, leather-skinned from a life spent working in the Southwest Texas sun, none of his features mine except his disposition. Stubbornly optimistic beneath a camouflage of pessimism, he is probably killing the engine on his battered work truck and starting to pair up cows and calves, listening to the rustle of the cattle—which I believe to be the stupidest animals on earth—grazing in the thick Bermuda grass, and chewing their cuds.

VI. Lobster Pot

6:02 a.m. Self, bleary-headed in a string-tied apron and strapped-on smile. Hating Aqua Vitae, but glad not to be staring at cows engaged in nature's most brainless activity—or arguing with my father about whether cattle are the most loyal, or the stupidest, animals on the face of the earth—I greet Barkeep as he makes his usual Sunday morning entrance in a sweat-soaked workout suit, military haircut, and stubbly beard.

Barkeep glances up at the Quote of the Day, smiling his tight-lipped ex-Airborne smile. "Eat your own shorts, buddy," he says. Barkeep, who spent his formative years in the Airborne Infantry and now tends bar at a place up Congress Avenue, has been dating one of the Aqua Vitae waitpeople—a lifer named Annie who has an invalid child. Where Barkeep learned his Latin, I have no clue.

"Not for a million dollars, Barkeep. I know where they've been." I meet him at the breakfast bar with a cup of Aqua Vitae Blend, a fresh creamer, and a glass of water with no ice. In the face of the Beethoven concerto, Chay and Jeremy have retreated to the patio, and I wipe down the counter while Barkeep settles onto his usual stool. "How would you like your free eggs?"

"Scrambled this morning," he says, "with a short stack of gingerbread-blueberry pancakes on the side."

"I'll have to charge you a dollar for the blueberries."

"*Alea iacta est,*" he says.

"Hail Caesar," I say. "I'll hang your ticket while you march on Rome."

6:05 a.m. I hang Barkeep's ticket, but there is no one in the kitchen. So I walk around to the flattop and throw the cakes down myself. I dimple the sizzling gingerbread batter with a handful of fresh blueberries, then head back around to the breakfast bar to refill Barkeep's cup. Barkeep drinks coffee faster and hotter than anyone I've ever seen.

While I splash hot, fresh Aqua Vitae Blend into Barkeep's cup, I make a visual inspection of the waitfloor. The purple Aqua Vitae pterodactyl, seen from this angle, seems to be swooping over Barkeep's shoulder. It's like a glimpse back through time into a prehistoric age—an age when work was done for the simple purpose of survival, and there were no mortgages, no student loan debts, no tables to wait, and no briefcases full of exams waiting to be graded.

6:08 a.m. There is still no one in the kitchen. So I walk around to the flattop and flip Barkeep's gingerbread-blueberry shortstack, then head down the line to start work on his eggs. When I look up from egg-beating, I see Himmler—Bruno the dishwasher's brother, the six-foot-six, shave-headed cook and Aryan Nations member who should've been here at 6 a.m.—hulking beside me, looking down.

"Hey, Teacher Joe. Thanks for getting things started. My brother says you tipped him ten dollars," Himmler says. "When the Aryan Nations avenge Waco, you will be spared. Now get your ass out of my kitchen and don't bring it back in."

"Hey, Himmler. Could you make sure the cakes and eggs on this first ticket come out hot and fresh, and together? I think my timing was a little off."

"Could you get your ass out of my kitchen? And get me some coffee while you're at it?"

"Thanks, Himmler," I say. "Coffee's on the way."

I set a cup of Aqua Vitae Blend on the counter at the very edge of Himmler's kitchen sanctuary and then make a refilling run—coffee pot in one hand and water pitcher in the other—by Barkeep at the breakfast counter and by all four tables of latenite leftovers still lingering on the waitfloor. By the time I'm back, Himmler is putting plates of cakes and eggs in the pick-up window.

I set cakes and eggs and syrup in front of Barkeep, then slip over to the hoststand, haul a stack of final exams out of my briefcase, head back over to the counter, and—Austin Community College coffee cup in one hand and red pen in the other—start making red marks on tests just as fast as my fingers will move.

"Who are today's victims?" Barkeep asks.

"Classic Civ 1613," I say. "The only thing they remember about Rome is that it had the first shopping mall."

"Trajan's Market," Barkeep says. "AD 112."

"A-plus," I say. "I'd give you a free two-egg breakfast, but you're already eating one. How is everything?"

"It's been better, Joe. Everything has been a whole lot better."

"Don't blame me!" Himmler shouts through the window. "Teacher Joe waited too long to start the eggs."

"I'm sorry, Barkeep," I say, noticing only now that Barkeep—who usually goes through breakfast food as fast as he does Aqua Vitae Blend—has hardly touched his cakes and eggs. "It's my fault. I can't seem to get caught up these days."

"It's not the food, buddy. It's Annie. We've been seeing a lot of each other lately. Truth be told, I'd like to ask her to move in with me. But she's having major problems with her son, Crockett, and I don't want her to think I'm asking her to move in just to help her out. I don't know what to say to her. She's independent, you know? If I ask her to move in, I'm a male chauvinist bastard. If I don't ask her to move in, I'm a commitment-phobic son of a bitch. I feel like there's no way to win."

I look hard into Barkeep's eyes that I notice only now are

102

bloodshot and baggy. I grope for words, but nothing comes. "*Me miseret*," I say at last.

"I'm sorry, too. But I still don't know what to say to Annie. I keep trying to think of the right thing, you know? *Cogito, ergo sum*." Then he translates for Himmler, who is leaning through the window and hanging on every word: "'I think, therefore I am.'"

"*Cogito, ergo doleo*," I say. "'*I think, therefore I am depressed.*'"

"*Cogito sumere potum alterum!*" Barkeep says, and smiles his tight-lipped smile. "'I think I'll have another drink!'"

"I could use a drink myself," I say. "I think we all could."

"Eat my shorts, buddy. I'm off the clock. And hey, speaking of Annie, isn't she here yet?"

"Not yet," I say. "Come to think of it, I guess I'm off the clock myself. But that's not keeping me from working." Then, suddenly remembering that I've got papers to grade, I slap a C-minus on another test.

"Say, Joe, you don't look so good yourself," Barkeep says. "What's the buzz?"

"I had a very bad dream that came true," I say.

"You and Martin Luther King!" Himmler shouts through the pick-up window.

"What was the dream?" Barkeep asks, ignoring Himmler.

"I was a lobster among tank lobsters, with my claws wired closed."

"You really could use a drink, buddy," Barkeep says. "Come down to Ego's sometime when I'm working, and have a couple of drafts on the house."

"Seriously?" I ask.

"Seriously."

"I still have to charge you a dollar for those blueberries," I say.

"That's okay, buddy. The draft beer's still free."

6:28 a.m. I put the graded exams into alphabetical order, place them back into my briefcase with four stacks of ungraded finals, and clear Barkeep's half-empty plates from the breakfast counter.

"Can I wrap this to go for you, Barkeep?"

"I think I'll sit here a while and wait on Annie," he says, sliding a five-dollar bill across the counter. "Keep the change. What was the final tally on those exams?"

"One A, two B's, ten C's, fourteen D's, and five F's."

"*Nil desperandum*," Barkeep says.

"Never despair," I say slowly. "Words to live by. If I ever get home today, maybe I'll share them with my wife."

103

VII. Kill, Kill, Kill Them All

6:33 a.m. I wipe down the counter, bus the four dirty tables that the latenite leftovers have abandoned in their flight from the coming sun, then set out a two-pound bag of Aqua Vitae Blend beans for Harry the Hippy, another of my regulars who comes in every Sunday morning, precisely at seven, to pick up his weekly coffee supply. By the time I'm done, Barkeep's cup is empty again.

"Hey, buddy," Barkeep says, "how about a little splash of high octane?"

I refill Barkeep's coffee, then haul another stack of ungraded exams out of my briefcase. The first test I grade is a borderline D-minus/F from a student I've had problems with the whole semester—he's gone to the head of the Humanities Department twice on my account, once to complain about my ridiculous attendance policy and once to complain about my unfair grading standards—and after struggling with myself for a full two minutes, and guiltily assigning the test a grade of C in hopes of avoiding an appeal and another trip to the head of the Humanities Department's office, it is all I can do to pick up the next exam.

"Wanna talk about it?" Barkeep asks.

"I'm in debt up to my eyeballs, I hate both my jobs, I never get to see my family, my sex life has stopped, I haven't gotten a good night's sleep since my son was born, and I started my morning by getting up late so I'm working this shift off the clock."

"That's not so bad. Anything else?"

"Yeah," I say, looking out the front window and feeling my heart sink into my filth-encrusted shoes. "A student I've been having problems with the whole semester, and who I just gave a C instead of an F on a Final Exam just to keep from ever having to see him again, is about to walk in the front door with what looks like his entire family."

"Okay, that's bad."

6:42 a.m. I lean through the pick-up window and tell Himmler we're getting a ten-top. His response would send a saint to Purgatory. Thinking of penance, I watch the family of my problem student drag tables together out on the waitfloor while I count out ten menus and silverware setups. By the time I've got everything together, they're all seated at a makeshift ten-top that takes up space enough to seat twenty. My problem student is at the head of the table. Once I've handed out menus and silverware, I talk to him first.

"Good morning, Mr. Wiles," I say.

"Good morning, Dr. Jasmine," he says. "Nice apron."

"Thanks. Can I start you out with some coffee?"

"First let me introduce you to my mother," he says, smiling at the handsome older woman sitting next to him in a black formal dress. She has diamonds in her ears the size of blueberries. "Mother? Meet Dr. Jasmine. He's the teacher I've told you so much about."

"You should be ashamed of yourself," the old woman says, her eyes blazing like her diamonds.

"My father would say the same thing, if he could see me right now. Would you like to start with some coffee?"

"Bring all of us coffee," she says. "Except the children of course. Bring them orange juice. You do have orange juice, don't you?"

"Yes, ma'am."

"Then hop to it."

6:45 a.m. I load eight cups of Aqua Vitae blend, two O.J.'s, and ten icewaters onto an oval tray and set them down on the Wiles's table, starting with the mother and working my way around to finish up with her son. "Are you ready to order breakfast?"

"We'll all have the lobster and eggs special," the mother says. "With buttermilk pancakes as our side orders."

"I'm sorry, ma'am," I say. "But we don't start serving lobster until 9 a.m."

"Ridiculous," the old woman says.

"But true," I say.

"We'll see about that," the old woman says. "Bring me a manager."

6:50 a.m. Manager Joe swings open the office door after at least thirty seconds of pounding. "This had better be good," he snarls.

"The host and the second brunch waitperson are late," I say, "and there's a ten-top on the waitfloor. They all want to order lobster."

The look on Manager Joe's face is grim. "The host was supposed to be Kurt. But Kurt's having girlfriend problems, and he won't be here for another hour."

"So what's new?"

"One thing that's new, Teacher Joe, is that Kurt will be written up when he comes in. This will be his final warning. Another new thing is that the second waitperson was supposed to be Annie, who was supposed to be getting a ride to work from Kurt because that piece of shit Beetle she drives is broken down again. But when I called and told her to find another ride, she told me that her crippled kid was sick. In short, you're going to be on your own for a while."

"What about the ten-top?"

"Tell your ten-top they're welcome to have the lobster. Tell them Himmler will be happy to start boiling them now. Tell Himmler I said so. Now get back out there and hold things together until I can get some more bodies in here."

6:55 a.m. In the time it took me to talk to Manager Joe, three more tables have seated themselves on the waitfloor. I deliver menus and silverware setups, and take their drink orders. Then I inform the Wiles party that they will indeed be eating lobster.

"The manager says you're welcome to order the special now," I say to Mrs. Wiles.

"I thought as much," the old woman says, her smile diamond-hard and bright. "Your lobster policy is almost as ridiculous and unfair as your attendance policy and grading standards. I plan to have a talk with the head of the Humanities Department first thing tomorrow morning."

6:57 a.m. When I run drinks to my three new tables, they all order the lobster with buttermilk pancakes as their side orders.

7:02 a.m. I hand the two-pound bag of Aqua Vitae Blend that I set up earlier to Harry the Hippy, who must've slipped in while I was taking my last round of orders. I take Harry the Hippy's money, and keep his change. Then I hang tickets for all four of the orders I just took, all at once, with a total of seventeen lobsters and thirty-four buttermilk pancakes among them. Himmler's response consists almost exclusively of the word *fuck*—coupling barnyard animals, vegetables, and assorted kitchen appliances to every imaginable orifice on myself and Manager Joe and our mothers, the customers and their mothers, even the purple pterodactyl and its mother, at a volume which raises the possibility that even the pterodactyl's mother will be able to hear.

7:03 a.m. The effect of Himmler's tirade on the customers is almost exactly the same as the one I observed when the weird keening scream was suddenly cut off during shift change. Everyone in the restaurant pauses. Blinks. Looks around. Even Harry the Hippy—a man who has lived longer and harder, and seen and done more than anyone else I know in Austin—looks shocked.

"*¡Increíble!*" Harry says, his face, above his braided white beard, looking as dazed as faces of the rest of the customers. "That's going to cost you some tip dollars, my boy."

"If not for my wife and son, my mortgage, and my student loans, I'd be saying the same thing."

"I hear you, buddy," Barkeep says. "I work with the public myself. What I always do, when I can't toss a customer out on his ass, is picture him in the most embarrassing scene I can imagine."

"Does it work?" I ask.

"It's always good for a smile."

"Can it, Himmler!" I hear Manager Joe bark, behind me. Then he goes on, much lower, "Why all the negativity toward mothers?"

"This world was built by a loving and perfect God that does not

106

accept mothers who won't take *no* for an answer."

"Are you saying you know the mind of God?"

"I'm saying the Apocalypse is near at hand, my friend, and I intend to go out in an orgy of blood and bowel-spurting."

"Find somebody else to insult."

"Who?"

"Anyone but the customers. And you, Teacher Joe," Manager Joe snarls at me. "How about giving a little service to the ones that just walked in?"

On the waitfloor behind me, I see three new tables seating themselves, and one that has already self-seated. "I'm on it," I say. Then I look at Harry the Hippy. "Can I get you a cup of coffee, Harry?"

"I've got to go. *Buena suerte*, my boy."

"Thanks, Harry. You, too."

7:15 a.m. I gather up menus, silverware setups, and a coffee pot. But before I head for the waitfloor, I stop back by the bar. "I talked to Manager Joe," I say to Barkeep as I top off his cup. "He says that Annie won't be coming in." Then I make a drink-taking and refilling round. I'm apologizing the whole way around, moving from coffee cup to empty coffee cup, trying to smooth the ruffled feathers of mothers and offspring who have not only been insulted by Himmler but also had their coffees run dry.

7:20 a.m. I put together the four new drink orders and make my way back across the restaurant, setting down coffees and icewaters and O.J.'s, and taking breakfast orders as I go.

7:25 a.m. I hang all four new tickets, again all at once, and hear Himmler break into a series of intricate variations on the use of the f-bomb the likes of which I've never heard. This time, most of them seem to be aimed at waitpeople who hang multiple tickets.

"At least none of them ordered lobster and cakes!" I say into a break in the string of expletives that comes as Himmler places plates of lobster and pancakes in the pickup window.

7:30 a.m. As I stack the Wiles order onto two oval trays, Himmler breaks into song. The tune is "Row, Row, Row Your Boat," but the words have been altered:

Kill, kill, kill them all
Kill them all real slow
Shackle them, flay their skin, cut off their balls
Then choke off their airflow.

7:32 a.m. Manager Joe, in the kitchen helping Himmler throw down enough food to fill all the orders I've taken, actually starts to sing along. Then I hear Barkeep take up the song as well.

"What are you still doing here?" I ask. "I figured you'd be on your way to Annie's by now."

"Moral support," Barkeep says in a pause between stanzas. "You looked like you could use a dose. Remember to picture them in as embarrassing a scene as you can think of."

I nod, heft both oval trays, and stagger toward the Wiles party.

7:33 a.m. I set the oval trays down on a couple of empty tables and start to unload them, setting lobster and pancakes down in front of Mrs. Wiles first, and then working my way around the table to end up with her son.

"It's about time," she says.

"Yes, ma'am," I say, handing out cracking tools and refilling coffees, the whole time trying to come up with a scene embarrassing enough to do the job.

7:37 a.m. As I load three more tickets worth of lobster and cakes onto the two oval trays and start back across the waitfloor, I notice that the customers have started to sing Himmler's song, even though it's them Himmler is singing about skinning, castrating, and killing.

7:38 a.m. I check the Wiles table as I pass by, and see that they are all happily chewing and swallowing. They are chewing to the beat of the song.

7:39 a.m. Suddenly, from out of the blue, I see them as cattle. I imagine the entire Wiles family as a black bald-faced herd grazing on Bermuda grass and chewing their cuds in the Southwest Texas sun. Then I remember my father—who is probably about to finish pairing up cows and calves right about now—and our long-running dispute about the loyalty versus the stupidity of cattle, and it comes to me that I have been wrong: cattle are not, after all, the stupidest animals on earth.

But just as I decide I'll have to call my father and admit he's right, I look back at Barkeep, who is still sitting there and singing Himmler's song, lending me moral support when he'd rather be seeing Annie—and it comes to me that my father has been wrong about cattle also: they are not the most loyal creatures on earth either.

7:40 a.m. I serve plates of lobster, scrambled eggs, and buttermilk pancakes to three more tables. Then I take up Himmler's song myself.

For the first time in I don't know how long, I feel myself smile.

Things Roman
in which Cecil tests his luck
(2007)

As he walked down to the river, Cecil Jubak couldn't help a rueful smile at the irony of it all. He guessed it was tough for most parents-to-be to decide whether they'd rather have a baby girl or a baby boy. But for Cecil—who luck, or God, or the merciless math of the gene pool had thrust into the role of grandparent-to-be this time around—the answer had always been clear: have boys, not girls.

Have boys, not girls was not a matter of favoritism for Cecil. He had nothing at all against other men's daughters, and he certainly wasn't one to hold a grudge against his own. It was just that boys were so much easier to raise. Boys were less emotional, they required less money in their free time, and they were less whiney. And when it came to the worry factor surrounding the three-letter word that had come to occupy more and more of Cecil's waking hours since his own daughters had reached dating age, there was no comparison—boys scoring about a one on his ten-point worry scale and girls at least a thirty-seven.

Have boys, not girls was not a matter of blind prejudice. Cecil could see that he was unfair. But as the births of Venus, Minerva, and Diana had reminded him in turn, life was unfair. He sat down in his green plastic thinking chair and watched the river flow past the weatherbeaten wood of his boat dock, feeling again the sad desperation that had grown to fill his heart as hope for a son had faded. This time it was a grandson his heart yearned to see delivered, but that didn't make his desire for a blue-swaddled bundle any less poignant. A male offspring had become for him like a desert mirage for a cowboy dying of thirst. And having grown up working on his father's cattle ranch outside Jordan, Texas, Cecil knew what a desert mirage looked like. In his imagination he gazed wistfully upon a strapping young man with whom he could share the wealth of arcane knowledge he'd gleaned since leaving the cactus-cursed desert plains for the river-blessed Hill Country: the tail-slap of a gar off the bow of the canoe, the croaking cough of a great blue heron startled off the nest, the sweet swish of a perfect swing chasing the ball as it arced off the tee.

Cecil's wife, Juno, said it was all a matter of luck. *Fortuna Brevis* was the term she used—a Latin phrase she said meant "fickle fortune" and referred to one aspect of the Roman goddess Fortuna, to whom the women of ancient Rome had prayed during childbirth and for whom Juno had wanted to name their third baby girl. But when Cecil found out that Fortuna was later connected with women of ill fame, he'd asked for a goddess of higher moral character and preferably some association with the great outdoors. Juno obliged by naming the child after the goddess Diana, who she said was also connected with childbirth, as well as with chastity—an irony that Juno would point out to Cecil more than once over the course of Diana's junior year in high school, and that he would come to appreciate in the fullness of time. Juno Jubak was as lovely and well-educated a lady as any who ever lived, and Cecil wouldn't trade her for a houseful of strapping sons. But like her mother, her grandmother, and the rest of her female-centric family, Juno had a strange fascination with all things Roman and a wildly emotional reaction to childbirth.

Indeed, it was this hysterical quality that was the first and most important reason Cecil was convinced it was better to have boys than girls. Boys were naturally less emotional about the problems that came their way, and this was strengthened as they grew by a society that viewed emotion as a mostly female trait. Anyway, it seemed that way to Cecil. For example, if a boy had a derogatory comment made about him at school—like he was pregnant, for instance; well, no . . . like maybe he had no balls—he would simply get into a fight with the offender. After a few punches, the problem would be solved. Girls, on the other hand, required much more emotional attention, as their natural reaction to the same situation would be to cry and then gossip. This would escalate into a huge problem between the girls involved, which would eventually result in more crying, which would occur at home where it would be the parents' job to deal with it. At San Saba High School, for instance, where all three of Cecil's lovely daughters had been on the Armadillos cheerleading squad—Venus and Minerva having since moved on to the university and become Longhorns, Tri-Delts, and Classics majors like their mother before them—a vicious rumor had gone around that the weight Diana, who was now nearing the end of her junior year, started putting on back during football season was due to pregnancy. The cheerleading uniforms were white, which of course emphasized the weight gain, with purple-and-gold pompoms that did not serve well to soak up tears during crying jags. Cecil's entire month of November had been spent trying to calm Diana's alternating fits of despair and bouts of rage—during which tear-soaked purple-and-gold pompoms were hurled across the living room with great frequency but little practical effect—while Diana alternately sobbed and snarled, "I swear to God it's just a rumor," into her cell phone, and Juno talked wistfully about irony and how quickly *Fortuna Brevis* could regress into *Fortuna Mala*.

Cecil shifted a little in his thinking chair and glanced up at the house, rebuilt out of native limestone in an imposing style that Juno had identified as Romanesque, after the last house—built in equally imposing Romanesque style out of wood, and the birthplace of Juno's grandmother and great-grandmother—had been destroyed in the great flood of 1938. It was not Cecil's home. Not really. He had married into it, and into the vast tract of acreage on the Colorado River that went with the Romanesque limestone manor. So he'd not been offended earlier that afternoon when his mother-in-law, Vesta, shooed him out the door and across the porch—Juno and Vesta called it a *portico*—with childbirth-hysterics already creeping into her voice. This was something Cecil was used to, Juno having insisted on giving birth to all three of their children in her own home, as her mother had done before her. And now, despite all her cell-phone-snarled protestations to the contrary, it was Diana's turn.

No, it was better to leave the house to the women—Vesta, Juno, Diana, the midwife—and retreat instead to the river out back, the one place on earth where Cecil truly felt at home. He had already gutted out three rollercoaster rides of boy-hope and girl-dread right here on this boat dock, in this same chair, watching the river roll by and hoping that instead of a pink swaddling blanket emerging from the back door, he would see a blanket of blue. His canoe lay upside-down on the carpet grass sward above him. A bucket of golf balls and his bag of clubs sat at his feet. These were the same companions he'd had for each of his previous experiences with labor. And even though this time it was his daughter, rather than his wife, who was having the baby, Cecil was far from panicked. He had the means to keep himself entertained.

Indeed, this was the second reason that Cecil was convinced it was better to have boys than girls. Boys did not require money to entertain themselves throughout their childhood, adolescence, and even adulthood. They could amuse themselves in clever and creative ways with almost anything. They could whittle sticks into baseball bats; make mud into paste, pies, or projectiles; and fashion countless other common materials into virtually anything. When boys reached high school age, all they needed was a rusted-out old truck and a job that would provide money to fix up said truck. Despite the myriad chores that came along with growing up on a cattle ranch, as a teenager Cecil managed to hustle and scrape together enough odd jobs to turn his pop's beat-up old castoff ranch truck into a red rocket that struck fear into the hearts of the street-racing crowd at Jordan High—and not a penny of that hard-earned cash had come out of his father's pocket. Girls, on the other hand, had to have money or toys that cost money. They required dolls and doll houses when they were young, and money to go to the mall when they were a little older. And then there were the cell phones. Cecil shuddered, remembering the cell phone bills Diana had racked up as "I swear to God it's just a rumor" regressed into "I'm going to raise the baby myself." More than $2000 in three months. What boy, Cecil asked himself, would ring up a bill like that?

He would never forget the day Diana introduced them to the father of her coming child—Cecil had heard Diana call him her "baby daddy" on her cell phone—a long, lanky Longhorn freshman named Frankie who she met while visiting her sisters in Austin and who Cecil had come to think of as Frankie the Snake. Cecil interrupted a rambling explanation of their future plans—or rather, the lack thereof—that he chiefly remembered for the repeated phrases "not in a relationship" and "no plans to marry" with the question: "Do you have a cell phone, Frankie?"

"Can't afford one," Frankie said. "I'm paying my own way through college on a baseball scholarship. Diana always calls me on my dorm phone. Why?"

Cecil levered himself up out of his green plastic thinking chair and whispered a fervent prayer to the Goddess Fortuna—although he was neither a Roman nor a woman—that this time the childbirth he awaited would result in a boy, not a girl. Juno had told him on more than one occasion that the sign of Fortuna's favor was a cornucopia. Cecil didn't have a cornucopia, but he did have a bucket of balls and a golf bag full of clubs which, it seemed to him, strongly resembled a cornucopia. And it came to him almost like a vision that a hole-in-one would be a sign from the goddess that the birth of a male offspring was finally at hand.

He picked up his golf bag and his bucket of balls and stepped up onto the carpet grass. He looked out across the river, trying to gauge the width of the stream. It looked like the water was down about a foot from the level it had hit after the last rains, but was still flowing muddy and wide—about thirty yards, he guessed. He pulled the sand wedge from his bag, dropped three balls onto the fairway-height grass, lined up the shot, and swung through the first ball.

He could feel that the shot was short even before he saw it arc shallowly up over the river and splash into the muddy water about five yards shy of the opposite bank. He shook his head, replaced the sand wedge, pulled out the pitching wedge. Then he lined up the shot and swung through the second ball, watching the arc of its trajectory carry across the river to plop into the mud on the far side.

Short again. He shook his head, replaced the pitching wedge, pulled out the nine iron. Then he lined up the shot and swung through the third ball, watching the arc of its trajectory carry across the river to bounce up off the back of the close-clipped carpet grass green on the far side and disappear into the pecan trees behind it.

Long. He dumped the bucket, whispered another fervent prayer, and took his time sending each ball in turn arcing across the river. Some of them bounced up off the back of the green and into the pecan trees. Others bit on the back of the green. But not a single shot came within easy putting distance of the pin—much less dropping in for a hole-in-one. When he finished the bucket, he picked up his golf bag and threw it into the river. Then he sat down in his thinking chair and tried to gauge the strength of the current while he contemplated women, luck, golf, rivers, and God.

Rivers had been lucky for Cecil, mostly. They had introduced him to women, improved his golf game, and brought him closer if not to God then to Creation at least. The day after he graduated high school, Cecil fled his father's brushcountry cattle ranch for the city of Austin to work construction during the boom. He arrived tanned and fit and wise enough in the ways of women to keep his mouth shut and listen while Juno talked about ancient Rome. He'd met her on the Colorado River during her time as a Longhorn, a Tri-Delt, and a Classics major—literally ramming his boat into the one she was riding in so he could get the chance to make it up to her by buying her dinner—and courted her on riverside picnics at Auditorium Shores. Marrying Juno gave him the farm in San Saba County that she'd grown up on and that they made thrive together, a collaboration in the truest and best sense: tireless physical labor on his part, unshakably patient guidance on hers, and lifegiving water from the river that made their peanuts and pecans flourish. When Cecil had time and the water was high enough, he packed his canoe with camping gear and ran the fifty-three miles of Colorado that lay between his boat dock and the free LCRA boat ramp at Cedar Point on Lake Buchanan. He'd grown to know every bend and trouble-spot, every sand spit and fishing hole. He'd grown to know the peace that came from paddling beneath towering limestone cliffs and circling bald eagles. But even so, the Colorado sometimes managed to surprise him. Like women and luck, the river was always changing.

Diana was the only one of his daughters Cecil ever managed to talk into running the river with him. She was thirteen years old at the time, still a little gangly but beginning to blossom into the graceful beauty that she would later come to share with her mother and sisters. As they paddled away from the boat dock—Cecil in the aft seat with the ice chest and water container, and Diana in the bow with her cell phone—Cecil felt sure he was finally on the verge of sharing the precious peace of the wild river with someone he loved. His hopes were dashed, though, by the lack of cell towers. In order to convince Diana to undertake the trip, he had to promise her cell service on every gravel bar and sand spit between their boat dock and the LCRA boat ramp. But he could only deliver on this promise at Flat Rock in Bend, hardly a day into their three-day trip—and even then, she could hardly hear. So his heavenly vision of shared peace on the river deteriorated into a hell of constant complaining that could best be described as a perpetual whine.

Indeed, this very whininess was the third reason that Cecil was convinced it was better to have boys than girls. Whining was bad enough when girls were very young; but once adolescence had been reached, the problem quickly escalated out of control. Adolescent girls would whine at the drop of a pin and would complain to anyone or anything that crossed their paths. Sadly, the problem persisted throughout most of adulthood as well, although it was greatly diminished—except during pregnancy. Boys, on the other hand, were much less inclined to whine and were easily made to stop their bellyaching if and when the occasional fit did occur. They were generally easygoing and carefree, no matter what came their way. A lack of cell towers would never cause a boy to whine on the river. Come to think of it, Cecil realized, no self-respecting boy would even bring a cell phone into a canoe.

At the thought of the canoe, Cecil sat bolt upright in his chair. He had suddenly remembered Juno telling him that, in addition to a cornucopia, the favor of Fortuna—who was sometimes represented with a boat rudder—could also be shown by the lucky guiding of a ship. Cecil had thrown his golf-bag cornucopia into the river in frustration at the lack of a sign that his earlier prayer might be answered. Maybe if he could guide his boat to the spot where the golf bag rested, and rescue the bag from the riverbottom, it would be a sign that his heartfelt plea for a boy might be answered after all.

In a flash, Cecil fetched a paddle and a boathook, and lowered his bright green canoe into the water. "Oh, Goddess Fortuna," he prayed as he paddled, "send me a grandson. End my years of boy-despair." He paddled and prayed, prayed and paddled, until he was directly upstream from the spot where he figured the golf bag had struck the water. Then he switched the paddle for the boathook, which he lowered and used to dredge the riverbottom as the canoe was carried downstream.

He came up with nothing but mud and weeds. But he kept paddling and praying, praying and paddling, fighting the current to get above the spot where his best judgment said the golf bag would've drifted to the bottom, then lowering the boathook and dredging for a golf-bag-sized snag.

Nothing again. And again. And yet again.

Until finally, so exhausted from paddling and dredging that he could hardly make his way back to the boat dock, Cecil was forced to admit defeat. He rolled the canoe as he climbed out of it, feeling so fatigued as he dragged himself out of the water that all he could do was watch his beloved ship sink to the bottom in the shallows just offshore—where it lay barely visible in the murk like the shadowy face of a hostile god.

Cecil lay on the weatherbeaten wood of the boat dock, soaked and breathing heavy, and feeling completely betrayed by women, luck, golf, rivers, and God. The only thing that hadn't let him down was his faithful chair. But in a fit of rage born out of a mix of girl-frustration and boy-despair, he lurched to his feet and lobbed the green plastic chair as far as he could into the muddy water.

Then he turned his back on river, golf bag, chair, and canoe—in short, on all he had come to think of as his—and faced the back side of the Romanesque limestone mansion he'd married into. As he sat there dripping, empty, at the end of himself, he saw Juno emerge from the back door with a blue-swaddled bundle.

He hardly had the strength to sob for joy.

Pink Elephants
after Ernest Hemingway
(2007)

The patio bar at Pat O'Brien's on the San Antonio River Walk was loud and crowded with patrons, their voices echoing up off the Spanish tile floor. The patio was long and narrow, and three of the walls were wood-paneled, stained dark like the bar. But the afternoon sun poured through the plate glass windows that filled the wall between the bar and the courtyard. Out among the courtyard tables, a fountain splashed and played in the afternoon sun. The American literature professor sat on a barstool nursing his second happy hour pint of Guinness. Next to him a bleach-blonde in a baby blue dress, which made a perfect counterpoint to the hot pink lipstick on her engorged lips, sucked the last of the hurricane the professor had bought her through double straws. Then she looked away, out into the courtyard.

"Another hurricane?" the professor asked, leaning closer to the blonde. "We could head over to the piano lounge. It's a bit more private. The music should be starting up any minute now."

"I don't think so." The blonde pursed her puffy lips and rose to leave.

"At least take my card." The professor drew a business card from the pocket of his silk sport jacket and offered it to the woman. "Maybe we could meet somewhere on the River Walk later for a nightcap."

"No thanks." The blonde drew a lipstick from her purse, narrowed her eyes at her reflection in the bar mirror, and retouched the coat of pink on her lips. Then she walked off in the direction of the piano lounge.

The professor watched her go, squinting into the afternoon light reflecting up off the polished Spanish tile floor. When he turned back to face the bar mirror, he saw a dark-haired woman sit down on the stool vacated by the blonde.

"She did you a favor." The woman made eye contact with the professor in the bar mirror. "You can do better."

"Excuse me?"

"You can do better than the blonde. Talk about augmentation gone wild. Her lips looked like pink elephants."

The professor sipped his Guinness and looked away into the

courtyard at the flames leaping from the basin of the signature Pat O'Brien's fiery fountain. Once darkness fell, a steady stream of tourists would have their waiters take pictures of them standing next to the flames that seemed to erupt from the water.

"Come on, don't get sore," the woman said. "We're both here for the same reason, aren't we?"

"Are we?" The professor looked back into the bar mirror, where he saw the dark-haired woman next to him signal the bartender.

"I'd like two Dulce Vida Tequila Añejos."

"Would you like them with water?" the bartender, a young woman with bright red hair pulled back into a ponytail and a white button-down shirt, asked.

"Just a splash." The dark-haired woman paid for the drinks and slid one of the glasses toward the professor. "No hard feelings," she said. "I didn't mean any harm when I said her lips looked like pink elephants. I've got a pink elephant connection myself."

"Tequila and Guinness? Are you kidding me?"

"Come on. Have you ever tried Dulce Vida Tequila Añejo? No? Then leave off the Guinness for a minute or two and savor this."

"Look, I don't mean to be rude. But we shouldn't even be talking right now. And you know that."

"I know, I know. But you're here. And I'm here. And it's happy hour. How about we agree not to even bring up . . . well, you know." She raised her glass toward the reflection of the professor in the bar mirror. "Let's make friends. How about another Hemingway reference? Will you please please please start talking?"

The professor grinned. "Do you know which collection Hemingway originally published 'Hills Like White Elephants' in?"

"No."

Men Without Women.

They both laughed, and the dark-haired woman slid her barstool a little closer to the professor. "You know," she said, "when they do a lip augmentation, the injection is either collagen from cow skin, or fat harvested from the belly or thighs of the injectee."

"Okay, so maybe you're right about me being better off without that particular woman."

"Let's drink to something. What shall we drink to?"

"How about pink elephants?"

They clinked their glasses together and took slow sips of the tequila. In the bar mirror, the professor saw the woman smile.

"What do you think of the Dulce Vida?" she asked.

"At the risk of overdoing the Hemingway allusion, it tastes like liquorish."

"That's the way with everything." Her smile disappeared. "Especially those things you've worked so hard, for so many years, to earn."

"I thought we agreed not to bring that up."

"You're right. It's just that . . . well, never mind." The dark-haired woman smiled brightly at the professor, as if to apologize. "You know, I really do have a pink elephant story. Would you like to hear it?"

"Sure." The professor sipped his tequila and turned to face the woman beside him.

"As a young girl," she began, "I was deprived of an imperative object: a pacifier. My father was against letting me have one. Luckily, though, for my first Christmas I received a stuffed elephant. I guess you could say this pacified me. Baby, as I originally named her, came to me dressed in a dainty pink pinafore with a matching bow atop her head. She became my constant companion.

"I literally took her everywhere. As you can imagine, the years of wear and tear left Baby looking a bit tousled, just as any child's favorite toy. But to me, she was beautiful despite the smudges and tatters. Then, one awful night that I will never forget, my parents took me and my two best friends, Venus and Minerva Jubak, to Mill Pond Park—"

"Venus and Minerva?" the professor cut in, grinning again. "You're putting me on, right?"

"Look, this may seem like a joke to you. But for me, it's serious. Do you want to hear the rest of the story, or not?"

"I apologize. Please continue."

"As I was saying, we went to Mill Pond Park in San Saba, where I grew up. I had Baby in tow, as usual. Venus and Minerva and I fed the ducks, splashed around in the spring-fed waterfall, and had a grand old time getting thoroughly soaked. When my parents and I got home, though, Baby was nowhere to be found. My father went back to look, but had no luck. I was about as distraught as a four-year-old could be. The most emotionally significant thing in my life was gone forever.

"Thankfully, a year before that, my parents had bought me a stuffed elephant almost identical to Baby. The only difference was that this elephant was a boy outfitted in green overalls. I dubbed him Other Baby, but I paid no attention to him because I was convinced he had cooties. After I lost my dear Baby, my mother had the idea to have Other Baby undergo a kind of sex-change operation. She removed the overalls and created a beautiful pink pinafore and bow exactly like the originals.

"At first, I was leery of the clean new Baby. But as time passed, the new Baby slowly took the place of the old, and has been closely guarded ever since. She still holds more meaning for me than anything else I possess. Her stitches, tatters, and tears represent more innocent times. Every night when I get into bed, Baby is there watching over me. She always makes me smile when something really bad happens to me . . . like when I get denied some hugely important thing that I really deserve."

The professor, who had been half-smiling and sipping his tequila, suddenly frowned. He turned away from the woman and set his glass on the bar. "I appreciate the drink," he said, rising, "but I think I should go."

"Not without telling me why."

Instead of answering, the professor reached for his briefcase that sat next to the barstool he'd just vacated. But as he turned to leave, he felt an uncomfortable pressure on his forearm. The dark-haired woman, he saw, had locked his navy sport jacket in a white-knuckled grip.

"Unhand me, madam," he said quietly but firmly.

"If you don't start talking, I'll scream. And that's no Hemingway allusion."

"Go ahead and scream. I've done nothing wrong."

"That's not what I'll tell the police and the Provost. I'll tell them you tried to use your position on the promotion and tenure committee to blackmail me for sex. You've got a reputation as a shark, particularly among the female graduate students. And everyone in the department knows you come to happy hour at Pat O'Brien's to hit on tourists."

"Jeanette?" the professor called down the bar, taking care to keep his voice calm and even. "Would you bring us two more tequilas, please?"

The bartender came over to the corner of the bar where the dark-haired woman was sitting and the professor was standing. "You want them with water?"

"Would you like yours with water?" the professor asked the woman who had not relaxed her grip on his arm.

"It's better with water."

"One with water," the professor said to the bartender, "one without."

The bartender brought the drinks, and the professor shot his down all at once.

"I won't discuss the particulars," he said. "But I will agree to talk in general about the proceedings." He met the dark-haired woman's eyes that were wide, almost wild. "That is, if you'll agree to release my arm."

120

She let go her grip and took a slow sip of tequila.

The professor paid for the drinks, set his briefcase back down next to the barstool, and took a seat. "What do you want to know?"

"I want to know why you voted no. I want to know why the committee voted no. I won the teaching award, for Christ's sake. How could I have been turned down?"

The professor sighed. "Look, it isn't about how well you teach. In essence, teaching is a side issue. It's about how much you publish, and where."

"I've got publications."

"A single book from a minor university press. And a few short stories. To put it simply, the committee felt that your history of publication was not of sufficient merit."

"But what about all that service? What about all those great recommendation letters? Hell, I've got letters from major authors..." She let her sentence trail off, downed the rest of her tequila, and signaled the bartender. "Could I get another one of these, please?"

"Make it two, Jeanette. The same as before."

"No," the dark-haired woman said. "This time, I'll pass on the water."

"Two more without water," the professor called. Then he turned back to the woman, who had covered her eyes with one hand. "The University of Texas at San Antonio is a research institution," he said gently. "They don't want letters from major authors. They want a major author."

The bartender delivered the drinks, and the professor paid. Then he slid a glass of tequila over in front of the woman, who removed the hand from her face and downed the drink in a single gulp.

"It isn't fair," she said.

"Of course it's unfair. It's academe."

The dark-haired woman sat and stared into her empty glass.

"How about a pint of Guinness?" the professor asked. "This ... what did you call it?"

"Dulce Vida Tequila Añejo."

"Right. Surprisingly, it goes pretty well with Irish beer. Jeanette, bring us a couple of pints of Guinness, please."

The bartender brought the pints, and the professor paid for them. Then he sat and sipped his Guinness and saw the dark-haired woman do the same.

"You're right," she said. "High-octane Mexican tequila goes surprisingly well with Irish beer."

"You know, I have a pink elephant story of my own. It isn't a story that I share with very many people. But I think that, in this particular case, it might help."

"I'm listening."

"My first full-time teaching job was at a community college. I got the job ABD, and spent two years teaching a 5/5 load and knocking out my dissertation. During that time, my now ex-wife and I had a daughter. We named her Catherine—my dissertation was on *A Farewell to Arms*—and we bought her a pink elephant for her first birthday. The elephant had a flower in its trunk, a daisy; and when Catherine was old enough to talk, she named it Horton after the elephant from *Horton Hears a Who*.

"I wish I could tell you whether the elephant was my daughter's constant companion. I wish I could tell you whether the elephant had more emotional significance for her than anything else she possessed. I wish I could tell you the names of her two best friends. But the only thing I can tell you truthfully is about all the nights and weekends I spent working on articles and books about a dead writer named Hemingway. I can tell you about all the articles I've published in the most prestigious journals, about all the books I've brought out from the most distinguished academic presses, about how my work is in every major library in the world.

"And I can tell you that when Catherine phoned me one Friday night, from the prestigious East Coast university I pressured her to go away to so that she could make a mark in life like her father, I was at a Hemingway conference in Italy . . . and I didn't take her call. She hanged herself in the restroom of her dormitory, at around 3 a.m. on that same Friday evening."

"Jesus Christ."

"You might as well put your faith in Santa Claus." The professor took a long gulping pull off his Guinness. "Hemingway once said that all thinking men are atheists. And I'm nothing if not a thinking man. Here is an inventory of all the fruits I've plucked as a result of thirty years of academic life: an endowed chair at a research university, a bunch of prestigious publications that maybe a hundred people will ever read, and a beat-up pink elephant with a daisy in its nose and stuffing coming out the seams."

"Is any of that true? Or are you just trying to make me feel better?"

The professor, who had glanced out into the courtyard at the flames leaping from the fiery fountain, turned back to the woman beside him. "Actually, my ex-wife kept the elephant. But the rest is fact."

The dark-haired woman sipped her pint of Guinness and said nothing.

"I confess that I'm guilty of being a shark. But I have never preyed on undergraduates. And I never even started on grad students until after my wife and I had split."

"I have a confession of my own," she said at last. "I came here knowing that you argued against me at the meeting this morning. I came with plans to pick you up, lure you back to my apartment, have sex with you, then accuse you of rape—to destroy your career like you did mine. But after your pink elephant story, I think I've changed my mind . . . even though I do still sort of blame you for getting me fired."

"They're not going to fire you. Anyway, not yet. You've got the rest of this year, and all of next, to look for another job."

"I could also appeal the committee's verdict."

"That's certainly your right. And I wish you the best of luck, whichever path you choose. And now, if you'll excuse me, I believe I hear the music starting up in the piano lounge."

"If you strike out, feel free to come back and finish your beer."

The professor picked up his briefcase and carried it through the narrow patio and into the crisp, dark air of the piano lounge. He drank a Dulce Vida Tequila Añejo at the bar and looked at the blonde with the pink lips, where she sat at a table drinking a hurricane with a man in a designer suit.

Then the professor went back out onto the patio. The dark-haired woman was still sitting at the bar, and she smiled reasonably at him.

"Did you strike out?" she asked.

"I never stepped into the batter's box. Still feel like taking revenge?"

"I feel fine. I can't say there's nothing wrong with me. But right now, I feel fine."

Mineral Spirits

in which Erin Johnson, denied tenure, eats pecan pie
(2007)

"Are you hungry?" Erin's father asks. The two of them stand on the front patio, watching the last of the guests pull away up the gravel drive. A blast of wind follows them back in the door, chilling the inside air and billowing her father's long salt-and-pepper hair. He keeps his black dress coat on as he leads her into the kitchen.

The house smells like death.

Not decay. The body was kept at the funeral home where they pumped it full of formaldehyde or whatever they pump bodies full of once the life goes out. No, it's the smell of food that reminds Erin of death and dying. The casseroles and pecan pies brought in the days since her mother finally gave in to the cancer are lined up like caskets on the kitchen counter. Their mixed aromas make the house that Erin grew up in, and that has sheltered three generations of Fisher descendants, seem as alien as her mother's grave. On the long return ride from the service in San Saba, she hoped that being back in the big house on the river would be like reentering the womb—a source of solace, support, inner peace.

It wasn't. "Are you kidding?" she shoots back. "The smell of those casseroles makes me feel as though I might never eat again."

"Juno Jubak made one of the pies."

Feigning interest for her father's sake, Erin studies the pecan pies. There are three of them, and she knows they should be a source of comfort. The house has been filled with the warm brown smell of pecan pie since she was a baby. But now it only reminds her of her mother's absence. Shakespeare called death an undiscovered country. In San Saba County, Texas, death is a country of casseroles and pecan pies.

The thought makes Erin's stomach churn. "Which pie is Juno's?" she asks at last. "I don't see—"

"I put Juno's in the fridge for later. She didn't seem to mind." He opens the refrigerator and sets the pie on the counter. Through the clear plastic wrap, Erin sees the signature *J* made from sugared pecan halves curling gracefully across the top. "You know how I love a cold pecan pie, especially one made by Juno Jubak. And I could use a little pick-me-up right about now. Shall we?"

"You go ahead," Erin says. Juno was at the service with her husband, Cecil, and they came to the house after. Erin remembers the way Juno looked in her black formal dress: long-legged, red-haired, ageless in the way of a great work of literature or art. They spoke for a while in the living room; but thinking back on their conversation now, barely an hour later, Erin can't recall a single word. "The smell of these casseroles is making me sick."

"I'll get them covered and into the fridge," he says. "It'll just take a minute."

Erin walks into the living room. Through the big bank of windows that make up the eastern wall, she can see the Colorado River flowing broad and muddy. The house sits on the San Saba County side, just above Bend. She sees a couple of houses across the river partially shrouded by towering pecan trees, and sees the wide flat rocks that line both banks. She tries to focus on all the times she sat on those rocks with her father, swimming or fishing or just watching the river flow by in the direction of Austin and the Gulf of Mexico while her mother tended the trees. But the smell from the kitchen keeps turning her thoughts back to her mother's grave.

"Hey, why don't we head up to the studio?" her father asks. "It's a casserole-free zone. Did you bring any of your painting gear?"

"I've got a canvas and some paints and brushes in the car."

"Bring them up. I'll get Juno's pie."

Outside, the first norther of the fall whooshes raw air through the pecan leaves and makes Erin glad she left her coat on. She fetches a pre-prepped canvas, a palette, and two clear plastic briefcases filled with tubes of acrylic paint and brushes from the trunk of her car, and carries the supplies up to her father's studio over the freestanding garage. As she steps into the chaos of paints and easels and canvases and prepping tools that her father works among, she catches the strong scents of oil paint and mineral spirits and the delicate aroma of Juno Jubak's pie.

"You're right," Erin says. "Casserole-free."

"That was a dream of Ellie's and mine, way back when." Her father smiles faintly. He has traded in his black coat and dress clothes for a pair of paint-smeared overalls. "In graduate school back in Austin, I was living in the attic of one of those big old houses west of campus and courting your mother. She was still an undergraduate then. We lived on a diet of cheap food cooked in casserole dishes and crock pots. We promised ourselves that when we finished school and started making money, we would never eat another casserole again. God, Ellie was beautiful back then. It's strange how much . . ." He lets the sentence trail off as he takes Erin's canvas and moves toward the worktable. "I've cleared a space for your paints and brushes. A bit of order amid the chaos."

"Thanks." On a shelf under one of the windows that faces the river, Erin sorts the paint tubes into groups of warm and cool colors. She places the brushes in a neat row according to size and shape. As she carefully folds her coat over a chair, she catches sight of the pie on a paint-spattered table in a far corner, half-hidden by easels and a profusion of canvases in various stages of completion. There are two forks, a knife, two glasses of milk, and no plates. This tradition of Erin's and her father's dates back to her early girlhood: splitting a whole pecan pie between them. It has never failed to make even the very worst of the bad days better.

"Why don't you help me prepare my canvas first? Then we can move on to painting and Juno's pie. Not necessarily in that order, of course."

"Oh Dad," she says, "why on earth won't you step into the twenty-first century and start buying pre-prepped canvases?"

"Because I'm actually a better canvas-stretcher than I am a painter."

"We both know that's not true. You've got paintings in museums and important private collections all across the country."

"You've sold a few as well, despite the fact that you continue to divide yourself between painting and writing." He takes a set of wooden stretchers and hammers them together. Erin knows that he made them himself out of native pecan, and they lock together perfectly. "But let me explain. For me, the meditative aspect of preparing the canvas is key to the evolution of the painting as a whole. While my hands are doing the prepping, my mind and spirit are composing the images that will combine with the canvas to make a work of art. It's all about focus, Erin."

Erin feels herself wince. Like the pies, the painting-versus-writing argument with her father is something that stretches back across years—and she just doesn't have it in her to take it up again today. "Those look like golden rectangles," she says instead, nodding at a couple of half-finished paintings next to the worktable. On one of the canvases a giant tree is being riven by a bolt of lightning. On the other two figures recline on a wide flat rock and watch a river flow past. "Do you use the Fibonacci sequence?"

"The what?"

"You know. The golden ratio. The divine proportion. The golden mean."

"I use my eye," he says, rolling a length of raw linen out on the worktable beside him and laying the stretchers on top. "And the better part of myself." He puts a starter tack into the middle of each side, then nods at Erin. "Lend me a hand with this, and you'll see. I'll do the stretching. You do the hammering."

"Just tell me when." Erin picks up the hammer and watches her dad work the pliers.

He moves from side to side, making sure to place the pliers right on the edge of the frame. He manipulates the pliers and the canvas masterfully, pausing at regular intervals to place a tack and say, "Now."

Then she hammers in the tack, attaching the taut canvas to the stretchers at the place he points to, and he moves on to the next side. Finally, he locks the wooden keys into the corners so that the entire canvas is stretched tight.

"Nice," Erin says.

"Let me slap a coat of gesso onto this, then we'll eat. That is, assuming you're determined to use that pre-prepped canvas."

"I always do. When I'm painting."

"What does that mean?"

"For the past few months I've focused on writing and publishing—well, on writing and trying to publish—and on putting together and submitting my tenure file."

"I guess we haven't talked much lately, and I'm sorry. Things here have been . . . well, you know how they've been. How's all that tenure stuff going?"

"About like nursing a cancer patient, I imagine." Erin looks out the window at the pecan trees shuddering in the raw wind. "Painting has kind of gotten lost in the shuffle."

"Well, you're about to be painting now. Even better, we're about to be painting together." He stirs together a bit of water and a can of gesso in a big blue bucket, then works a coat onto the canvas they stretched. Next he lays the primed canvas flat on a bare patch of floor directly beneath the ceiling fan and turns the fan on high. "Now we can focus on pie."

"Aren't you supposed to put on more than one layer of primer before you start painting?"

"*Supposed to* and *painting* don't belong in the same sentence."

Neither do *publishing* and *tenure*, Erin thinks. But instead of talking, she sits down at the little paint-spattered table in the corner. Her father slices Juno Jubak's signature sugared-pecan *J* down the middle. Then they each take a fork and dig in.

"This really is a work of art," Erin says after a mouthful of pie and a sip of cold milk. "It's like a chiaroscuro. The flavors and textures are a study in contrast. Sweet and spicy, crunchy and gooey. The recipe is perfect."

"It's not just the recipe," her father mumbles around a mouthful, "that makes the pie perfect."

"All right. What, then?"

"You tell me. What makes the Jubak pie perfect?"

For a long while the only sounds are the wind in the trees, the low hum of the ceiling fan, and father and daughter enjoying Juno's creation. Savoring every bite, Erin thinks about her father's question. Both families, the Fishers and Riesens, were original settlers of San Saba County; and both have grown and sold native pecans on the banks of the Colorado for better than a hundred years. Like the Fishers, the Riesens rebuilt their big Romanesque style house on the river after the great flood of 1938. Because of the birth of daughters instead of sons, the last names of both families changed: the Fishers became Johnsons, while the Riesens became Jubaks. Like Erin, the three Jubak daughters went to school in San Saba; the elder two, Venus and Minerva, were Erin's best friends. But the recipe that Juno uses to create her signature pecan pies is unique—a Riesen family secret passed down from mother to daughter since San Saba County was organized and Edward Riesen proclaimed it the Pecan Capital of the World—and Juno Jubak is acknowledged, albeit grudgingly, as the pecan pie queen. Erin's mother tried for years to replicate the recipe, to no avail. Erin finds herself wondering if Juno has shared the secret with her daughters yet, or whether they'll have to wait until death comes to claim Juno Jubak the way it claimed Ellie Johnson.

The thought of her mother dying makes Erin's stomach churn again. "Hard work, I guess," she says, setting down her fork. "The best ingredients. Mastery of craft."

"No." Her father finishes his half of the pie, starts in on what's left of hers. "It's love."

"Love? I'm sorry, Dad, but that's the corniest thing I've ever heard."

Erin's father gives her a long, measuring look over the rim of his milk glass. "You said a while ago that putting together your tenure file was a lot like nursing a cancer patient. And for your sake, I hoped it was true. But now I'm not so sure."

"I don't follow."

"Caring for your mother, helping her fight the cancer, was the most beautiful thing I've ever done. It wasn't a job. It was a labor of love. There was no part of it that didn't bring us closer, make the bond between us stronger. I was totally focused on her. As gorgeous as Ellie was during our first days together in Austin, she was never more lovely to me than at the end."

"What does any of that have to do with a pie?"

"Nursing your mother gave me the same feeling I get when I'm painting, the same feeling your mother always got when she was tending her pecan trees, the same feeling I'll wager Juno Jubak gets when she's in her kitchen." He sets down his fork, takes another long drink of milk. "Ellie always said that working with the trees made her feel like her own roots reached the center of the earth and her branches touched the sky. Did writing, or trying to publish, or putting together your tenure file— anything at all connected with your tenure application—make you feel that way?"

"Dad, I didn't get it."

"Get what?"

"Tenure. The committee shot me down. It isn't official yet. I'm not even supposed to know. But I spoke with one of the people who reviewed my application. I'll never forget what he said: 'The committee felt that your history of publication was not of sufficient merit.'"

"Oh Erin, I'm sorry. I wouldn't have brought it up if I'd known. But this isn't just about tenure. Is there anything in your life that makes you feel like your roots reach the center of the earth and your branches touch the sky?"

Erin stands up and walks over to the painting of two figures reclining on a wide flat rock and watching a river flow past. "Is this you and me?"

"It will be when I'm finished."

"When I was a little girl, and you and I would sit on the rocks by the river while Mother tended the trees, I felt the way you just described. Grounded, but reaching for the sky. Like one of Mother's towering pecans." Erin walks over to the painting of the lightning-split tree. "Now I feel like this."

"I've felt that way myself since your mother passed."

Erin looks back at the painting of the two figures on the rock, this time studying it carefully. "I don't see Mother here. Are you going to add her in?"

"A long time ago, your mother and I made a bargain. You know how she hated being photographed. She felt the same way about being painted, only moreso. But when I was young, and we were in that first crazy physical phase of being in love, I needed to paint her more than I needed to breathe. So she agreed to pose for me once, in any way I asked her to, if I promised never to paint her again while she was alive."

"And?"

"And what?"

"You can't just stop there. Tell me what happened."

"There's not much to tell. Your mother posed. I painted her. And I kept my word."

"Do you still have the painting? I'd give anything to see it."

"Of course I still have it," he says, smiling faintly again. "But it's not something I'll ever share."

"Was that part of the bargain?"

"No. That's one of the roots that keeps me grounded." He gets up, walks over to the canvas he primed with gesso, gently touches the surface. "This feels dry enough to get started on. And I've been waiting thirty years to paint your mother again. Let's paint her now, together."

"All right."

He sets up two easels next to the worktable and places their canvases on the easels. "While we're at it, there are a couple of things we need to talk about."

Erin takes her time squeezing small blobs of acrylic paint in order from warm to cool onto her disposable palette and mixing them carefully with a Grumbacher number two flat brush. Her father picks up a terra-cotta tile, squirts a massive glob of black oil paint onto it, then picks up a brush and attacks his canvas. Because he didn't sand the primer, the texture of his painting is bumpy and irregular. And he works fast, framing a face and moving on to mark the nose, the eyes, the ears, and the hair with rough lines of thick black.

The texture of Erin's painting, on her pre-prepped canvas, is smooth as she underpaints with red earth, pauses, then builds up the light with white and yellow ochre and a touch of raw umber, mixing variegated shades of warmer grays. She starts with an oval in the middle part of the canvas, carefully mixes slightly darker grays on another part of her palette with a different flat brush, shades in the two eye sockets precisely in the middle of the oval. Next she shades in the ears. She pauses, reflects, switches to a fan brush and shades in the beginnings of eyes just beneath the eyebrows. She measures carefully, making the gap between the eyes the same distance as the width of each, the size of the ears the same as the gap between the tip of the nose and eyebrows. She blocks in the lip line halfway between the chin and the tip of the nose. Then she stands back and looks at her father's canvas.

He is working with colors now, laying the paint on thick and mixing it right on the canvas. He doesn't seem to be measuring anything at all—just applying layers of paint, switching brushes, shaping details as he blends the colors. For the cheeks he starts with red, then grabs some yellow and puts it in right over the red, the darker colors underneath and the lighter colors on top. Blues and greens he lays down under the arch of each eye. Instead of pausing and reflecting, he just keeps putting on paint. Finally, as if sensing Erin watching him, he steps back.

"What do you think?" he asks.

She looks from her father's painting to hers and back again. "They're so different."

"You and I are very different people, Erin. You've always approached life much more like your mother than like me—methodically, rather than by the seat of your pants. You look like her, too. Sometimes it's strange to me how much you two resemble each other. Well, resembled each other, I guess. It's hard to think of Ellie in the past tense."

"Is that one of the things you wanted to talk about?"

"No," he says, completely absorbed in the figure of Ellie taking shape on his canvas. "I'm thinking of selling the place. These pecan trees of your mother's need a lot of looking after, and I wasn't cut out for tending trees. You can't manage a pecan-growing operation by the seat of your pants." He shifts his gaze out the window. "Unless you'd like to move back here and take over, I was thinking of heading down to the realtor's office on Monday and listing the land and the house for sale. But the final decision has to be yours. You're the last of the Fishers, Erin."

She shrugs, setting her palette on the corner table next to the remains of the pie. "I've never felt any real connection to the land or the trees. Anyway, not the kind Mother felt. For her, tending the trees was a labor of love. For me, it would just be labor."

"This isn't something to decide on impulse. Take your time. You can stay here with me for as long as you like. We'll throw out the casseroles and live on pecan pie."

"I have to get back to work, Dad."

"But doesn't being denied tenure mean that you don't get rehired? What can they really do to you?"

"I'll get a year, after this one, to look for other teaching jobs. That's a benefit of being tenure-track. Unless I give them cause to terminate my contract, that is. I think not coming back to work would qualify as grounds for termination."

"Well, you've got a couple of days anyway. Stay here with me until Monday and think it over." He picks up a brush and attacks his canvas again.

Erin picks up her palette and goes back to daubing paint. She is moving to darker shades now. She mixes blue and white in one area of her palette; she mixes yellow and blue in another area, to make a green the color of the pecan leaves outside; and in another, she blends yellow and red to make a sunset orange. She puts the paint on the canvas in ever-thinner layers, daubing it on carefully, stepping back and looking. Adjusting.

As Erin continues to paint, she thinks of the pecan operation—of the trees and the land, and of her mother's 365-day-a-year labor of looking after both—and the figure of Ellie Johnson gets darker and darker. Pecans have always been the family's real livelihood, despite Erin's father's success as an artist. Her mother put everything into running the pecan business and caring for the trees: fighting casebearers, shuckworms, weevils, aphids, and webworms; dealing with the crop damage caused by crows; hiring mechanical shakers and sweep machines come harvest time; culling lightning-split trees. So many responsibilities. But her mother discharged them all without complaint, even after the onset of the cancer.

The figure taking shape on Erin's canvas definitely resembles Ellie. But the face looks old. Old, and in pain, Erin thinks. And something, somehow, isn't right. The proportions are off. Erin looks carefully at the partially finished face. It's the septum, she realizes. The fleshy gap between the nostrils is too wide. She mixes a whitish yellow and lightens up the dark crease where the nostrils meet the upper lip. Then she steps back again—and runs smack into her father.

"I'm sorry, Erin," he says. "While my brushes are soaking, I was watching you work."

Erin blinks, feeling herself jerked back into the present moment. She smells the strong scent of the mineral spirits her father is using to clean his brushes. When she looks over at his canvas, she sees that the painting is finished.

"She's gorgeous," Erin says. "I don't remember ever seeing her look so young." Striking in its use of black, and dark colors, the painting puts her in mind of Picasso's African Period—and yet, it is totally her father's. The work shows Ellie naked from the waist up. Long hair the color of pecan bark swirls around the shadow-dappled skin of her face and body. Her breasts are high and firm, the textured sinews of her arms flex as she stretches them upward, and her eyes are the color of the sky. "Mother was always a tree spirit. You've captured that perfectly."

"Not even close," he says. "But I've got the main ingredient right—and the rest of my life to perfect the recipe. Let's have a look at yours."

Erin's painting strongly resembles Ellie also, but older. More introspective. Instead of reaching for the sky, Erin's version of her mother seems to be looking deep into herself. "Mine's not as good as yours," she says.

"It isn't finished yet. But they complement each other. Both are ethereal, and yet concrete at the same time. Like ghosts that have taken on solid form." He looks from the painting to Erin, then back at the painting again. "To be honest, I see as much of you in it as I do of Ellie. The colors and the texture remind me of stones more than trees. Hard pastels, if such a thing is possible. Are you painting your mother, or yourself?"

It does seem to Erin as though the figure in her painting has taken on the hard gray tones of the rocks that line the river. "You said a while ago that I was the last of the Fishers. I don't think that's true. Mother was the last of the Fishers, Dad. You and I are mineral spirits. We love the river rocks more than the trees. Maybe it is time to sell this place."

"That brings me to the second thing I wanted to talk to you about," he says. "What would you say to the two of us going into business together? We could use the money from selling the pecan operation to open our own gallery on the River Walk in San Antonio. As you said earlier, my work will lend a bit of *gravitas* to the enterprise. And yours will bring a breath of fresh air. You've had shows on the River Walk, and you've got paintings in a couple of galleries down there. Surely you must have connections."

"I have, and I do." She hesitates, struggling to match feelings with words. "I've always believed that writing was my first, best destiny—that writing was the thing that would put me on the map, if I was ever going to get there. But after the tenure committee's verdict, and our pie and painting session this afternoon, I don't know what to believe."

"Just because we open a father-daughter art studio doesn't mean you have to stop writing. You'd be shifting your focus, that's all. And we'd still be next to a river. What do you say?"

Erin looks at her father's painting of her mother, a tree spirit in the flush of youth. Then she looks at her own painting that she realizes now is indeed a self-portrait, a mineral spirit at a crossroads. "I'll make a bargain with you," she says, "the same way Mother did. I'll agree to sell this place on the Colorado River and open a studio with you on the San Antonio River Walk, if you'll agree that the first painting we hang will be the one you did of Mother all those years ago in Austin when she was young."

"I don't know. I feel like I'd be breaking a promise to your mother."

"Ellie's gone, Dad. But I'll be here until Monday morning. My offer stands until then." She looks up into her father's eyes that seem lost in his picture of Ellie. "In the meantime, I'd like to take another crack at painting—but Mother this time, instead of a tortured self-portrait. Do you think I could talk you into prepping another canvas?"

Her father smiles, and his eyes meet Erin's. "Done," he says.

Goodbye to Carthage
in which Joe sees the future
(2008)

"If there were no such thing as love, would we invent it?" I ask. Again.

And for the second time in as many minutes, not a single one of the twenty-five students in my Intermediate Latin II class says a word. We're studying Book IV of the *Aeneid* in the original Latin, and I'm having about as much luck engaging student interest in Virgil's epic as I might have sailing the Trojan fleet up the San Antonio River.

"Come on. Love is the one thing that poets, like Virgil, have been telling us we can't live without since the time when poems were first sung. Did we invent it—flash love into being like lightning, emotional electricity generated by the first humans worthy of the term? Or did we only discover it? Was love always there—a white space on the universal chart awaiting a boat and two intrepid travelers?" I glance from face to face. "What would Dido say?"

Still no answer.

"Really? Has no one in this room ever fallen crazy in love, and gotten burned? When Aeneas sails away from Carthage toward his destiny in Rome, Queen Dido climbs onto a funeral pyre and falls on his sword! If we could transport her out of the *Aeneid* and into this room, what would Dido say about love? Did we invent it? Did we only discover it? And more importantly, can we live without it?"

"What do you say, Dr. Jasmine?" a young woman in back asks.

The honest truth is that I have no clue. But seeing interest finally kindle in every eye in the room, I know I have to say something. "As your Latin professor, the only thing I can really teach you about *amare* is how to conjugate it," I say at last, clinching the corners of my mouth up into a rueful half-smile. "But as a human being? Like a lot of the people in this room, I've fallen crazy in love. And like Dido in the epic, I got burned. Even so, given the opportunity to invent love, or to discover it all over again, I'd grab that chance with both hands—and it would take a hell of a lot more than the will of Jupiter to make me let go."

To my complete surprise, the girl in the back row starts clapping. The other students take it up, the applause building until it sounds like a fireworks display, and I find myself groping for a way to transfer their interest in my personal life to Virgil's epic poem—the only way my three-year Visiting Assistant Professor gig at the University of Texas at San Antonio will turn into the tenure-track position I've applied for is with student support.

"Thank you," I say as the applause dies down. "Over the weekend, I want you all to think about the question of love as it plays out in Book IV of the *Aeneid*. But connect it in some meaningful way to your own life. Come to class on Tuesday with a 250-word personal narrative—in Latin— on whether you see yourself as Dido or Aeneas, and why."

Then I snag my dog-eared copy of the *Aeneid* and sprint for the parking lot. I'm picking Sara up at the Mystic Café at 11:30, which gives me exactly a half hour. But as I pull into traffic, sending camping gear clanking around the back of my beat-up Xterra, instead of the quickest route to the River Walk or the chances of finding a parking spot downtown so close to noon, I find myself thinking about love. Despite the student applause—or maybe because of it—I feel like a fraud.

Could I write that personal narrative myself? The Latin would be the easy part. But love . . . Where to begin?

* * *

A little over three years ago, my wife Elizabeth filed for divorce and ran off to Boulder with a Brazilian bicyclist, leaving me alone in Austin with our son, Jacob, and his newly diagnosed Autism Spectrum Disorder. I will never forget the last words she said to me before she walked out the door: "I don't love you. I don't think I ever really did love you. Goodbye."

I felt the best part of myself die as the door slammed shut behind her. What do you do when you hear those words from the mother of your son, the woman you've been working two jobs to try and build a life for, the person all your days begin and end with?

Dido faced that question. The last part of it anyway, the part that really matters.

I didn't have a funeral pyre or a sword. But the double-barrel 12-gauge I inherited from my father stood in a corner of the hall closet. Loaded. Waiting. I took it out and held it, cold and heavy on my lap, in the rocking chair where Elizabeth nursed baby Jacob. After forty-five minutes of banging his head on the floor—it was the symptom that finally led us to the autism diagnosis—Jacob now lay in his bed sleeping the sweet sleep of exhaustion, at peace in the oblivion that only children and suicides can sink into. I stroked the shotgun in my lap and thought: two shells, two of us. Sweet oblivion. God forgive me, but I thought of nothing else all through that darkest and most awful of nights. Until the coming day lit the living room window gray as the ghost of an epiphany, whispering that it was time to move on. And I put the shotgun back into the closet; resigned my position at Austin Community College; quit my weekend job waiting tables at Aqua Vitae Café; and at the age of forty, took five-year-old Jacob and moved back to the Southwest Texas ranch that I swore I'd left behind forever when I turned eighteen.

The old home place had run down in the years since my father died. The paint on the house was faded, the barbed wire fences rusted and slack. But the arid plains with their cactus and mesquite, the daily rhythm of tending to horses and cattle, the spectacular sunrises and sunsets and the cavernous silence, they were all the same. My mother was grayer, but still strong as ever, and wise enough to let me work through the hurt on my own.

After months of soul-searching, grueling physical labor patching fences and putting things on the ranch back into order, and struggling to find the right treatment for Jacob's Autism Spectrum Disorder—mild Asperger's, thankfully, with every indication that he will grow up a fully functional, independent adult—I landed the Visiting Assistant Professor job at UTSA and made another start. I could live without love, I figured. Anyway, without romantic love. I had people to care for, a career to build.

I was done playing Dido. It was time to be Aeneas instead.

* * *

The word *catharsis* flashes across my mind as the mélange of coffee and incense that fills the Mystic Café permeates my senses. It was here at her combination coffee and divination boutique that I first met Sara Ripa a year ago. Full-figured, dirty-blonde, her eyes deep green as a river flowing in a limestone bed, Sara flashed a crooked grin at me—and I spent the rest of the afternoon convincing her to come out for a hurricane at Pat O'Brien's on the River Walk when she closed up shop. We sat beside the trademark fiery fountain in the courtyard, listened to live jazz, shared first-date-edited details about our lives; but what I remember most about that evening was the electric spark in Sara's eyes.

As I catch sight of her now at the takeout counter in an iridescent yellow robe, she flashes that same crooked grin—and I feel the part of myself that was dead for two years quicken with life. "Hello, love," I say.

"Are you ready to spend a couple of days on the Brazos River?"

"No, I'm not. Not yet. I've got to get out of this outfit first and finish packing Ariel's overnight things. She's spending the weekend with Belinda. And there's something I need you to help me out with while I get ready to go."

"I'd rather help you out of that outfit."

"No such luck." Sara ducks through the bead curtain that separates the takeout counter from the rest of the shop. "Come on."

I follow her through the funky coffee bar/alternative bookstore, then on through another bead curtain into the tarot salon. Natural light filters in through the sliding glass door to the balcony overlooking the river, and the round glass-topped table that dominates the little room is occupied by a dark-haired woman in a loose-fitting robe like Sara's, but red.

"Hello, Belinda," I say. "How's the fortune-telling business?"

"Brisk. With the exception of the next half hour, I've got palm and tarot readings booked all day." She nods to the empty chair across from her. "Have a seat."

"Well, um . . . I'd love to sit and visit. But Sara and I are about to —"

"Joe," Sara interrupts. "This is the thing I need you to help me out with."

I look from Sara to Belinda and back again, realizing that I've just walked into an ambush. But after a long moment spent running through possible options—the best of which by far involves a sit-down with Sara's former mother-in-law—I take the chair.

"Would you prefer palm or tarot?" Belinda asks as Sara ducks back through the bead curtain.

"I'll leave that up to you."

"Tarot then. But first, tell me about your botched proposal."

It is another ambush. But times ten—about like my asking Belinda to tell me what it's like working for her dead son's widow—and the blush stinging across my cheeks feels like a slap. "It sounds as though Sara has told you already."

Belinda's dark brown irises, flecked with gold highlights, are fixed on my face. "I'd like to hear it from you."

"I don't know if I feel comfortable sharing it with you." I shift my gaze out onto the balcony, the place where Sara and I first made love. We were celebrating the one-month anniversary of our first date. A full October moon silvered the river beneath us and Sara's skin, so warm under my fingertips, was the color of the water. "For Sara's sake," I say, glancing back in at Belinda, "okay. But when I'm finished, you have to promise to answer a question for me."

"Agreed."

"For the record, I don't think *botched* is a fair description of my proposal attempt. Everything was going perfectly until the ring went into the Brazos."

"Sara has told me about the ring and the river. It's the context I'm interested in."

"Context? I was proposing marriage, for Christ's sake."

The ghost of a smile plays across her lips. "Indulge me," she says, "with details."

"Okay. We were up in Granbury visiting the Clarks, a couple who have a cottage overlooking the Brazos. The invitation came because of an article I published about the Latin Settlement, which was a utopian community founded in the Texas Hill Country by a group of German Freethinkers. They wanted to replace civil law with brotherly love and goodwill, and tried to make Latin their official language."

"Brotherly love and goodwill?" She raises a perfectly plucked eyebrow. "How did that work out?"

"Better for me than for them. The Latin Settlement is long gone—but the publication was a big deal, career-wise. So was the visit. I've expanded the essay into a book; and Dr. Clark, a prominent Texas historian, helped get it accepted by a major academic press. Sara was the real star of the show, though. She and Mrs. Clark hit it off at dinner on Friday, and it was obvious that Dr. Clark was completely smitten. When dinner was over, I took Sara to the Groggy Dawg for drinks on their floating deck. As we sat looking at the full moon reflected in the water, I got down on one knee to propose. But when I pulled the ring out of my pocket, it did a double back-flip, bounced off the wooden slats of the deck, and plunked into the river."

"And you honestly don't think *botched* is a fair description of that?"

I feel my cheeks burn again. "Does it really matter what I think? Sara called my losing the ring in the river an *omen*. And she's been distant ever since. That's why I planned this weekend canoe trip. We're going to run the Brazos above Granbury. I'm hoping that some time alone on the wild river will remind her of why I proposed in the first place, and why she was going to say yes."

"Is that all?"

"No. I'm going to ask her to marry me again. But I'd appreciate it if we could keep that between ourselves."

"Is that what you wanted to ask me?"

I pull a bright yellow waterproof case out of my pocket and set it on the table between us. "Actually, I'd like you to bless the new ring."

The only thing that betrays Belinda's surprise is a slight twitch of one thin, dark eyebrow. "Are you sure?" she asks. "I am, after all, your prospective fiancée's former mother-in-law. What if I put a curse on it instead?"

"Sara has told me about your son's accident, and I'm sorry. But I'm not sorry to be in love with Sara, or to be doing everything in my power to make her and Ariel happy." Despite the gravity of the situation, and my decidedly mixed feelings about Belinda, I have to fight back a grin as I picture Sara's fiery-haired sprite of a daughter, six years old and already lovely like her mother. "I think Ariel really loves me. And I know that Jacob, like his father, is crazy about Sara. I honestly believe we can all be happy together, a real family. And that includes you. I'm not jealous of your relationship with Sara. You're good for her, and good for Ariel."

Belinda takes a deep breath, lets it out again. "Sara has serious misgivings, and I'm not sure that a canoe trip alone can allay them. That said, I rather like you. I didn't expect I would, but I find that I do. So I'll do the blessing." She picks up the case and opens it, whispering in a language I can't place. She removes the ring, kisses the oval-cut emerald that is exactly the color of Sara's eyes, holds it against her heart. Then she replaces the ring in the case and returns it to me.

"Thank you," I say. "Do you mind if I ask you another question?"

"Go ahead."

"If there were no such thing as love, would we invent it?"

"Excuse me?"

"I guess what I'm really asking is: Can we live without love? Before I met Sara, I thought the answer was yes. Now I'm not so sure."

Belinda smiles a close-lipped half-smile. "You have a good heart, no matter how things may turn out with Sara. So instead of reading your tarot, I'm going to teach you to see the future. If you're interested."

"I've never been very good with cards."

"To be honest, neither is Sara." Her half-smile blossoms into a spray of good-natured laughter. "But like your intention to propose again on this river trip, that fact must remain between you and me. One of the simplest methods of fortune-telling is the interpretation of pendulum movements. Here is how it's done. First, attach a key—the older the better—to one end of a seven-inch cord. Next, hold the other end of the cord so that the key dangles freely. Get the pendulum to hang as still as possible, then ask a question that can be answered *yes* or *no*. In a moment the pendulum will start to move. If the key swings in a north-south direction, the answer is *yes*. If it swings east-west, the answer is *no*. Incidentally, instead of a key, you might use a ring."

"I understand. Thanks again. For everything."

"Good luck," Belinda says. "Something tells me you'll need it."

* * *

September has brought rain to the cedar-studded limestone crags of the Texas Hill Country, and everything is green. Just outside of Llano, Sara reaches over from the passenger seat and brushes her fingertips across the back of my hand. "It's beautiful here," she says.

"Wait till we get on the Brazos. Like John Graves wrote in *Goodbye to a River*, the best way to get to know this country is from a canoe."

"I've never read *Goodbye to a River*. And Joe, you don't have a canoe."

"Trust me. I'm borrowing a boat from an old friend of mine in San Saba. And as for the book, I brought along a copy to give you when we get to the Brazos. It's packed in my rucksack. If you'd like, I can stop and get it out now."

"Let's talk awhile instead. I need to explain about Belinda. About why I had you meet with her, I mean, before we left."

"You don't have to—"

"Joe, I need you to understand how I feel about the possibility of being married to you, and why it makes me afraid."

"Why on earth would the possibility of being married to me frighten you?"

Sara looks away from me, at the limestone hills passing outside the window. "I'm afraid you'll leave."

"Sara, I would never do that. That's what the marriage vows mean."

"But you're divorced."

"Elizabeth is the one who left. You've seen the effect that had on Jacob's and my life."

"You can't promise you'll never die. Like David did."

"Sara? Will you look at me?"

She shakes her head, keeps looking silently out the window.

"Okay, you're right. I can't promise that I won't die on you. But I give you my word that, unlike David, I'll never drive drunk—and that will certainly lower the odds. And I can tell you this for a fact. My mother and father were married thirty-nine years before the old man passed. If my mother had thought the way you're thinking right now, they'd have gotten none of those years. And she wouldn't have Jacob to take care of this weekend, while you and I are canoeing the Brazos."

Still looking out the window, Sara interlaces her fingers with mine.

* * *

I catch sight of Cecil Jubak's green canoe—riverworn and sunfaded—angling up over what there is of downtown San Saba traffic, and I swoop into the parking space next to his big black Expedition. The historic county courthouse looms above us, all red bricks and white Ionic columns. I glance at the clock in the cupola as I bolt from the Xterra: 2:45. My plan to re-propose to Sara this evening calls for the two of us to be on the river by 5 p.m., but my talk with Belinda has us running late.

Cecil shakes my hand, the grin swallowing half his face. He and I have been friends our whole lives—even served as best man at each other's weddings—and although our last couple of decades have been spent mostly apart, we've seen each other when we could. His grip feels as firm as ever; but crow's feet crinkle the corners of his eyes, and his hair is getting thin.

"Do I look as old as you do?" I ask, grinning back.

"Not even close," he says and belly-laughs. "But then again, you haven't raised three daughters. And you haven't spent the past year being kept awake all night by your new grandson. I'm too damn young to be a grandfather, Joe. And too damn old to be a substitute parent, I can tell you that."

"Marrying Juno was the smartest thing you ever did, and we both know it. And it never would've happened if I hadn't introduced the two of you that day on the river."

"As I recall, it was my idea to paddle the boat over."

"*Paddle over*? You rammed into her canoe. But it was me who knew Juno from Latin class."

I introduce Cecil to Sara, and the two of them visit as we transfer the boat onto the Xterra. By the time we've got it tied down, the courthouse clock reads 3:15.

Cecil runs a hand along the flank of the canoe. "Take good care of this boat. I plan to point it down the Colorado with my grandson as soon as he's old enough to paddle." He glances up at the courthouse clock, then stares away southward and westward—the direction I drove out of this morning long before the coming sun paled the eastern sky. "Do you remember that pact we made back in high school?"

"To get the hell out of Southwest Texas, you mean, and never come back? I think about it every time I cross the cattleguard onto the ranch. You've done well for yourself, Cecil. Better than I have."

"Bullshit. You got an education, Dr. Jasmine. You've got your boy. And that's a lovely lady you're spending the weekend with." He shakes my hand again. "See you Sunday afternoon. With my boat intact."

* * *

At the Highway 16 bridge just below Possum Kingdom Dam, Sara takes pictures of the green ribbon of the Brazos while I unload the ice chest and stuff supplies into waterproof bags. Then we take the canoe off the top of the SUV together and drag it down the cement ramp. Once I've stowed our gear in the boat, we're ready to go. I check the time on my cell phone before I double-bag and stow it. 5:45 p.m. Almost an hour behind schedule.

I wade into the cool water and steady the canoe as Sara steps into the front. Then I pull the heavily laden boat out toward the main channel. As I hop into the back, I feel the boat start to roll—the last time I paddled a canoe was on the upper Colorado with Cecil, ten years ago—and for a heartstopping moment, my plan for a perfect evening swings wildly toward a thorough soaking for Sara and myself and all our gear. But I manage to dig the paddle into the graveled riverbed and shove us forward, and the boat trues out as we merge with the current.

We scrape through a couple of quick riffles into a broad channel, fast-moving and clear, and I settle into an easy rhythm. The current carries us along past desert-varnished bluffs, and I identify the trees on the banks for Sara: salt cedar, mountain cedar, pecan, hackberry, elm, and ash. The river alternates between broad, gravel-bottomed shallows and deep, clear holes full of fish. At first, Sara is an awkward paddler. But she soon gets the feel of things in the front of the canoe and learns to trust me to do the steering from the back.

"What was that you and Cecil were saying earlier about a pact?" Sara asks once she's sure enough of her balance to turn around and face me.

"Cecil's father used to own the ranch next to the one I grew up on.

143

We played together as kids, worked together from the time we were ten, went to school together from kindergarten through twelfth grade. Our senior year, we made a solemn promise to leave Southwest Texas as soon as we graduated and never come back."

"But you are back. You and Jacob."

"No, I'm on the Brazos River with the most beautiful woman in Texas."

"You know what I mean. You didn't keep your promise."

An accusing undertone has crept into Sara's voice. I understand that she's talking now about our possible future together, rather than about Cecil's and my distant past. "When Elizabeth left, just after Jacob's initial autism diagnosis, she told me that she didn't love me, and that she never had. The best part of me died that day. Forever, I thought, until I walked into the Mystic Café and looked into your eyes. Moving back to the ranch made falling in love with you possible." I find myself remembering that awful night with the shotgun. "In a way, it saved my life."

Sara nods, faces forward again. I dig in with the paddle and try to make up for lost time. The sun has long since slid behind the bluffs, and we still haven't come across a suitable place to set up camp. If we don't find a campsite soon, I'll have to set up in the dark—which will put an end to my carefully laid plan to propose.

A little after 7:30, I catch sight of a broad peninsula of pea gravel that slopes gently up to the base of a limestone cliff. It is exactly the kind of spot I've been looking for, and I feel a rush of relief as I grind the front of the canoe up onto the shore. Once I've beached the boat, I pull the copy of *Goodbye to a River* that I brought for Sara out of my rucksack and walk over to where she has stretched out on a wide flat rock that angles down into the water.

"Here's the Graves book I told you about," I say. "Would you like to rest and read a bit while I set up camp and start dinner?"

After pitching the tent, breaking out the camp kitchen, and making our air-mattress bed, I build a fire and crank up the gas cookstove. I sauté spicy Italian sausage and garlic and onions and green bell peppers in olive oil, boil a bit of pasta, and plate it up with some fresh sliced tomatoes. Then I call Sara over.

"It smells delicious," she says.

I open a bottle of cabernet and we toast our first night on the Brazos next to the blazing fire. The river whispers in its gravel bed, the fire pops and crackles, a light breeze carries the keening of distant coyotes along the canyon. My spicy Italian stir-fry tastes as good as it smells.

When we're finished, Sara snuggles against me. I find myself wishing for a full moon reflecting up off the river, but the moon is still hidden behind the bluff. Except for that, everything feels exactly right. I pour each of us a second glass of wine and pull the ring case out of its hiding spot.

"Sara," I begin as I kneel beside her, "I'd like—"

"Joe, if you're about to propose again, please don't."

"Ouch." I close my eyes. For a gut-wrenching moment I am in that living room in Austin again, and Elizabeth has just walked out the door. I take the deepest breath of my life. Then I open my eyes and focus only on Sara, who sits staring into the fire. "Does that mean you don't want me to propose at all?" I ask with—I hope—no hint of desperation in my voice. "Or just that the present moment isn't quite perfect?"

"I don't know. But not now. Not tonight."

I take our dinner dishes down to the river and force myself to concentrate only on the simple motions of scrubbing, rinsing, drying. Finally, as the moon starts to peek over the cliff above me, I carry the kitchen gear back up to camp.

Sara glances up at me as I enter the circle of firelight.

"I'd like to share something with you," I say, "if you'll let me. It happened in my Latin class earlier today." I explain about Aeneas and Dido, and about the questions I asked the students regarding the origin of love. Then I tell her about the girl in the back of the classroom who turned the tables on me—and about the students' reaction to the answer I gave.

"They actually applauded you?"

"Every student in the class. But the most important thing wasn't the applause or my improved prospects for a tenure-track job. It was what I said about love. Jupiter himself couldn't make me let go of what you and I have, Sara."

"I believe you. And I love you. But I'm not ready for another proposal. Please don't pressure me."

* * *

By the time I climb into our air mattress bed, Sara is asleep. And as I lie staring up into the darkness, I am afraid to touch her. The evening certainly hasn't turned out according to plan, and I feel completely at a loss as to how to proceed. I drift off to sleep amid tangled thoughts about Sara, about love, about the questions I asked my Latin class; and in my dreams, Dido and Aeneas are paddling away from Carthage together in Cecil's canoe. Behind them, the North African coast lies low and dark in the moonlight; ahead of them, the Mediterranean Sea is an open possibility glittering beneath the rising moon. But not long after they've said goodbye to Carthage, a storm blows up, giant waves start to break across the boat, and suddenly they are both in the water—and the faces of Dido and Aeneas have become Sara's and mine.

I awake drenched in sweat with Sara still sleeping beside me. I ease out of the tent without waking her and make coffee as dawn breaks above the bluff. Then I start breakfast. By the time the eggs are scrambled and the toast is starting to brown, Sara has emerged. I hand her a cup of coffee as she sits down beside the little fire I revived from last night's coals.

"Thank you," she says, looking at the mist rising off the river instead of at me.

"I'm not going to pressure you, Sara," I say. "About anything. You know how I feel. Let's just enjoy the river and each other's company."

After breakfast I strike camp and shove the canoe into the water. We spend the morning alternately floating with the current and paddling against a moderate headwind through wide, gravel-bottomed shallows and deep pools lined with huge gray boulders. There are high banks with limestone cliffs behind them on one side; on the other, the low banks are thick with trees. The silence is broken only by the splash of our paddles, the songs of the various bird species that make the river their home—cardinals and Rocky Mountain bluebirds and great blue herons—and the occasional scream of a bluff-loving hawk riding the spiraling wind currents as it looks for prey below.

"I did some research yesterday before class," I say at last, "and found some information that you might be interested in."

"More freethinking Germans?" Sara asks. "I thought you were done with that book."

"Actually, your last name. The word *ripa* is Latin for *bank*, like the bank of a river. I've told you that before. The origin of the word *river* was *riparia*, and for the Romans it represented specifically the banks of the river instead of the stream. But in the Early French it became *rivere*, and represented both the banks and the water between them. This was the source of our modern English word, *river*."

Sara turns to face me. "So am I the river, or the riverbank?"

"For me, you're both. You're the current that carries me by day and the safe place where I rest in the evening." I stop paddling and lean forward in the canoe. "I've been doing a lot of thinking about those questions I asked my Latin class. And I've come to the conclusion that love is something you discover—a white space on the map of human existence—

and here we are in a boat, two intrepid travelers on a voyage of discovery. Together."

Instead of saying anything, Sara flashes a crooked grin. In the light reflecting up off the river, her green eyes catch fire. Then she turns and starts paddling again.

We stop for lunch on another pea gravel peninsula, then we battle a fierce headwind for most of the afternoon. As the Brazos twists and turns, the headwind occasionally becomes a tailwind; but since the wind is blowing out of the south, it mostly stays in our faces. This part of the river consists of wide lakelike sections with almost no current, alternating with a series of shallow rapids, and I begin to understand what Graves meant when he wrote in *Goodbye to a River* that dams were the death of wild streams. Sometimes the channel is so shallow Sara and I have to get out and push the canoe. The bluffs are taller here, rising to three hundred feet, and Indian blankets and blackeyed Susans make the walking lovely. But Sara has not brought a good pair of water shoes, and after a couple of wading sessions, she is limping noticeably. When I ask if she'd rather sit in the canoe and let me pull her along by the bowline, though, she shakes her head and keeps walking. We finally reach the Highway 4 bridge—halfway to the Sunday pickup I've arranged with a local river outfitter—around 7 p.m.

We push on a little farther, looking for a good place to spend the night. But we finally give up and take out on a patch of gravel beneath a high sandbank. We're both tired, and the wind is gusting hard enough now to make setting up camp difficult. With Sara's help, I finally get the tent pitched and the camp kitchen set up. But neither of us has the energy to lug the heavy cooler and the rest of the gear to the top of the bank. So I haul the canoe up to the base of a salt cedar, flip it, and tie it off. We pull the bags up next to the canoe. Then we drag ourselves back up the sandy slope to the campsite, eat a cold supper, crawl into the tent, and fall asleep in each other's arms.

In the night, a particularly fierce gust rips the raincover off the tent. I have to get up, chase the raincover down, and anchor it with the paddles. Otherwise, we sleep like the two exhausted travelers that we are.

* * *

I awake at dawn the next morning, still a little tired but glad we didn't get the downpour that the gusty winds portended. With the raincover off the tent, Sara and I, and all our bedding, would've gotten soaked.

147

My relief is short-lived.

When I walk down to check the equipment, I discover that disaster struck in the night. While we were sleeping, it must've been raining upriver. The water level has risen at least a foot, and the cooler and the bags we didn't carry up to the top of the sandbank have been swept away. The canoe lies on the bottom, half-filled with riverwater—but still there—at the end of the bowline I tied to a tree.

I stand and stare at the half-sunken canoe, taking stock. Instead of panicked at the wreckage of my grand plan to re-propose to Sara, I just feel numb. The only thing I can really think to do is make a pot of coffee with water from the river before I wake Sara and break the news.

She takes it in with a quiet calm that is as welcome as it is unexpected. "Run through it with me," she says after a slow sip of coffee, "and don't sugar-coat it. Tell me exactly what we're up against."

"We have no food except the breakfast stuff we carried up to the campsite last night. The beer and wine are gone, too. And our supply of drinkable water is really low. One of the things Cecil and I learned back in our canoeing days was to always keep a clean cooler on a river trip, bagging all the food in sealed containers so the icemelt is not only fit to drink, it adds freshness to the plasticky water from the five-gallon jug. Now that ice is gone."

"There's something else," she says ruefully, pulling her feet from underneath the blanket she has wrapped herself in and laying them on my lap. Both are splotched with an angry web of blisters that stretches from her toes to her heels.

"Oh, Sara," I say. "I am so sorry."

"It's my fault, not yours," she says, her muscles tensing as I gently examine the blisters. "You offered to pull me in the canoe, but I turned you down. I wanted to prove that I was as tough as you."

"You're tougher. By far. I would've been sitting in that canoe with my feet up, watching you pull. But will you at least let me doctor these blisters? I've got some stuff in the tent that will make them feel better."

As I rub on the ointment, the tension in Sara's muscles starts to ease. "Anyway," she says, "we still have the canoe. So we're not going to have to find our way out of the middle of nowhere on foot." Her expression is half grimace, half crooked grin. "On *blistered feet*, I guess I should say."

"And we've got the cookstove, so we can boil riverwater for drinking. It's not much of a consolation, but it's better than nothing."

We drink the coffee and eat bran muffins as the sun comes up.

Despite everything, the sunrise is gorgeous. The sky has cleared and the wind has slacked off. Once I've packed up camp, I flip the canoe, drain most of the water, and drag the boat ashore to dry. I search the river-bottom for our missing stuff, but the only thing I get for my trouble is a thorough soaking.

We get back on the river around 9:30 and paddle against a light headwind for most of the morning. We pass a stone mansion atop a towering bluff and a wooden cabin at the top of a flight of steps that climbs about ten feet above river level. The cabin seems deserted, but a sign nailed to the porch reads: COMING ONTO THIS PROPERTY IS NOT WORTH GETTING SHOT. It's an easy decision not to try climbing up there in hopes of refilling our much-depleted water supply. Instead, we push on.

We stop for lunch on a rocky outcrop. I pull the canoe up onto the warm limestone ledge and spread a tarp for Sara, who settles onto the silver canvas and slathers more ointment on her bare and blistered feet. Then she opens the Graves book on her lap.

"You know," I say, "there is one positive thing about the river having risen in the night. We didn't have to get out and walk a single step this morning."

"You're right. And I don't believe that will be the only positive thing," Sara says thoughtfully, looking up from *Goodbye to a River*. "I have a good feeling about today."

"Good enough for another proposal?" I ask with a tentative grin. "The new ring wasn't in the bags that washed away last night. So there's no reason to say *goodbye to an engagement*."

Sara groans. Then she laughs out loud. "No," she says. "I don't guess there is."

We eat the last remaining bran muffins and continue on. The Brazos runs deeper and narrower here between wooded banks, and the current carries us along past trotlines marked with brightly colored ribbons. When the river broadens again, though, the wind picks up. Soon we're fighting a headwind that gusts out of the south. To lighten the load on Sara, I dig in with the paddle and settle into a river-churning rhythm that eats up the miles and takes my mind off the empty state of my stomach and our lack of food supplies.

Finally, around 5 p.m., Sara breaks the silence with a shout that nearly makes me flip the canoe. "Joe! Look! Isn't that our cooler?"

Snagged between two scraggly cedars in an eddy at the bottom of a little rapid—scuffed and open-lidded, but intact—our green ice chest sits bobbing in the river. The ice has melted, and the sausage and sandwich meat have definitely turned. But the vegetables look fine. Even better, most of our beer has somehow remained inside. I secure the lid and tie the cooler onto the back of the canoe.

"It looks as though the river gods have finally smiled on us," I say.

"I told you I had a good feeling about today."

A little later we find the best river campsite I've ever had the good fortune to come across—a broad alluvial plain covered with stones ranging from pea-gravel up through big river-smoothed boulders half the size of the canoe. The flat white expanse is littered with dead trees that make gathering firewood easy. While Sara sits down with her Graves book, I quickly fetch enough deadwood for a bonfire, then put the beer into the river to cool.

As I'm anchoring our pale ales with rocks to keep them from floating away again, I catch sight of a blue-flagged trotline that starts to jerk and sway in the water. I swing my eyes along the line a little farther out from the bank and see a dark shape just beneath the surface. Then the big fish slaps the water with its tail and disappears again amid a swirl of bubbles and a great jerking and swaying of the trotline.

I hesitate a moment, taking a quick look around for approaching johnboats. Seeing nothing, I haul the long, heavy section of twine in hand over hand until I feel the catfish floundering against my legs. Then I reach down, catch it by the gills, and pull it out of the water. I steady its slippery, struggling bulk against my waist just long enough to pull the hook from its jaw before staggering up onto the rocky bank with my prize.

"Sara? Come and look at this!"

"What is it?"

"Dinner," I say, holding the fish up for her to see. It takes both hands. "Anyway, the main course."

Sara sets her book down and hauls herself gingerly up onto her feet. "How did you catch it?"

"I took it off a trotline."

"Isn't that stealing? I won't eat stolen food. Besides being wrong, it's bad luck."

"Sara," I say. "Love, if we don't eat this fish, we won't be eating much of anything between now and noon tomorrow when he reach the take-out point. The meat in the cooler, and all the dairy stuff, spoiled when the ice melted. All that's left are a few vegetables."

"Joe," Sara says earnestly, "our luck has just started to turn for the better. The last thing we need now is to tempt fate."

"You're right. But what about this: we keep the catfish, but use the spoiled sausage in our cooler to re-bait every hook on that trotline. It'll be like trading a dozen fish for the one we're taking."

"I don't know."

"There's nothing catfish like better than rotten sausage. I guarantee you we'll be doing whoever runs that trotline a favor."

"I guess I can live with that."

I slip the bowline of the canoe through the catfish's gills and put the fish back into the river. Then Sara and I take the sausage from the cooler and bait every hook on the trotline I pulled from the stream. Finally, I wade back out into the channel, cut off the end section of the twine, and anchor the re-baited trotline with a rock. On my way back to shore, I pull two newly chilled pale ales from the river.

"Now that the river gods have been fed, how about us?" I open the pale ales, pass one to Sara. "Let's cook that big catfish before he pulls our canoe out to sea."

"Only if you let me do the cooking for a change."

"Done."

I clean the catfish while Sara chops garlic, onions, green bell peppers, and tomatoes into the frying pan. Then she adds in the catfish chunks and some olive oil, and sautés it all up into a delicious dish that we share next to a blazing fire. The full moon hangs low and lovely overhead, silvering the surface of the river before us and the white stone plain behind us so that we seem to be floating on a pool of liquid moonlight. The gusty wind settled down at sunset, leaving a gentle southerly breeze that is just enough to keep the mosquitoes at bay. If there is ever going to be a third proposal attempt, the moment has come.

I take the ring from its hiding place and kneel beside Sara. "If love is a white space on the universal map," I say, "then you and I have discovered it together. Marry me, Sara."

Sara takes the ring and holds it up so that the emerald comes alive in the firelight. "It's lovely. Better than a diamond by far."

"For the ancient Romans, the emerald was sacred to the goddess Venus. They believed it sustained love and could also reveal the truth of a lover's pledge."

"Oh, Joe, I want very much to say *yes*. But you know how I feel about omens and about fate. And you have to admit that the omen we got during your first proposal attempt wasn't exactly promising."

"The Romans also cherished the emerald as a stone of prophecy." I pull out the piece of twine that I cut from the trotline after we re-baited the hooks. "I'm willing to let the river gods decide, if you are."

"What do you mean?"

"Let me share with you something that your former mother-in-law shared with me when we had our talk." I explain to Sara about the pendulum method of fortune-telling that Belinda described back at the Mystic Café. "A north-and-south movement means *yes*," I say, "and an east-and-west movement means *no*. What do you say?"

"You'll really abide by the outcome, no matter what?" Sara turns to face me, and with her back to the fire, her skin shines as silver in the moonlight as the river we've run together.

I think about fortune and fate, about Aeneas and Dido, about the headwind Sara and I fought against all afternoon. "You said that you wanted an omen," I say, taking the ring from Sara and tying it to the end of the string. "And I want to show you that I'm as good as my word. If the pendulum swings north-and-south, we get married. If the pendulum swings east-and-west, it's no go. I'll make that most solemn promise, and I'll abide by the outcome, if you will."

"All right," Sara says. "I do promise."

I meet Sara's eyes and lower the pendulum into the gentle southerly breeze. "I do, too."

Tragic Voices
after William Shakespeare
(2008)

They were now, as they had always been, real to him—as much a fact of life as the southerly breeze that cooled his front porch. Their elocution excellent, their projection perfect, the voices spoke to Roger in lines from Shakespeare's greatest plays.

Sometimes, when the sky was clear-blue and bright feathers flashed as birds came to the feeders in front of the old Tudor-style house, the voices spoke lines from the comedies that made Roger smile. Other times, when he was walking the two miles from the ranch into Jordan and feeling beaten down by the weight of the Southwest Texas sun, the voices spoke lines from the histories that stirred Roger's spirits and steadied his stride. Then there were the times when the voices spoke lines from the tragedies. The tragic voices made Roger feel things he didn't like to think about.

Nowadays, the tragic voices mostly spoke when squirrels were stealing the seed Roger worked so hard to put out for the birds. The lines came from *Othello*, *King Lear*, *Romeo and Juliet*, and *Hamlet*. They urged him to do "murder most foul" to the wily thieves. To drown out the voices, Roger picked up his drum major baton and marched circles around the feeders humming Mendelssohn's "Wedding March" from *A Midsummer Night's Dream* at the top of his lungs until the squirrels fled. Only then could he return to the porch and watch feathers flash red and blue and yellow and gray as the birds came back. Only then would the tragic voices go quiet.

He was watching the bird feeders now. There were three of them in front of the big Tudor-style ranch house that his father had designed himself back before the tragic voices goaded Roger into shotgunning his parents. He and his father had built the feeders together. They were miniatures of the big house—tiny Tudor cottages with decorative half-timbering, prominent cross-gables, and steeply pitched roofs—and the birdseed went into the top. The roofs flipped up on hinges, and there were troughs on either side of each cottage that the seed trickled into. The houses sat atop steel poles, and steel crosspieces were welded onto the top of each pole so the birds could perch and eat from the troughs. Roger's father, an amateur architect and lapsed Catholic, had set the center pole a foot higher than the others and jokingly called the trio his "Golgotha Revival." But Roger's mother, a professional homemaker and Hardshell Baptist, had not found that funny in the least. She'd insisted that Roger refer to the feeders as "Tudor aviaries" instead.

A pair of mourning doves settled onto the middle feeder, and Roger smiled, hearing the comic voices speak one of Hermia's speeches from the opening scene of *A Midsummer Night's Dream*. Hermia swore to elope with Lysander "by the simplicity of Venus's doves, by that which knitteth souls and prospers loves, and by that fire which burned the Carthage queen, when false Troyan under sail was seen." Roger settled into his rusty metal lawn chair, feeling the westering sun's heat radiate up off the concrete porch as the sky turned gold. The calls of the doves blended with the comic voices, and Roger's world was as bright and hopeful and full of love as the triple wedding that graced the end of his favorite comic play.

But then a squirrel scampered out of the brush and shinnied up the pole that held the middle feeder. Roger's smile faded as the comic voices turned tragic, and *A Midsummer Night's Dream* darkened into *Romeo and Juliet*. Juliet began speaking in harsh tones about that "dove-feathered raven," that "wolvish-ravening lamb," and Roger's thoughts turned as bloody as the dagger she sheaths in her own sweet flesh in the final act. The squirrel reached the crosspiece of the feeder and the mourning doves flew up, their high-pitched distress cries blending with Juliet's dying voice as they circled away into the sinking sun.

Roger's world narrowed to the voices, which had moved on to *King Lear* now—bleak, blood-spattered, lovely *Lear*—and Roger's thoughts, like the setting sun, turned the color of blood. He heard again the tragic voices goading him into murder all those years ago: Regan and Cornwall in the grisly third act, whispering poison, spurring Roger to take revenge. He remembered the smell of burnt gunpowder as he blasted three holes into his traitorous father's chest. He remembered the change in his mother's eyes—disbelief to terror, terror to loathing—as she tried to drag the body down the hall that led from the stairway to the back door, leaving a smeared bloodtrail on the parquet floor. He remembered clicking three more shells into the magazine, pumping one into the chamber, firing the shotgun again and again and again. He remembered the muzzle flashing fire in the dim hallway as the fear in his mother's eyes dissolved into gore: "Out vile jelly! Where is thy luster now?"

Wait.

Roger saw something moving in the brush at the edge of the clearing in front of the house. It was not a squirrel. No, it was a boy. It was that same boy with that same BB gun who had shot one of Roger's birds the week before. A cardinal. Roger had not seen the boy shoot the bird. But he had seen the boy with the gun. And then he'd found the cardinal at the base of the left-hand feeder with a hole in its chest.

Roger picked up his drum major baton and brought the heavy metal head down hard against his palm. He saw the blood-red sun sink below the line of hills on the western horizon. The tragic voices spoke from *Othello*: "Turn out the light, and turn out the light." He slipped off the porch and crept through the thicket, careful to avoid the thorns on the mesquite and prickly pear. He came quietly up behind the intruder just as the boy raised the BB gun and fired a shot.

Roger drew a quick breath, swinging the drum major baton hard at the boy's head as his eyes followed the arc of the shot. But instead of a dead dove falling gracefully to earth, he saw the squirrel on the middle feeder go ass over teakettle as the BB knocked it off the crosspiece. It flopped like a pratfalling clown when it hit the ground, then skittered away into the brush.

"Don't kill me!" the boy said, cowering back. He held the BB gun against his chest and looked up at Roger, who stood with the baton frozen in the air about three inches from the boy's contorted face. "You can have my gun. It's a Red Rider. My father gave it to me."

Roger looked at the gun. In his mind the squirrel went back-flipping off the feeder again, and he heard the voice of Puck speak in *A Midsummer Night's Dream* about the "crew of patches, rude mechanicals." He heard Puck promise to lead them "about a round through bog, through bush, through brake, through brier." Instead of Quince, Snug, Bottom, Flute, Snout, and Starveling, Roger saw the squirrels being played for fools. And for the first time since his parents died, he thought about the squirrels and laughed.

"Sweet Puck!" Roger said, holding his hand out for the gun and feeling the warm, sweat-damp stock slide into his fingers. "This falls out better than I could devise."

"My name isn't Puck," the boy said. "It's Jacob."

"And mine is Roger. Did you climb through the fence from the Jasmine place next door?"

The boy nodded. "My father and me live there with my grandma now."

"Jacob Jasmine? I knew your father all too well, once upon a time.

155

Joe Jasmine wasn't a very nice young man. Especially to me. In fact, he and his best friend, Cecil Jubak, did everything they could to make my high school days a living hell."

"My father is too a nice man! He takes care of my grandma and me."

"Hmm . . . I knew your grandparents too, back when your grandpa was alive. Unlike your father, Big Joe was a fine gentleman who was never anything but kind to me. How would you like to earn your gun back, Jacob?"

"Depends on what I've got to do. I've got another BB gun. It shoots harder than this one, but you have to pump it up."

"All you have to do is come back tomorrow. I'll tell you a funny story about a fairy king named Oberon, a fairy queen named Titania, and a man named Bottom with a donkey's head. There's a fairy named Puck who plays pranks on Bottom and his friends. You can play Puck, and I'll play Oberon. And we'll make those squirrels rue the day they ever saw a bird feeder. "

"I don't know. My grandma says I'm not supposed to come over here. And anyway, I'm kind of low on BB's."

"Well then, don't tell your grandma," Roger said. "As for BB's, I'll go to town and get the biggest box they've got. And some other stuff besides."

The next morning, Roger walked into Jordan and bought a box of 5000 BB's and a greasebucket. The greasebucket was heavy and awkward to carry—every bit as awkward as the twenty-five pound bags of birdseed he bought each month—and lugging it the two miles back out to the ranch house exhausted him. He fell asleep in his lawn chair, watching the birds.

He was startled awake by a crackling in the brush and opened his eyes to see Jacob walking across the open space in front of the house. The boy was carrying another BB gun, and the squirrels—who had climbed all three poles during Roger's long nap and were now busy robbing all three feeders—fled at the sight of him.

"Welcome, good Robin!" Roger called out, his heart fluttering like a sparrow's wings at squirrels' discomfort. "See'st thou this sweet sight?"

"Robin? I thought I was going to play Puck."

"So you are. Robin Goodfellow is called Puck for short. I see you've kept your promise about bringing the other gun. I've kept mine as well." Roger brought out the BB's and let Jacob show him how to fill up both guns, even though the lever-action Red Rider was exactly like the one that Roger used to shoot as a boy.

"You said you were going to bring some other stuff."

"So I did. But that's for later."

"What are we going to do right now?"

"Now we wait. And I'll tell you the story I promised."

They sat on the porch, Roger in his rusted-out old metal lawn chair that was once yellow but had faded almost white in the Southwest Texas sun, and Jacob on a gray plastic milk crate that Roger brought out from the kitchen. Roger started the story of *A Midsummer Night's Dream*. But no sooner had the drugged Titania fallen in love with the donkey-headed Bottom than a pair of squirrels emerged from the brushline. One of them started shinnying up the middle pole, and Roger stopped the story.

"What now?" Jacob asked.

"Committ'st thy knaveries willfully!"

The boy glanced sideways at Roger, his eyes dark brown and confused like the eyes of a puppy that's been petted then spanked.

"Go ahead, Puck," Roger said gently, smiling into the boy's eyes and then glancing up just as the squirrel reached the crosspiece. "Take the first shot."

Jacob slid a BB into the chamber, pumped the gun five times, then steadied his aim on his knee and squeezed off a shot. The squirrel on the crosspiece leaped three feet into the air, tried to grab the crosspiece on the way down, missed, and spun slow arm-flailing circles all the way to the ground. Then both squirrels ran back into the brush.

"Trip away; make no stay!" Roger called after the fleeing squirrels.

Jacob laughed out loud, and Roger wondered briefly why Shakespeare never included squirrels in any of his plays. Squirrels were certainly naturals at low comedy.

They spent the rest of the afternoon just like that. Roger let Jacob do all the shooting, Jacob let Roger do most of the talking, and they both spent a lot of time laughing out loud. When the boy hit a squirrel on the ground, it would grab the spot the BB had struck and leap into the air before skittering like greased lightning back into the brush. When he hit a squirrel on a pole, the squirrel would flip backwards with its arms all aflail until it hit the ground and half-ran, half-staggered back under cover. In between squirrels, Roger told the story of the rest of the play. After the triple wedding had taken place and the squirrels had pretty much given up on raiding the bird feeders for the day, Jacob told Roger that it was time for him to head home.

"I wouldn't want my grandma to come looking for me," he said.

"Why not?" Roger asked.

"My grandma says you're crazy, and that you killed your parents. She says you sit out on the porch with a shotgun waiting for folks to come up to this broken-down old house so you can shoot them, too. But I don't believe it. You haven't shot a single squirrel all day."

"I guess I haven't," Roger said.

"Hey, what about the other stuff you bought?"

"Other stuff?" Roger asked. Then he remembered the grease-bucket. "Oh yes. Come back tomorrow, and we'll try something new."

Jacob took the pump gun and left, leaving Roger the lever-action Red Rider. He cradled the gun on his lap and swung his chair around to face the house that he had grown up in as an only child after his two older sisters married and moved away. He guessed the old place did look broken-down. Most of the upstairs windows were busted and some of the shingles were missing from the roof, evidence of hailstorms and dusters that had come and gone in the years since the tragic voices goaded Roger into shotgunning his parents, and he was sent off to the San Antonio State Hospital to be made sane. Roger remembered telling the doctors about the tragic voices. He also told them about the comic voices and the voices from the histories, but it was the tragic voices the doctors were interested in. Their official diagnosis was paranoid schizophrenia with auditory hallucinations. They gave him a prescription, and the voices stopped. Roger also had psychotherapy, which meant that he talked and talked, sometimes to the doctors and sometimes to other patients he didn't like very much. It turned out that his father had sexually abused him when he was a boy. The doctors said Roger had repressed that until the therapy brought it out. Once he'd spent enough time talking, and promised to take his pills, they let him go.

Of course, Roger came back home. His sisters went to court to keep him from ever contacting them again, so he had no place else to go but the ranch. Roger guessed he and Jacob had that in common. The next nearest human habitation to the Jasmine place was in Jordan, and the Jasmines lived another mile past Roger's house. He figured the boy would be back the next day all right, grandma or no.

Late the next afternoon, after the sun had swollen and cooled from a white-hot point to a great golden circle and Roger was beginning to wonder whether the boy would come after all, he heard the brush crackle and saw Jacob step into the cleared space.

"My gentle Puck," Roger said, "come hither. I was beginning to think you wouldn't come."

"It was hard to get away from my grandma. My dad went on a

canoe trip this weekend, so she's watching me extra close. I think she knows something's up."

"As I recall, your grandma is pretty sharp."

"Not that sharp," the boy said. "She keeps going on about how you shot your parents and went to the loony bin, and how you'll shoot me, too. And I know that's not true."

"What if part of it was true?"

Jacob glanced sideways at Roger, but didn't meet his eyes. "What part?"

"It's true that I shot my father. And when my mother tried to help him, it's true that I shot her, too. But I wouldn't shoot you, or your grandma, or anybody else. I promise. I will never do you any harm. I don't even have a gun anymore. The doctors wouldn't let me."

"Doctors?"

"It's true about the loony bin, too."

"Really? Did they hook up wires to you and shock you, or burn you with cigarettes, or tie you up and leave you in the dark?"

"Nothing like that. I hear voices in my head. Sometimes they try to get me to do things. The doctors asked me questions about that, and I talked about it. Then they gave me some pills and asked more questions, and I talked a lot more. Finally they told me that if I promised to always take my pills, they would let me go."

"What kind of pills?"

"The kind that make the voices go away," Roger said.

The boy met Roger's eyes and smiled a slow, cautious smile. "I take pills, too."

"What do yours do?" Roger asked gently.

"Help me focus. I've got Asperger's, and the doctor told me that I have trouble controlling my impulses. The medicine calms me down."

"It certainly sounds like we have a lot in common," Roger said.

A couple of squirrels scampered out of the brush, and one of them started up the middle pole. Jacob raised his gun and sent the would-be thief backflipping to the ground. They spent what little time they had left that afternoon pelting squirrels with BB's. Just before the boy left, he asked again about the other stuff Roger had bought, and Roger promised that if Jacob would come a little earlier tomorrow, they would bring it out.

Which was just as well. It turned out, upon Jacob's early return, that after a couple of days of getting pelted, the squirrels had gotten used to the BB's. When the boy missed, they shook their tails at him and chattered as if they were mocking him. When he hit them, they backed off and came on again. They managed to get to the feed by keeping the pole between themselves and the porch, wincing when the BB's pinged off the stainless steel pipe, but still climbing.

"Jacob," Roger said at last, "it's time for the greasebucket."

"The what?"

"The other stuff I bought. We're going to grease the poles."

Roger fetched the greasebucket from the kitchen. The thick black goo felt cool and smooth as he pumped it out of the bucket onto their hands.

"It looks like frosting." The boy licked a bit of grease off one of his fingers and made a face.

"How does it taste?" Roger asked.

"Disgusting."

They slathered all three poles from base to crosspiece. Then they wiped the goop off their hands and settled back onto the porch to watch the show. It wasn't long before a pair of squirrels scampered out of the brush and approached the center pole. The squirrels sniffed around the base at first, skittering back to the brushline when they smelled the grease. But after chattering back and forth, they ambled out again. The lead squirrel stood up on its hind legs and tried to grab the pole, leaping back when its paws sank into the grease. Roger and Jacob laughed out loud as the squirrel frantically licked its paws and wiped its mouth on the back of its arm. Then the second squirrel scampered over to the left-hand pole and did exactly the same thing as the first—with the same results.

"They don't like it either," Roger said.

Finally, one of the squirrels leaped up onto the pole and tried to grab hold, only to slide slowly and comically back down. When its tail hit the ground, it let go of the pole and writhed around in the dirt trying to lick and wipe the thick coat of goo off its belly. Jacob laughed so hard at the sight of it that he fell off his crate, and Roger laughed until there were tears in his eyes.

Over the rest of the afternoon, squirrel after squirrel scampered out of the brush and repeated the leap-and-grab-and-slide of the first pair, much to the delight of Jacob and Roger. As the sun sank huge and gold toward the line of low hills to the west, the boy said it was time to go.

"This is the best day I've had in a long time," Jacob said.

"It's the best day I've ever had," Roger said. "I'll see you tomorrow."

After Jacob left, Roger sat on the porch and watched the sunset spread in gold and orange and red glory across the sky. It felt as though all that beauty was inside his chest. Mourning doves settled onto the feeders, and Roger listened to them calling out to each other. For the first time since he'd stopped taking his pills, the voices were quiet in the presence of the birds. But unlike before—when his life had felt so empty without the voices that he'd stopped taking the drugs—Roger felt content. He had his memories of the day with Jacob to keep him company, and the promise of another day filled with greased poles and sliding squirrels and laughter.

But the squirrels had a surprise for Jacob and Roger. When the boy arrived the next day, the two of them slathered the poles with a fresh coat of grease. The first pair of squirrels emerged from the brushline, the lead squirrel did that same leap-and-grab-and-slide from the day before, and Jacob and Roger laughed out loud. But the second squirrel took a running start, leaped almost up to the crosspiece of the left-hand feeder, bear-hugged the pole, and managed to shinny up the rest of the way by sheer force of will.

Jacob looked at Roger. Roger looked back at Jacob. Then they both looked at the squirrel that was alternately feeding on birdseed and wiping off grease. Neither of them was laughing.

"Time for a BB," Roger said after a while.

"I didn't bring my pump gun."

"Use the Red Rider," Roger said, handing him the gun.

The boy levered a BB into the chamber and pelted the squirrel. But after flinching and almost falling off the crosspiece, the squirrel pulled up the rooftop lid on the feeder and climbed into the birdseed as if he were going to bathe in the stuff. A bunch of seed spilled onto the ground, and the other squirrel started to feast.

The boy levered another BB into the chamber and pelted the squirrel on the ground. But the squirrel put the pole between itself and the porch, and went right on eating the fallen seed.

Roger was dumbfounded.

But just then, Jacob turned to Roger. "We could electrify the poles!" he said excitedly.

"What? How?"

"Run extension cords from the house," the boy said, his eyes all afire. "Shock treatments! That'll teach those squirrels a lesson."

"There's no electricity."

It was Jacob's turn to be dumbfounded. "How can you have no electricity?"

"I have two older sisters," Roger said. "My father left them all the money my parents had, and the insurance, and the cattle which my sisters sold. He left me the land and the house. When I came home from the hospital, I was on my own. The money from the oil wells on the ranch was set aside to pay the taxes on the land and keep the place up. But the wells don't pump much anymore, and I have to live on that money, too. The place fell into disrepair. The house is a wreck. And the electricity and phone have been cut off."

"But how do you cook? How do you light the house?"

"I've kept up with the gas bill. Come on, I'll show you."

Roger led the boy inside the house, through the living room that was empty except for the mattress Roger slept on, and into the kitchen. A white gas stove with the words DETROIT JEWEL in silver letters on the oven door stood in the corner. Next to it, underneath the window that faced west, was the chair Roger sat in when he ate his meals. The chair had been beautiful, once upon a time, with a richly patterned cover done in green and gold. Roger's mother had ordered it from England. But now the cover was tattered and the stuffing laid bare. On the far counter, next to the door that led to the stairway, Roger's bottles of pills were stacked in neat rows. On the other counter to their right were candles and a kerosene lantern.

"I cook on that stove," Roger said. "It runs on gas. And I light the house with the candles and the lantern. I only use the kitchen and the living room. In the winter, I pull my mattress in here and sleep next to the stove."

"I thought you promised to take your pills," Jacob said, pointing at the dozens of neatly stacked bottles full of untaken meds.

"It was so lonely without the voices before you came."

"So you lied. You broke your promise."

Roger saw that look in Jacob's eyes again, like a puppy that's been petted then spanked, and he remembered his promise not to do the boy any harm. "I'd never lie to you, Jacob," Roger said. "You're my best and only friend."

The boy looked away from Roger, out the window that was gold now with the light of the setting sun. "I have to go," he said.

"Will you come back tomorrow?"

"There's no electricity to shock the squirrels. Grease and BB's won't work. So what can we do?"

"My father used bottles of fox urine."

"What? No way!" Jacob said. But his eyes were afire again, like they'd been when he suggested shock treatments for the squirrels.

"Really," Roger said. "He had to order it from England. Come back tomorrow, and I'll show you."

The next day, Jacob was back early. Roger had just finished lunch, and was thinking about a nap on the porch, when he heard a tap on the half-open window and looked out to see the boy pointing at the feeders with a gun. It didn't look like a BB gun.

"What's that you've brought?"

"My dad's 12-gauge. It used to be my grandpa's. I snuck it out of the house to use on the squirrels, just in case."

"Come on in," Roger said, hearing the voices start to whisper in the back of his head at the sight of the shotgun. "But leave the gun outside. Bring the milk crate in with you instead."

The questions started as the boy settled onto the crate next to Roger. Jacob was very curious to know how they got the fox urine into the bottles. When Roger told him they used catheters, and explained how a catheter worked, the boy was amazed. He imagined catheterizing foxes. He imagined vast warehouses full of foxes in cages with catheters poking through the bars and running into a huge urine vat.

"I don't think it was as fancy as all that," Roger said. "The bottles my father used to get in the mail were pretty small. He had to be careful not to waste it. It was very expensive."

"What do you mean?"

Roger explained how his father had tried it first on the cat, with no effect. Roger's father guessed that the cat was too far removed from the wild. So he'd sprinkled towels with the urine and tied a towel to the base of each feeder. The squirrels ambled up to the feeders, sniffed the towels, then ran to the edge of the yard and disappeared into the thicket. They chattered back and forth for a while. And then they raced back, leaping over the towels and climbing the poles to get to the feeders.

"Just like with the grease," Jacob said.

"Yes," Roger said. "Just like that."

"Do you think there's any left?"

"Any fox urine? We can go see. My father used to keep it in the shed out back. But we'd better take this." Roger picked up the drum major baton that leaned out of sight in the corner on the far side of the stove. "I haven't been out there in a while."

"We could bring my dad's gun."

"I think we'd better stick with this instead."

"What is that?" the boy asked as Roger led him out the front door and around the house. "Can I hold it?"

Roger handed the baton to Jacob. "It's a drum major baton. I used to be the drum major in high school. The drum major is the person who leads the band."

"It's heavy."

"My father had it made out of stainless steel. He was very proud that I'd been named drum major. In fact, as a graduation present—and a reward for being accepted into Harvard to study English Literature—he sent me to England for the summer. I went to Stratford-on-Avon and studied Shakespeare."

"Who's Shakespeare?" the boy asked, swinging the baton like a club as they walked around the back of the house and headed toward the shed.

"Shakespeare was a famous playwright and poet from England, my father's favorite dramatist. And mine. The play my father liked best was *King Lear*. Would you like to hear his favorite quote?"

"Sure."

"It's from Act I: 'How sharper than a serpent's tooth it is to have a thankless child!'"

"Weird."

"Not all that weird, really, if you knew my father," Roger said, pulling the heavy latch on the shed door. "Do you know what irony is, Jacob?"

"No."

Roger swung open the door. "Well then," he said, "come on in and see for yourself. But first, hand me the baton."

Jacob handed the baton back to Roger, who led the way into the shed. It was brightly lit near the open door, but dark among the piles of tools, boxes, and farm implements stacked against the far walls. Before Roger could start toward the murky space in the back, something near the door caught the boy's attention.

"Wow! Are those rattlesnakes?"

The sunlight fell on three buckets of snakeheads that lay on a bench near the open door. The sun-bleached skulls seemed to glow with a light of their own.

"What's left of them," Roger said. "My father used to kill rattle-snakes, cut off their heads, and put them on stakes around the birdfeeders to keep away the squirrels. There were snakeheads everywhere, fangs bared."

"Can we try that?"

"I thought you wanted to look for fox urine."

"Snakeheads are way cooler than fox pee. Let's do this instead."

They couldn't find any stakes to put the heads on. So Roger pulled a ball of twine out of a box, and he and the boy carried the buckets of snakeheads, the baton, and the twine to the front of the house. They strung the snakeheads onto three pieces of the twine and wrapped them around the poles, arranging each head so that the fangs stuck out like thick bristly armor. Then they retreated to the porch to watch and wait.

After a while, a pair of squirrels emerged from the brush and approached the center pole. They got within sniffing distance of the snakeheads and paused for a moment before fluffing their tails up and running like reddish-gray streaks back into the brush. The boy laughed out loud, but Roger just chuckled uncomfortably. Sitting on the porch, watching the squirrels run from the snakeheads, Roger heard the tragic voices whisper his father's second favorite quote from *Lear*: "Why should a dog, a horse, a rat, have life, and thou no breath at all?" The quote came from the final scene, and the irony was sharp indeed when applied to Roger's own situation. In his family's real-life version of the play, Regan and Goneril were faithful, and Cordelia was a boy who killed the king.

"Look!" Jacob said, pointing and laughing.

Another pair of squirrels emerged from the brush. Unlike the first pair, these two got to the base of the center pole before retreating. The next pair was bold enough to touch noses to a snakehead before their fluff-tailed run back under cover. All the while, the boy was laughing at the squirrels' discomfiture; but try as he might, the best Roger could manage was a kind of nervous gurgle. The tragic voices were speaking louder now, and the sight of the gun—a break-action double-barrel shotgun—leaning against the wall underneath the kitchen window, was making Roger feel things he didn't like to think about.

Finally, a pair of squirrels made a run at the center feeder, and the lead squirrel didn't even slow down. It climbed the outstretched fangs like a ladder until it reached the crosspiece, flipping back the rooftop lid on the feeder and slipping inside. Birdseed slopped onto the ground, and the second squirrel began to feast. And suddenly, the tragic voices spoke loud from the fifth act of *Lear*: "a dog, a horse, a rat . . ."

Roger snatched the gun from against the wall and shot the squirrel that had poked its head up out of the top of the feeder. It somersaulted backward and fell heavily to the ground. The second squirrel retreated to the brushline, where it sat chattering at Roger until he lowered the shotgun. Then it scampered across the yard, hugged the dead squirrel to its chest, and started to pull the body away from Roger exactly like his mother had done after he killed his father.

Roger raised the shotgun and walked toward the center feeder.

165

Instead of running, the squirrel stared up at Roger. He sighted down the double barrels at the look of terror and loathing in its eyes, and emptied the second barrel into its face.

Then he swung the gun around toward the porch.

The look in Jacob's eyes was pure horror. He stared at Roger for a timeless moment as Roger sighted the shotgun at the boy's face and pulled the trigger. But the gun didn't fire. Roger kept pulling the trigger over and over and over again—waiting for the muzzle to flash and for the terror in the boy's eyes to dissolve into gore—until Jacob leaped off the porch and sprinted across the cleared space, hitting the brushline at a dead run.

Clutching the sweat-damp stock of the shotgun, Roger heard the tragic voices howl the rest of his father's second favorite quote from *Lear*: "Thou wilt come no more, never, never, never."

Jelvis

in which May Belle grapples with Jesus, Elvis,
Wanda Mulebach's love life, and a ghost from her past
(2010)

According to Wanda Mulebach, the high school secretary's desk, which she had occupied for the past eight-and-a-half years, was shaped like a capital *J*.

She'd repeated this "life-or-death detail" three times in the five minutes since May Belle Stiles's arrival in the principal's office. It was beyond May Belle why Wanda was so insistent—particularly since the desk was actually shaped like a capital *L*—but it was May Belle's first day at the high school, and she thought it best not to argue. Wanda, the outgoing secretary, was training May Belle to take over.

Massive, made of solid oak, the desk served as a barricade between the students who came in from the main hall and what Wanda called "the beating heart of Jordan High." The only way for the students to get at that beating heart—which, according to Wanda, was the master clock—was to get past the secretary at her desk. Encased in metal and bolted firmly onto the wall that divided the principal's office from the main hall, the master clock controlled the bell system, which in turn controlled everything else. The clock currently read 6:30 a.m. The first bell, which would send all the students scurrying for their homerooms, would not ring until 8:05. Beneath the high school's beating heart, Wanda had hung two pictures. One of them was of Jesus. The second was of Elvis. Jesus was blue-eyed, blonde, and pale-skinned. Elvis was blue-eyed, dark-haired, and tanned.

"When you come in every morning, just remember *J for Jesus*," Wanda said. "*J for Jesus* is step one." Then she ducked under the desk.

L for loony, May Belle thought but didn't say. Instead, she studied Wanda's broad backside and wondered what her front side was up to under the desk.

"You don't have to unlock the doors until 6:45," Wanda said, her voice muffled by a half-ton of solid oak. "So the first step in your day should be to crawl under the desk and turn on the computer. That way, it has time to load while you make the coffee."

May Belle saw the monitor on the desk flash as the computer went into the start-up sequence. Then Wanda's ample bottom was replaced by

167

her tanned, makeup-caked face.

"When you crawl out from under the desk, just remember *J.C.*" She fluttered turquoise eyelids at the painting of Jesus, and May Belle noticed that Wanda's eyes, underneath all the makeup, were puffy—as though maybe she'd been crying on her way to work. But May Belle just put it down to mixed emotions over her last day at Jordan High and tried to focus on the task at hand. "Those are steps one and two in your day. But instead of *Jesus Christ*, think *J-shaped desk* and *coffee.*"

May Belle nodded. At least she knew now why Wanda was so insistent about the desk being shaped like a capital *J*. "What about Elvis?"

"Elvis?"

May Belle pointed at the pictures under the master clock.

"*E* is for *e-mail*, of course. But that is step three. We'll get to step three after we make the coffee."

Wanda led May Belle into a little shelf-lined room filled from floor to ceiling with supplies—notebooks, binders, paperclips, boxes of paper, cans of coffee, bandages, pens, pencils, chalk, markers, paper towels, a seemingly endless array—along with a sink, a stainless steel coffee urn, and a small refrigerator. Wanda filled the urn from the sink, scooped coffee into the grounds basket, then carried the urn out and set it on the corner of the desk farthest from the hallway door.

"Everyone who drinks coffee comes to the office and shares." She plunged under the desk again, this time with the coffeemaker cord, and then reappeared. "But that is all we share. When we get to step four, which is *D for doors*, the first thing we have to do is lock up the supply room. No one is allowed in there but me, and now you."

"What if the teachers need supplies?" May Belle asked.

"They have to buy them. I have a price list in the desk."

May Belle glanced at the painting of Jesus. "What about Christian charity?"

"That's what the coffee is for. Everything else must be paid for in cash." The luscious aroma of coffee brewing filled the office as Wanda moved on to the next step. "Like we talked about before, *E* is step three." She nodded at the picture of Elvis. "But instead of *Elvis*, think *e-mail*."

May Belle was thinking about coffee. She'd had her customary single cup, scalding black, on her back porch an hour ago along with her customary single Camel unfiltered cigarette. Normally, that was all she allowed herself until the afternoon. But training with Wanda already had May Belle aching for seconds on both. Since the campus was smoke-free, coffee would have to do.

But the coffee was still brewing. And Wanda was still talking about e-mail. Seated at the desk now, she showed May Belle how to open the online e-mail program—despite the fact that May Belle had been using the exact same program for years in her job as the superintendent's personal secretary—and then showed her how to prioritize messages: principal not showing up, teachers not showing up, no-show teacher lesson plans.

"Remember that voice-mail messages are converted to e-mails," Wanda said. "If the high school principal calls in sick, you have to call the middle school principal for all the discipline issues that arise. We'll have plenty of chances to talk about discipline issues after the first bell. If a teacher calls in sick, you have to call a sub immediately. You can only call subs from the list of approved substitutes, which is in the desk. The no-show teachers are required to e-mail their lesson plans for the sub."

"What happens if they don't?"

"Sodom and Gomorrah. Teenagers nowadays are full of lust. Without a lesson plan, the sub walks into a roomful of sex-crazed adolescents with nothing to occupy their minds but each other's private parts." Wanda shuddered. "If the no-shows don't e-mail a lesson plan, you have to call them up and make them send one. There is a list of teacher phone numbers in the desk. Remind them that a written reprimand will go into their permanent file if they don't send that lesson plan. Three written reprimands and they're out of a job. Got it?"

If physical attraction was such a terrible thing, May Belle found herself wondering, why did Wanda go to the trouble of tanning and slathering on makeup? This question led in turn to another that was becoming more and more pressing: How long could it possibly take for the brew cycle to finish on that coffee urn? But what she said was, "I think I've got it."

"Good. It doesn't look like we have any no-shows today. That means it's time to move on to step four. When you get done with e-mail, just remember *J.C.* and *E.D.*" Wanda nodded at the supply room door. "And now it's time for a little pop quiz. What is step four, and what is the first thing you have to do when you get to it?"

"Step four is *D for doors*. And the first thing I do is lock up the supply room."

"Excellent! When Superintendent Sumps told me that you were taking over the high school secretary's job, I thought to myself: May Belle Stiles has certainly got the *cajones* for it. Now I see you've got the *cabeza* as well." Wanda pulled a ring of keys from the top desk drawer and handed it to May Belle. "The key with the gold jacket is to the supply

169

room. The key with the green jacket opens the outside doors. The key with the maroon jacket is the master classroom key. If there are any no-shows, you have to unlock their classroom doors so the subs can get in. But today it's just the supply room and the outside doors. Do you feel like you're ready to do this step yourself?"

Still stuck someplace between her *cajones* and her *cabeza*, May Belle managed to reply in the affirmative.

"I'll tag along just in case you have any questions," Wanda said.

The mascot for Jordan was the Cowboys, and the school colors were maroon and white. All these elements had been incorporated into the interior design of the high school building: the lockers were painted maroon, the walls were painted white, and maroon-colored wooden cut-outs engaged in various cowboy activities—bull-riding, bronco-busting, calf-roping—covered the walls between the banks of lockers. It struck May Belle that her dear departed Rooster would have loved the cut-outs. He had been a cowboy's cowboy—a horse breaker, cowhand, and competition roper by trade; a bare-knuckled scrapper by disposition; and the best two-stepper who ever lived. The thought of Rooster reminded May Belle about Wanda's *cajones* comment. She'd never met anyone with more *cajones* than Rooster.

"Actually, I do have a question." May Belle turned to face Wanda, who had been dogging her steps and watching her every move. "What did you mean about my having the *cajones* to do the high school secretary job?"

"Are you kidding me? You're a legend. The way you beat the snot out of that boy who assaulted you in the breakfast line? The one they used to call Boxer? Everybody in Jordan knows about it. You've got *cajones* alright. The kids are scared to death of you."

"Bobby," May Belle said. "His name is Bobby Lindell."

"Whatever. I heard his mama went in front of the school board to personally thank you for beating some respect into that hellion. Some-times the only thing that will set a bad boy straight is a good thrashing. It's just like Proverbs says: 'He that spareth his rod hateth his son: but he that loveth him chasteneth him betimes.' Not that I believe an angry hand should ever be laid on a woman, of course. But the day they took corporal punishment out of this school was the day it started to go downhill."

May Belle hoped she didn't look as stunned as she felt. Being a legend was not something she had ever aspired to. That was Rooster's department, and he'd achieved a good deal of success both as a compe-tition roper and a bare-knuckled scrapper. The dancing had been just for

May Belle. The fact that she'd become a legend for slapping a ten-year-old boy was deeply disturbing. As she finished unlocking the outside doors and headed back to the office, she thought about her altercation with Bobby Lindell. She remembered him hurling the worst possible insult at her that a man could use to stain a woman's honor, then smacking her upside the head with a handful of scrambled eggs. She recalled slapping him with all the pent-up fury that was in her. But by far the most vivid image in her mind was the dark red blood from his mouth spattering her apron. Despite the legend, and what Bobby's mother said to the school board, *cajones* had nothing to do with it. She'd lost control.

By the time they got back to the desk, the coffee had finished brewing. The smell was irresistible. "Could I have a cup of that?" May Belle asked.

"Of course," Wanda said. "Where is your cup?"

"I didn't bring one."

"There are Styrofoam coffee cups in the supply room. They cost ten cents."

"I didn't bring any money, either. I didn't think I would need it."

"I'll buy you a cup, and even fill it with coffee for you, if you'll answer a question for me," Wanda said. "That's a penny for your thoughts, times ten."

"Sold. As long as I get the coffee before I have to answer the question." May Belle took a seat in the secretary's chair while Wanda headed into the supply room. The beating heart of the high school now read 7:05 a.m. That meant she still had a whole hour left until the first bell—an hour she would have to spend training with Wanda. She hoped those cups were jumbo-sized. Her eyes wandered down from the master clock onto Wanda's pictures. Both Jesus and Elvis had maroon plastic frames that the fluorescent light turned the color of blood.

"What do you think of them?" Wanda asked.

Startled, May Belle turned to see Wanda reaching a tiny Styrofoam cup across the desk. It struck May Belle that Wanda's eyes looked even puffier than they had earlier, and that she'd spent an awfully long time in the supply room. "Is that the ten-cent question?"

"You said you wanted to have some coffee before we got to that. I thought we might warm up with the pictures before we move on to the harder stuff."

"Harder than Jesus and Elvis?" May Belle asked. "Are you sure you really want to hear my thoughts?"

"I want to hear the legend speak."

"Alright." May Belle took a cautious sip of the coffee, which was surprisingly strong and good. It would've been perfect, she thought, if she'd had an unfiltered Camel to go with it. "Truth be told, I never really got bit by the Jesus bug. My parents, rest their souls, raised me Southern Baptist. They dragged me to Sunday school and Sunday sermons, both. But I guess it just didn't take. And Rooster never believed in much of anything besides rodeo and country music." She took another slow sip of coffee. "I never particularly cared about Elvis, either. I've always been more into Texas singers like Willie and Jerry Jeff, and of course, George Strait. King George grew up right here in Southwest Texas. He was a rancher and a competition roper before he was a singer. Rooster roped against him a couple of times, back in the day. Did you ever meet Rooster?"

"I never did. But I've heard a lot about him from my husband, Beau. Rooster was Beau's hero, growing up. In fact, I guess he still is. Beau always says he wishes he could be the kind of cowboy Rooster was."

Lean and wiry, his skin creased and sun-leathered, a picture of the love of her life flashed into May Belle's mind so clear and so sharp she felt as though her heart had been pierced by a bullet made of ice. The breath caught in her chest, and for an eternal moment there was in all the world only Rooster and the pain fading to bittersweet as the ice slowly melted and respiration became possible again. "There'll never be another like him," she said at last.

"Okay, so you don't care for Elvis's music," Wanda persisted, apparently having abandoned the Jesus angle for the present, but unwilling to move on to the ten-cent question. "But what about his movies? Don't you like any of them?"

"Well, I liked that one real Western he did. *Flaming Star*. It was set on the Texas frontier."

"You mean the one where Elvis is Pacer Burton, half-Kiowa and half-white, persecuted by the white settlers that he lives among until he dies to save them when the Kiowas go on the warpath?"

"That's the one. Elvis was always a little too pretty for me. That is, before he got so fat. I like my men to look manly. Elvis sure enough looks the part in *Flaming Star*."

"You know, May Belle, Jesus was persecuted by the very folks he died to save, the same way as Pacer Burton. So Jesus and Elvis had something in common."

May Belle shifted uncomfortably in the secretary's chair. "So what's the ten-cent question?"

"Does beating somebody up—somebody who really deserves it, I mean—make you feel better? I know a good thrashing can set a bad boy back on the straight and narrow path. You proved that when you beat up that Boxer kid. But did it help you find peace within yourself?"

"Absolutely not. Since that day in the breakfast line, I've come a long way. But not because I slapped Bobby Lindell. After it happened, I became secretary to Superintendent Sumps. He should have fired me, but he gave me another chance instead. Dr. Sumps handles things with his heart and his head, not with his fists. He always does whatever is best for the person he's dealing with, and he's always smart in the way he goes about it. He only uses his power when he has no other choice. That's the reason I agreed to come over to the high school with him this semester while he fills in for Principal Toston. Honestly, I used to be a little bit afraid of kids. Now I'm not afraid of anything. But that's because I've learned to use my heart and my head, and not my fists. Those are the three steps I always remember when I have to handle a problem: *corazon* first, *cabeza* second, *cajones* last."

"Some legend you are!" Wanda snapped, pressing her lips so tightly together that furrows of bright red lipstick formed in the corners of her mouth. "Let's just focus on the steps you need to learn to handle your job as high school secretary. I believe we were up to step five, which is entering the previous day's absentees into the computer. To show you this step, I need my chair."

May Belle vacated the secretary's chair and stepped back as Wanda huffed her way into it. May Belle had no idea what to think of Wanda, of whom all that was currently visible was a ramrod-stiff back and bleach-blonde hair. In fact, May Belle was sure of only two things at this particular moment: she'd certainly earned her ten-cent cup of coffee, and she needed an unfiltered Camel like she needed air.

"Each absence has to be listed as excused or unexcused," Wanda mumbled, rapid-fire. "To be excused, a student must bring a note. Enter *E* for *excused*, *U* for *unexcused*, *A* when they have a verbal excuse but no note. *A*'s automatically turn into *U*'s after three days if the student doesn't bring a note. If the student does bring a note, you have to go back and change the *A* to an *E*. *T* equals *tardy*. Three tardies in one day means the student gets In School Suspension. Five tardies in one week also means a trip to ISS. All ISS trips get entered into the Discipline module of the computer. Got it?"

"Could you slow down a little bit?" May Belle asked.

"Attendance is done every period," Wanda continued, her face buried in the computer screen. "You have to keep a running total throughout the day. If a student misses a period, the secretary calls the room the student is supposed to be in next; if the student isn't there, then the secretary calls the student's home; if the student isn't there, then the secretary calls the Constable. Calls to the Constable must be documented in the Discipline section under *LGP*, which means *left grounds without permission*. Got it?"

"Not exactly."

"What part didn't you get?" Wanda asked without turning her head.

Before May Belle could gather her scattered thoughts into a coherent sentence, a wave of students and teachers surged into the building. The kids headed straight to their lockers; but the teachers came into the office, coffee cups in hand. After hitting the coffee urn, they stopped to visit. All the teachers welcomed May Belle to the high school, saying things like: "There's a new sheriff in town," and "Where's your tin star, Marshal?" Then everyone would laugh, except for May Belle and Wanda. A tall and lean-muscled man with a thick salt-and-pepper mustache who introduced himself as "Nick Bynum, the good chemistry guy," shook May Belle's hand and then jerked back, flashing her a cheesy grin and shaking his fingers as though she had crushed them. "Whoa, take 'er easy there, Pilgrim," he said. All the teachers laughed again.

Finally, the first bell rang. Every eye in the office snapped up onto the master clock, which read 8:05, and May Belle suddenly understood why Wanda called it "the beating heart of Jordan High." The students in the hall stopped what they were doing and scurried off to their classrooms; the teachers around the desk refilled their coffee cups and hurried off in the same direction.

By the time May Belle and Wanda were alone again, May Belle had framed her confused thoughts into words. "If I said something to offend you, I apologize," she said. "You can have your ten cents back, if you want it."

"I don't want my ten cents back," Wanda sniffled. "I want my husband back." She looked up from the computer screen, streaks of mascara running down her rouged cheeks. "I was hoping you could help with that, you being a legend and all."

It struck May Belle that Wanda hadn't looked up from the computer since she huffed her way down into the chair. She must've been crying for half an hour, and nobody in the office had even noticed. May Belle glanced away, up at the master clock. But instead of the office's

174

beating heart, she saw her vision of Rooster again—still lean and wiry and sun-leathered, but this time spinning her around and around as they danced to George Strait—and she found herself missing him every bit as much at that moment as she had in the raw days just after he passed.

"I want my husband back, too," May Belle said gently. "But for me, that is impossible. Let's see what we can do for you."

"Really?"

"If you'll walk me back through all that data entry, slow and easy, I'll do what I can to help you figure out this husband thing. But first, I need to know what the problem is. And second, I need to be back in that chair."

As they switched places, Wanda pulled her handbag out of the desk. "To tell the truth, I was just hoping you could teach me enough about fist-fighting so I could beat the snot out of Beau." She pulled a handkerchief and compact out of the handbag, wiped the mascara from her cheeks, then started to reapply the makeup that her tears had washed off. "I don't want to hurt him, just to get his attention. He's been acting like a bad little boy, and I think a good thrashing might set him straight."

"Do you remember what I told you about the three steps that I always take to handle my problems?"

"*Corazon, cabeza, cajones?*"

"Exactly," May Belle said. "Why don't we take a look at steps one and two before we move on to step three?"

"Okay, okay. I do love Beau. But Beau is a total TV sports junkie. His favorite is football, but he'll watch anything that involves competition. He's got a half-dozen television sets spread around our new house. He's even got a TV in the garage. They're on all the time, and it's driving me crazy. Worse, it's ruining our marriage."

"I don't mean to overstep," May Belle said, "but it sounds to me like you need to turn off those TV's and spend some serious alone time with your husband."

"Alone time?"

"You know, sex. Physical intimacy with the man you love. Doesn't the Bible say to be fruitful and multiply?"

"We're not . . . fruitful anymore. We used to be. That was back when there were only two TV's in the house, one in the living room and one in the bedroom."

"Why in the bedroom?" May Belle asked. "Do you have trouble sleeping?

Just then, the tardy bell rang. The high school suddenly went silent.

"This is just between us." Wanda lowered her voice to a breathy whisper and leaned in close to May Belle. "But back when Beau and me used to be fruitful really often, sometimes I would get him to put on an Elvis movie first. While Beau was getting busy, I was fantasizing that he was the King."

Extremely conscious, all of a sudden, of the tight space behind the secretary's desk, May Belle focused her gaze on the computer screen and started entering data. "I guess that explains the TV in the bedroom," she said.

"Sometimes it was Elvis in *Jailhouse Rock*. That striped shirt and those little black pants with the white stitching over his man parts made him look like a bad boy alright. And sometimes it was the Elvis of the *68 Comeback Special* in that black leather suit. But even the husky Elvis of the later years in that white sequin jumpsuit with the cape, was enough to send me into . . . well, you know."

A batch of e-mails came pouring in, interrupting Wanda's Elvis fantasies and May Belle's attempts at data entry. The e-mails were from the teachers that she'd visited with earlier, and they all had spreadsheet attachments. "What's all this?" she asked.

"We covered it earlier," Wanda said. "Don't you remember? Each teacher takes the roll every period and delivers it via e-mail to the office. The secretary compiles it on a daily attendance summary sheet, then in the morning it gets entered on the computer during step five."

"Well, should we do that now? Or should we keep entering yesterday's absences?"

"There's not really a separate step for the running roll. It's all a part of step five, which kind of goes on throughout the day. Since we can't start looking for class-cutters until second period, there's really no rush. So I guess it's your call. Which would you rather do?"

"Why don't we move on?" May Belle said. "I think we're done with all that Elv—"

May Belle was cut off by the entrance of a boy with shaggy red hair, a black leather jacket, and a patch of peach fuzz under his lower lip. He placed a slip of paper on the secretary's desk, took a measuring look at May Belle, and stepped back.

"You'll have to excuse me, May Belle," Wanda said. "This looks like a write-up slip, and that looks like Blaise Holybee. We've got our first discipline issue of the day." Wanda took the slip of paper from the desk and scanned its contents. "You called Miss Gurr a *what*?"

Blaise mumbled something unintelligible and looked up at the master clock.

"Don't you look up at that clock," Wanda said. "You look down here." She pointed at the picture of Jesus. "Don't you think Jesus is sad about what you said? Don't you think He is just heartbroken?"

Instead of Jesus, Blaise's eyes were on May Belle.

Wanda also turned to face May Belle. "All write-ups, along with the punishments, must be entered into the computer under the Discipline section," Wanda said. "If it's something minor, the secretary either gives a verbal warning or assigns ISS, especially if it's a talking-back thing. Anything more serious, like calling Miss Gurr a *stuck-up* . . ." instead of saying the word, she showed the write-up slip to May Belle, "gets referred to the principal for further action."

May Belle glanced at the slip and read the word written on it in all capital letters. It was the same awful name that Bobby Lindell had called at her all those years ago—the worst insult a man can hurl at a woman's honor—and for a slow-motion moment she was back in the cafetorium, the gooey egg mess that Bobby had flung at her hanging like a glob of spit in her hair. Feeling the fiery wrath from that terrible day building inside her again, she slammed down the note and glared at Blaise Holybee. "What gives you the right to say something like this to Ms. Gurr?" she snapped.

"Well, I . . . I mean she—"

"It doesn't matter why!" Wanda cut in. "What we've got to do now is call the principal. Well, I guess in this case, the acting principal. May Belle, could you please call Dr. Sumps?"

May Belle found herself, strangely, looking at up the blood-colored frame on Wanda's Jesus picture. The sight made her remember the way her altercation with Bobby Lindell had ended—with blood from his mouth spattered onto her apron—and the promise she'd made to herself afterward never again to lose control. "No, I won't," she said through clenched teeth. "Superintendent Sumps is spending the morning at his main office. That's why he's not here now. In fact, Dr. Sumps plans to use his own office as much as he can while Principal Toston is on medical leave. Dr. Sumps said that he wanted me to handle everything except emergencies myself."

"This boy has put his immortal soul at risk." Wanda cut her eyes back and forth between Blaise Holybee and the Jesus painting. "Wouldn't you say that qualifies as an emergency?"

May Belle picked up the note. Re-read it. "I'd say that Mr.

Holybee's sad stunt in Miss Gurr's class qualifies him for three days in ISS. *Sad*," May Belle said again, meeting the boy's terrified eyes and feeling the last of the wrath drain out of her. "That's all this is." There was something liberating in defusing the hateful word that he had tried to weaponize; instead of a victim, she felt like an EOD technician who'd just disarmed a bomb. "You should be ashamed of yourself. Your stepdaddy is a combat veteran. And after all he's done for you and your brothers, he deserves better than this. You think about that while you're in ISS."

Blaise sidled along the wall toward the main hall. "Yes ma'am," he said as he reached the office door. "I will." Then he turned and fled.

"Being a legend has its uses after all," May Belle said as Wanda stared at her, wide-eyed. "If you really want me to help you get your husband back, I need to ask you something. I don't want you to take it the wrong way. But have you always been this religious?"

"No. I used to be a Jezebel."

"What happened?"

"A miracle," Wanda said in a dreamy voice, her puffy eyelids fluttering at Jesus.

"What do you mean?"

"I mean exactly that. About this time last year, Beau and me were on our way home from Graceland. Right outside of Dallas, traffic was backed up. We stopped just over a hill. All of a sudden there was a scream of brakes. Then a big rig barreled into the back of our Suburban and rolled over on top of us. As we were laying there in that wreckage waiting to be rescued, I promised Jesus that if He would save Beau and me, I'd dedicate my life to Him. Not only did Beau and me get saved, but we got a big cash settlement because that trucker had been driving seventeen hours without a break. That settlement paid off the note on our house, and it's the reason I don't have to work at the high school anymore. It was a miracle all right. Jesus even brought my wayward sister Tammy home to nurse Beau and me back to health. And I've kept my promise to Him."

May Belle looked past the blood-colored frame into the blonde, blue-eyed face of Jesus on the office wall. She'd never put much stock in miracles. To her, what other people called Divine Providence seemed more like accidents. Sometimes the causes of those accidents could be explained by the laws of science, and sometimes they couldn't. But if human ignorance was the source of divine power, May Belle would pass.

"Don't you believe in miracles?" Wanda asked.

"For both our sakes, let's just agree to disagree about miracles. That way, instead of spending the rest of our morning arguing, maybe we can work our way through this husband thing."

"Okay," Wanda said. "How?"

"By being fruitful. You can't make fruit without pollinating a flower. You don't need to beat the snot out of Beau. You need to get his attention another way."

"What way is that?"

"Take him out dancing. It always worked for Rooster and me. Whether we were two-stepping to something upbeat, or waltzing to something slow, pressing our bodies together to the music was enough to make Rooster and me fruitful in spades. All you need to do is take Beau out to a rodeo dance, and the rest will take care of itself."

"He'll never go. Beau wasn't much on dancing before the miracle. And since then, about the only thing he does besides driving around the ranch and checking the cattle is watch TV."

"Then dance at home," Wanda said. "And not to Elvis, either. Put on some George Strait. 'Amarillo by Morning' is a good one. It was Rooster's favorite. Mine was 'Let's Fall to Pieces Together.' I guess it still is. I don't have any settlement money to wager, but I'll bet my bottom dollar that one of those songs will work for you and Beau."

"What if we don't have any George Strait?"

"Can you cover the desk a minute while I run out to my car? And while you're at it, can you write me up a list of the steps in the high school secretary's day that we haven't gone over yet?"

Without waiting for an answer, May Belle bolted out of the office and into the parking lot. When she got to her car, she rustled through the trash on the passenger side floorboard until she found her *George Strait Greatest Hits* CD. Then she headed back to the secretary's desk.

"What on earth are you up to?" Wanda asked as May Belle burst back into the office, out of breath and about to die for a cigarette.

"Giving you a gift." May Belle handed Wanda the CD. "Play this for Beau the minute you get home. Turn off all those TV's, and make him dance with you. Go right now."

"I can't leave you here alone on your first day."

"How many steps are left?"

"Five. But the last one is just *G* for *go home*."

"I think I can handle it," May Belle said. "And if not, I'll give Dr. Sumps a call. He was high school principal for six years before he took over as superintendent."

"But—"

"Go!" May Belle said firmly. "Just answer me a question first."

179

"Anything."

"I don't believe in an afterlife," May Belle said slowly. "I think the only life we get is the one we have now. Then the lights go out. But if you're right, what do you think Jesus will look like?"

"Honestly? I've always believed that there is a strong resemblance between Jesus and Elvis." She pointed up at the two pictures under the master clock. "They have the same eyes. See? And the same strong jawline and chin. I don't think that's a coincidence. I mean, think about it: The Holy Land? Graceland? Pilgrims going to both places? It can't be an accident."

"Hmm . . ." Gazing up at the framed faces, May Belle found herself imagining Jesus coming back dressed like Elvis in his later years: the jumpsuit, the cape, the pompadour. "Jelvis?" she asked at last. "It does have kind of a ring to it."

"It kind of does."

"Now go home! Before something else comes up. Put on George Strait, turn off those TV's, and don't take no for an answer. But this time, don't pretend Beau is Elvis. Just let Beau be Beau. And make that be okay. Let Beau send you into . . . well, you know."

Even through the makeup, May Belle could see Wanda blush. "I know," she said. Then she put the CD into her handbag and headed out of the office.

As Wanda disappeared down the main hall, May Belle looked back up at the pictures which did indeed so strongly resemble each other at that moment they seemed to blend into a single face. She found herself wondering what Rooster would do if he met Jelvis come again. Probably, she thought, give him a cowboy hat and invite him to a rodeo.

Symmetry
in which Beau and Wanda revisit the Parable of the Good Samaritan
(2010)

Out of whack. Off-kilter. Unglued.

Whatever you wanted to call it, Beau knew how *broken* felt. And from the look of her, so did the massively pregnant Black Angus heifer eyeing him suspiciously from six feet away. He'd found her off by herself on the lee side of a low hill, struggling to give birth. The calf appeared to be hung up inside her. But he was trying to get close enough to see exactly what ailed her, if he could just put her at ease—to see whether the labor was actually dystocic, that is, or if she was just having a rough go her first time out.

"Besides my back, what ails me is my sister-in-law, mostly," he said in his soothingest voice, despite the bitter feelings about Tammy. "She moved into the house to nurse Wanda and me after our accident. But then she stayed."

As if in answer, the first-time mother made a low moaning noise, a sound of hurt and confusion mixed together.

"I hear you," he said softly, edging closer. "I can't claim to've suffered through labor, but I can sure enough relate. I've felt hurt and confused myself every day since the wreck."

He cleared her distended belly, near enough now to lightly touch her hip. Then he ran a gentle hand along her pin bone, working his way around until the calving situation came into view. Among the blood and amniotic fluid, partially obscured by her tail, Beau made out what looked to be a single hoof poking out of her birth canal—there should've been two hooves and a nose—and when she pressed back against him, desperate for relief from any quarter, he felt a contraction jolt through her. She was dystocic, alright. And the clock was ticking.

"Easy girl," he murmured. "We're gonna get that calf out of there."

But as was the case with his sister-in-law's hoped-for eviction, Beau wasn't sure yet how to make that happen. He'd dropped hints to Tammy during the early morning physical therapy sessions she'd been coaching him through, and he'd tried talking to Wanda about it last night in bed. But Tammy was either completely clueless or absolutely set on staying, or both. And Wanda's only response was to recite the Parable of

181

the Good Samaritan from the Gospel of Luke, which meant the subject was closed. Instead of pushing, he'd flipped the TV onto a Spurs game on TNT.

Beau pulled out his pocketwatch and timed the next contraction: a little over three minutes. She was deep into the delivery stage already. He looked around, weighing his options. In the near distance the rest of the gentle Black Angus cattle he'd added to the herd his father built speckled the winter-white coastal Bermuda of the 200-acre pasture. Farther away Beau made out some of the older brindle crossbred cows his father was so proud of—hardy and self-sufficient, at home in the brush— grazing near the barbed wire fence that divided the pasture from the tangled thicket that covered most of the 6000-acre Mulebach ranch. In addition to improving the herd with purebred stock in the years since his father passed, Beau had almost doubled the size of the spread. The cattle pens, with their headgate and the specially rigged maternity pen he'd set up for calf-pulling, stood a mile away on the far side of the brush. There was no way the heifer could walk it, and no time to fetch a trailer.

He turned and looked up at the house that he and Wanda had built atop the highest hill on the ranch and that they'd paid off with settlement money from the wreck. Even if he drove up there and called the vet, it would be the better part of an hour before Dr. Clayton arrived. By then the calf would be dead, if it wasn't dead already. Wanda wouldn't be home from her secretary job at the high school until the afternoon. And the thought of having Tammy help with the delivery was about the equivalent of cutting his ears off with a dull knife.

In the horse pasture next to the house, he saw the charcoal-dappled white coat of Lobo Blanco with his head down, grazing for all he was worth. The sight of the roping horse made Beau yearn to be out riding through the cattle again. He'd always been one to talk through the things that weighed heavy on his mind or his heart, and there was no better listener than Lobo Blanco—who in addition to being smooth-gaited and blessed with instinctive cow sense was smarter than a lot of the people Beau knew, including his sister-in-law. But despite months of intense physical therapy, the fused vertebrae at the base of his spine, the left hip that had been partially replaced, and the permanent pins in his left leg still made it impossible for Beau to ride a horse. On chilly winter mornings like this one, it was painful even to get behind the wheel of the pickup.

The heifer moaned again, bringing his attention back to the matter at hand. He was going to have to pull the calf himself, and it was going to have to happen right here. Right now. He opened the tailgate, removed the halter and ropes and buckets from the bed; then he took the dish soap, Vaseline, and disinfectant from behind the seat and nestled them into the dry grass beside the two buckets. Next he gritted his teeth and hauled out the five-gallon water jug. As he awkwardly splashed water into both buckets, a flare of pain in the small of his back shot down into his left hip, sparking a fire that smoldered in his left thigh while he mixed disinfectant into the water in one bucket and sank one of the ropes into it.

"So much for the easy part," Beau said softly, picking up the halter and gently rubbing the soft black fur on the heifer's belly, then on her neck, easing his way toward her head. "This is where it gets interesting." He slipped the open halter over her nose, pulling the webbing up and tightening the buckle on the crownpiece in a single smooth motion before stepping back.

She shook her head and yanked on the lead rope, sending a blaze of pain down Beau's left side. But then another contraction hit, and all thought of the strange contraption on her head faded into the agony of trying to force out the stuck calf.

Beau wasted no time making the lead rope fast to the headache rack on the truck. Next he cut a piece of twine from the ball in the glove box and tied the heifer's tail up across her back, looping the other end of the twine around her neck. As the contraction faded, he tilted his hat back and wiped off the sweat that had started on his forehead despite the sharp January air.

"Well? Are we good with this?"

The heifer stood calmly next to the truck, having apparently accepted both the halter and the tail-tie.

"Good girl." He shucked his jean jacket and rolled up his sleeves. "Now let's see what we've got."

He worked a dish-soap lather into a hand towel and scrubbed the heifer's hindquarters, rinsing off the bloody mess with the clean-water bucket. Then he washed and rinsed his hands and arms, shivering with the shock of the cold as he dipped them into the disinfectant, and mentally preparing himself for what was to come. The process of giving birth to something as big as a calf was all about symmetry. If the calf was properly aligned in the birth canal—in a forward presentation, a dorsal position, and a normal posture—as long as the cervix was sufficiently dilated, and the calf wasn't too big, both cow and calf generally came through just fine. In this particular case, something was out of whack. And there was only one way to set it right.

He lubed his hands and arms with Vaseline and then slathered the perineal area, carefully working his cupped fingers inside the birth canal. She wasn't fully dilated, that much was clear. And Beau still couldn't tell whether he had a front hoof—which he hoped was the case—or a back hoof. He started manually dilating the cervix as quick as he could without adding to the heifer's distress.

"At least it won't take rocket science to fix what ails you," he murmured through clenched teeth, the smoldering fire in his lower back flaring red-hot because of the awkward position he was in. "I've got a titanium ball for a hip joint, titanium pins holding my left femur together, and a fused lower spine. Try that sometime." Beau smiled a grim smile. "Better yet, try nine months of physical therapy with my sister-in-law."

Once the cervix was open, he worked his hands inside the uterus, pausing during the next contraction that tried to force his arms out with the stuck calf. He found another hoof, and felt the fetlock and knee bending in the same direction—which meant the calf was facing forward—and the angle of the bend told Beau the calf was definitely right-side up.

"We've got a forward presentation and a dorsal position," he said softly, "so we're two-thirds of the way home. Once we get this calf out of you, you'll be on easy street. I'll still have a fitness-Nazi for a therapy coach, her two hyperactive boys bouncing off the walls of my house, and a Jesus junkie for a wife."

He didn't need the heifer to remind him that the *Jesus junkie* bit wasn't fair. Beau knew in his heart that Wanda had turned to religion in the aftermath of the wreck the same way he'd turned to watching sports on TV. She was as upset by what she called his *sports-habit* as he was by her being *born-again*. But the fact was that staring at athletes' bodies— powerful, graceful, pain-free—as they excelled on the television screen carried him back in time. In high school Beau had won the tie-down calf roping event at the Texas State Finals two years in a row, and he'd been winning roping matches and finishing in the money at rodeos across the Southwest ever since. Until his left side got crushed. The TV helped Beau remember what he was born to do and forget what the wreck was keeping him from. He wondered sometimes whether Wanda's churchgoing did that for her, too. But the honest truth was that he had no clue. After eleven years of symmetry, their marriage was as off-kilter as this heifer's parturition. And Beau had no idea how to set things straight again.

He couldn't seem to find the calf's head, which meant an abnormal posture. Instead of sharing this with the heifer, he pressed deeper with his right arm and finally felt an ear, then a mouth. And pushing his thumb past the calf's front teeth, Beau felt the mouth close around his finger and felt the tongue move in a suckle reflex.

"He's still alive! Or she is," he said, frankly surprised. "Although judging from the size of this bruiser's head, he's a bull. If I can just work his head up into a normal birthing posture, we may be able to get him out of you in time to keep him in the land of the living."

The heifer seemed to agree with every fiber of her being.

He pushed the exposed hoof back into the uterus, took a firm grip on the calf's muzzle, pulled it toward the opening in the pelvis. But before he could make sure whether the calf was properly aligned, another contraction started, and the first-time mother—so calm and so sensible up to now—panicked, shoving herself backwards and swinging her hindquarters around to slam Beau against the truck. He felt a white flash of pain in his lower back as the door handle dug into his spine and felt his head smack hard against the door frame. Then his left hip seemed to explode. He tried to get his arms free, but the pressure from the uterine wall trapped them tight against the calf and he hung there, crushed between the heifer's shuddering body and the door until the contraction faded finally, and he was able to separate himself.

He slid down the side of the pickup, breathing heavy. From spine to knee his bones sizzled like they were made of molten metal. When his tailbone hit the ground, he felt the heifer step on his left leg. And suddenly, Beau was back inside the wreck. He felt again the shock of impact, the explosion of pain, the crushing weight that pushed the air out of his lungs as the big rig rolled over onto the Suburban. He remembered fighting to breathe. He heard Wanda's voice—high-pitched, panicked— pleading with God. Making promises. Telling Jesus that she wasn't ready, that Beau wasn't ready, that she'd do anything if God would just give them more time. "If you'll only keep us from dying, Jesus, I'll go to church twice every Sunday and on Wednesday night. I'll give up the whiskey-drinking and the kinky sex. I'll bear witness to everyone I meet that you're the only thing on earth that matters." After two hours of agony on Beau's part and nonstop praying on hers, the Jaws of Life pried them out of that pancake of metal and flesh. And Wanda kept every promise.

Something cold and wet against his cheek brought Beau back to the pasture. The heifer nudged him again, and he managed to prop himself up against the door. He realized, vaguely, that he was missing his hat. He sat perfectly still, feeling fuzzy, the fire in his bones fading to a dull burn as he looked around for his Stetson. Beau silently cursed the heifer for her stupidity. He cursed the long-haul trucker who'd been at the wheel for seventeen hours without a break before plowing into the Suburban. He cursed Wanda for focusing so completely on fulfilling her promises to Jesus that there wasn't room in her life for anything else. They hadn't made love since the wreck. He cursed Tammy for her piercing screech and drill-sergeant demeanor during therapy sessions—"Harder!" "Faster!" "Dig, dig, dig!"—and her need to take total control of everything in the house except her boys.

But mostly, Beau cursed himself. After all, this was the heifer's first calf. She hadn't known any better than to panic. He, on the other hand, knew from long experience that a dystocic cow's hormone levels were sometimes so wacky, and her pain so intense, she decided he was an enemy to vent her frustration on instead of a source of relief. Once again, Beau could relate. He'd certainly treated Tammy like an enemy, something he knew deep down to be unfair despite her coaching style and her take-over of what was supposed to be his castle. The reason Tammy had left her own home was to escape an abusive husband—a rancher named Needham she met and married while attending Howard Payne up in Brownwood, but who took to beating the living hell out of her and their young sons with increasing frequency and fervor. She filed for divorce not long after moving in with Wanda and Beau. Despite the negative impact on their marriage and on Beau's daily life, it was hard to blame Tammy for wanting to feel like she was in control for a change.

He felt the heifer's nose cold and wet against his cheek again, reminding him that he had things to do besides sit on the ground and feel sorry for himself. Hope for a live delivery was fading fast for her and her calf. In order for there to be any chance at all, Beau knew that the time had come to get to his feet. He started to haul himself up, only to feel an intense muscle spasm in his left hip. But just as he was mustering the resolve to make another effort, he caught the dull rumble of what could only be a vehicle approaching across the pasture.

Less than a minute later, Wanda rolled up. "Beau!" she yelled, stepping out of her black BMW and running over to where he sat. "Are you hurt?"

"I don't know," he said slowly, trying to figure out whether he was broken inside or just bruised. Despite all the Jesus business, and the possibility that he'd just crippled himself again, he felt his breath catch at the sight of his wife. "But I'm sure glad you're here."

"What happened?" she asked, kneeling beside him. "Why are you sitting on the ground?"

"A little while ago, I got caught in the middle of a wrestling match between this pregnant heifer and the truck. And right now I'm looking up at the best-looking woman in the county, who just happens to be my wife."

"You're scaring me. Did you hit your head? Your eyes look funny, and you're not acting like yourself."

"I was out for a minute, I think. And I seem to've lost my hat."

"I'm taking you to the hospital. Right now."

Beau shook his head, as much to clear the cobwebs as to respond to Wanda. "That unborn calf has minutes to live. And if I'm crippled again, I don't want it to've been for nothing. I was about to climb up the side of the truck and try to pull the calf myself, come what may."

"I'll run up to the house and get Tammy."

"There's no time. Now that you're here, we can do this together."

He looked up into Wanda's eyes, which he noticed for the first time in he didn't know how long were cornflower blue, and saw that they were full of tears. "But I've never done anything like this before," she said. Then she glanced down at her skirt suit. "And I'm wearing Christian Dior."

"I guess the first thing to do, then, is take off your jacket and heels. After that, we'll get you washed up. We don't want to lose the heifer, whether we save the calf or not."

"The mother is in danger, too?"

"When we pull the calf, we have to take it slow and easy, or we'll hurt her on the inside. Maybe bad enough to kill her. And if we don't keep everything sterile, and she gets an infection, she won't be a mother for long."

"Okay, what now?" Wanda's teeth chattered as she stood, wet from washing and in her stocking feet, in the chill January air.

"The calf is coming frontways and right-side up. His head was bent back, though, which is why he got hung up. I tried working him into a normal posture, but the heifer panicked and slung me against the truck. If I managed to get him aligned, our job will be easier. But I can't see her hindquarters from where I'm sitting. It would help if you could turn her around."

Wanda took the lead rope and swung the heifer 180 degrees about.

"That's better," Beau said, clearly making out two hooves this time instead of just one. "The hooves are perfectly presented. But I still can't make out the calf's nose. I'm afraid you're going to have to reach inside her."

"Oh, Beau," Wanda said, dropping the lead rope. "No."

"You can do it. Just cup your hands and go right around the hooves. Then all you have to do is tell me what you feel inside the birth canal."

"I'm sorry." Turning her back on the heifer and on Beau, Wanda started toward the BMW. "I'll go get—"

"I'll make a deal with you," he called after her, his voice sounding every bit as ragged as he felt. "If you'll help me with this, and if the cow and calf both live, I'll give up TV."

Wanda stopped short and turned to face him. "Do you really mean that?"

"As God is my witness."

"He most certainly is," she said. Then she walked slowly and deliberately back. "Sweet Jesus, please help us to safely deliver this calf."

"Amen," Beau said. He didn't know whether it'd help any, but he guessed it couldn't hurt.

Wanda set her lips and reached inside the birth canal. "It's warm!" she said as if this fact surprised her. "And I think I feel a nose."

"Where?"

"Inside the heifer."

"I mean, where in relation to the hooves?"

"Right above them. And a little bit behind. But the calf still seems to be stuck."

"He's lined up alright. But he's too big for this first-time mother. We'll have to pull him. But first, we need to put the heifer down on her right side. He'll come through the pelvis easier that way, and it'll help her push."

"And how on earth am I supposed to throw a full-grown cow?"

"You're a natural," Beau said. "Just take that rope next to the disinfectant bucket and ease the end with the honda around her flank. Put the other end through the honda and pull it tight. Then all you have to do is pull the rope in the direction you want her to fall."

"It can't be that simple."

"Trust me. At this point, I'm surprised she's even able to stand."

Wanda clenched her jaw, picked up the rope, and threw the heifer. "I did it!" she said.

"All you need to do is trade that skirt suit and heels for jeans and boots, and you'll be ready to rodeo."

"Is that really what you want, Beau?" There was a timid tone in her voice now, a lost and searching sound that Beau hadn't heard in a long time.

It commanded his attention. He looked up at Wanda in her stocking feet with the rope clenched in her hands, her arms from fingertips to shoulders covered in blood and amniotic fluid. She'd never looked lovelier to him than at that moment. "What I really want," Beau said slowly, "is for things between us to be back like they were before the wreck."

"I want that, too," she said, tears welling into her eyes again and mascara starting to streak her cheeks. "I left work early today, to try and reconnect with you. I brought a George Strait CD and Chuckwagon barbeque. I planned us a nice romantic date."

"It's chilly for a picnic," he said, feeling his own eyes start to sting. "The forecast called for sleet. But let's get this calf pulled, and if I haven't come completely unglued, we'll see what we can do. Okay?"

"Okay."

"To begin with, take that rope in the disinfectant bucket and tie it to the calf's front legs. Use both ends. Wrap the loops above each fetlock and take a half-hitch below the joint." While Wanda busied herself with the rope, Beau slid his way carefully around to the business end of the heifer. His back was sore. His left hip and leg ached. But he didn't feel any shooting pains, and everything seemed to be functioning. "The uterus is contracting down on the calf from all directions," he said, once the ropes were on tight and Wanda was sitting on the ground beside him, "so the best way to get him out of there intact is to pull first on one side, then on the other. We'll walk his shoulders out first, then we'll see about his hips."

"Should I start?"

"Go ahead. Brace your feet against the heifer's hindquarters and give a steady tug on the rope. She won't be going anywhere until we get that calf out."

Wanda set her feet and leaned back against the rope, getting leverage. "I can feel him moving!" she said as the calf's left fetlock slowly emerged. She almost fell over when the leg suddenly slipped out all the way to the knee.

"You did great!" Beau said quickly. "Just hold what you've got." He set his feet against the heifer's hindquarters and pulled on the rope, keeping the pressure steady until the right leg came through, along with the calf's head.

"There he is!"

"Part of him anyway," Beau said, guiding the calf's shoulders out of the birth canal. "And everything looks just like it's supposed to. Next we'll rotate him so the widest part of his hips aligns with the widest part of the heifer's pelvis. This is usually where the mother takes a break. The umbilical cord is compressed, and while she's resting, the calf should start to breathe on his own."

"So what should we do?"

"Check the calf and wait. If his breathing is good, once we've rotated him, we might not have to do anything at all." Beau gently took the rope from Wanda's hands. "We might even have time for that picnic."

"I've been thinking all day about our first real date. You took me

189

to the Chuckwagon for barbeque, remember? That's why I brought the take-out." She shifted her gaze from Beau's face down onto the calf's. "Then you took me parking out on your daddy's ranch."

Beau leaned forward and cupped a hand over the calf's nostrils. "Of course I remember," he said. "And it's our ranch now."

"You spread a blanket in the bed of your truck, wrapped your arms around me tight, and talked about the constellations and how the old-time cowboys used the Big Dipper to time their night watches on cattle drives. It's been a long time since you held me like that."

"Too long," Beau said. But he was thinking about what happened after the talking had ended, and the fireworks began. They'd spent the rest of the night making love in the bed of his truck. It had been a long time since they'd done that as well—and he was trying to find a way to say so, when he realized that he couldn't feel any breath coming out of the calf's nose. "Wanda, honey, do you have a hand-mirror in your car?"

"I've got a compact in my purse."

"I don't believe this calf is breathing. But I'll need a mirror to be sure."

Wanda was on her feet in an instant. And in less than a minute, Beau was holding a black fold-out makeup mirror under the calf's nose.

"If he's breathing at all," Beau said, "the mirror should fog."

"I don't see anything," Wanda half-whispered, half-sobbed. "We took too long. He's dead."

"Maybe not. I need you to take hold of his neck while I grab his front legs. When I give the word, twist him to the right with all you've got. We've got to rotate him forty-five degrees. Then we'll get back on the ropes and finish the delivery."

"I'm ready."

Beau took a deep breath, got to his knees, and wrapped his arms around the calf just below Wanda's arms. "Go!" he said, feeling the calf slowly swing around in the birth canal as the two of them applied torque and pressure. "That's got it! Now grab the rope and pull. Just like before."

Wanda plopped down beside him, braced her feet, and leaned back for leverage as they pulled on the rope together. To Beau's surprise, the calf fairly shot out of the birth canal, sending Wanda flat onto her back with the newborn in her lap.

"Are you okay?" Beau asked.

"Poor baby," Wanda said, hugging the calf against her. "Please don't be dead."

Beau reached past Wanda's arms and carefully cleared the mucus from the calf's nose and throat. "Now I need you to rub him. Hard. Like you're trying to scour off his fur. That should stimulate him to breathe."

Wanda dug her fingers into the calf's soaking-wet coat and started working them back and forth. "Like this?"

"Perfect. Keep it going. I'll be right back." He limped around to the passenger side of the pickup, his body feeling bruised but not broken, and took a foot-long piece of garden hose out of the glove box. When he got back to Wanda, he held the mirror up to calf's nostrils again. "Still nothing."

"Oh no," Wanda moaned. "Oh no."

"We're going to have to try artificial respiration. I need you to stop rubbing so I can get this into his nose." Beau worked one end of the tube into a nostril, then straightened the length of hose and knelt beside the calf. "When I tell you, cup one hand around his muzzle, and with the other plug the open nostril while I blow. Ready, go!" He breathed into the hose, watching the calf's chest slowly expand as his lungs filled with air, then Beau removed the hose to let the air flow out. He breathed into the calf again. And again. Until finally the newborn kicked, threw his head back, and started breathing on his own.

"He's alive!" Wanda shouted, startling the new mother and Beau. "He's alive! We did it!"

"Shh . . . It was you who did most of it," Beau said, his voice a hoarse whisper. "And I'm proud of you and our teamwork. But now we need to back off so that this new mother and her calf can bond. It looks like they're both going to be okay."

"Do you think it would hurt anything if I washed up first?"

He looked at Wanda, then down at himself. They were both as wet as the newborn calf. "I'll join you," Beau said.

They cleaned off as best they could. Then he wrapped his jean jacket around her shoulders and they climbed into the truck. Beau turned the heater on full blast, and as their shivering slowly subsided, they watched the new mother get up and start licking her calf.

"It's beautiful," Wanda said.

"It is," Beau said. "But it's not over quite yet. We've got to wait and see whether he's strong enough to get up and suckle. That was a rough delivery, so it may take a couple of hours."

"Will she keep licking him until he nurses?"

"Yes. I guess we've got time for that picnic now. Although, truth be told, I don't feel much like eating barbeque."

"I don't feel much like eating barbeque either," Wanda said, still staring at the calf. "We could listen to George Strait. I've got his greatest hits CD in the car."

Beau reached over and took Wanda's hand that still felt chilly. "You asked me earlier if I remembered our first date. The place I took you parking that night, the place where we were completely together for the first time, was at the top of the highest hill on the ranch." He gestured with the hand holding Wanda's up at the house they'd built. "Why do you think I picked that as the site for our new home?"

"I guess I knew that, but it sounds good to hear you say it. And I'm ready to be with you in that way again. But it seems like all you've done since the accident is watch TV."

"I made you a promise about that today," Beau said. "A promise I aim to keep. But it seems to me like all you've done since the wreck is go to church, read the Bible, and pray."

"Those are not things I'm willing to give up," Wanda said, but she squeezed his hand as she said it. "And maybe you don't have to completely give up TV either. We just have to make a space for ourselves in between."

"How are we going to make a space for ourselves if our house is full of Tammy and those boys?"

"You're forgetting the Parable of the Good Samaritan."

"Am I?" Beau took a deep breath, held it, then let it out again. "Seems like I remember the Good Samaritan taking that robbery victim to an inn and paying his room and board. Maybe we could do something like that for Tammy."

"You mean help her find a place of her own?"

He nodded, cautiously hopeful for the first time since the wreck. "We could pay her rent until she finds a job."

"She and those boys are the only family I've got besides you." The timid, searching tone that had shaken Wanda's voice earlier was long gone. "We'll have to see how Tammy feels about it first. And if she says no, she stays."

"If that's the cost of getting you and me moving in the right direction again, so be it. I'll abide by her decision. And yours. But I think birthing that calf proves I don't need a fitness coach anymore."

"Oh Beau, look!" Wanda said. "Look!"

Through the tiny flakes of sleet that had started to fall on the windshield, he saw the calf heave shakily to his feet and start nursing while the new mother nudged his hindquarters in encouragement. "Our job here is done," Beau said. "Shall we head on up to the house and have that talk with Tammy?"

Wanda slid across the seat and leaned into him, her body pressing seamlessly against his right side, the side that had never been broken. The sleet glittered on the windshield like stars. "Let's stay and watch a while," she said.

Troubadours
in which Arthur and May Belle share the Queen of the Night
(2010)

It isn't just the fact that she's a stranger.

No, the fracking boom that's fired up on the Eagle Ford Shale, and the building boom that followed, have brought a lot of unfamiliar faces to Jordan. And I couldn't be happier to see them. A lot of the roughnecks and construction workers come into the Second Chance Café. I serve the best chili in Southwest Texas, in three varieties—a three-alarm shredded beef with fiery red peppers, a two-alarm ground venison with jalapenos, and a one-alarm ground beef and pinto beans with mild green chiles—with thick slices of homemade sourdough bread on the side. There are half-pound burgers and wedge fries, chicken fried steaks, spicy catfish stew, spicy-battered fried catfish filets with hushpuppies, and ice-cold beer to wash it all down. I serve the beer and run the register, hire perky girls from Jordan High School to serve the food, and the hungry young men come in droves. But that doesn't explain the dark-haired woman in the corner, casing the place with nervous eyes.

I noticed something odd about this particular stranger the minute she walked in out of the seething summer air lugging a black backpack in front of her instead of clutching a purse at her side, as if trying to hide the baby bump I spotted in an instant. She lowered herself carefully into the corner chair at table 15, ordered decaf coffee and a water, asked for the Wi-Fi password, and started watching everything that went on. No small-talk, not even a hello—which was unusual in and of itself in a little town like Jordan—and with a jittery edge in her voice, along with an undertone of something else. Hostility? Secrecy?

Something. Enough to set off a blip on my people radar.

As the restaurant filled and emptied with a mix of roughnecks in dirty coveralls and locals herding kids—Beau and Wanda Mulebach rocking their brand-new baby son in his car-seat carrier in the booth at 25; Corlis and Rosemary Holybee pulling 41 and 42 together to make a six-top, their little daughter so delicate in pink as she toddled into her booster seat beside those three big shaggy boys—the skittish stranger kept her back against the wall, her baby bump beneath the table, and her backpack at her feet. She drank decaf and water but ate nothing, seemingly absorbed in her cell phone but glancing up every time someone walked in, and eyeing the other customers and me around the edge of her phone screen.

Now it's after ten. I've already flipped the OPEN sign in the window that faces the state highway around to CLOSED, and let Lydia Rodriquez, the head cook, and Jenny Thompson, the late-shift waitress, go home. The only people left in the Second Chance Café are myself, standing guard at the cash register, and the dark-haired woman in the corner with the unpaid check for her coffee face-down on the table.

"Ma'am," I say at last, "I'm going to have to ask you to settle up. The café closed at 9:30, and it's 10:15."

Instead of replying, the woman starts tapping with both thumbs on her cell phone screen, rapid-fire.

"Ma'am?"

The only answer is more tapping, and the echo of my voice off the green-and-white checkered floor tiles.

I'm not the jumpy type, but I've taken in two thousand dollars tonight if I've taken in a dime, and the roughnecks and construction workers mostly pay cash. The pregnant woman's baby daddy could be lurking outside like a wolf spider ready to burst into the café and shove a gun into my face. And the state highway that bisects downtown Jordan runs straight down to Eagle Pass and Piedras Negras, so the pair could be in Mexico inside of an hour.

When the woman reaches into her backpack and starts fumbling around with something bulky, the blip on my people radar balloons to fill the entire screen. I snatch the telephone off the counter, start dialing Jim Thompson's personal cell—Jim is Jenny Thompson's father, chief deputy at the sheriff's office that's just a block away—and glance over into the corner, certain that I'll see the business end of a pistol pointing back at me.

But what the dark-haired woman holds instead is a black leather wallet. Empty, from the blank way she's staring down into it. Tears are streaming down her cheeks. And it comes to me as I set the receiver back into its cradle that the emotion I heard in her voice earlier, underneath the jittery edge, wasn't hostility or secrecy. It was heartbreak. The rush of relief that comes hard on the heels of that realization fades slowly into sympathy. I walk to the waitstation, pour myself a cup of high octane, and carry both coffee pots over to the corner table.

"Do you mind if I join you?" I ask.

"Are you the manager?"

"Manager. Cook. Cashier. Bartender." I pull out a chair and sit down. "I own the place. Although sometimes it feels more like the place owns me."

"I can't pay you for the coffee," the woman sniffles.

"I kind of figured that," I say gently, "from the look on your face when you opened your wallet." I know enough about heartbreak not to mention the tears that are dripping now from the woman's chin down onto her wrinkled shirt. "Can you sing?"

"Excuse me?"

"In the middle ages, there were poets who traveled the South of France singing songs about courtly love in return for their room and board. They called themselves *troubadours*." I reach the decaf pot over, refill the woman's cup. "I thought maybe . . ."

"I'm afraid I don't sing very well. And I don't really know much about poetry."

"Me either. But I've traveled the South of France. My favorite place was Cannes on the Cote D'Azur." I sip my coffee, a rich French roast ground fresh from beans I have custom roasted at a shop called the Mystic Café on the San Antonio River Walk. "After my husband died, it was my lifetime goal to retire there and open a restaurant on the Boulevard de la Croisette just off the beach. I was going to call the place the Café le Coq after my late husband—his nickname was Rooster—and there was going to be a big red neon gamecock out front that would be visible a mile out at sea." I feel myself smile, thinking about Rooster and about the turquoise water and powdery sand. "I opened the Second Chance Café here in Jordan instead."

"I don't understand."

"I guess what I'm trying to say is that sometimes things don't work out like we planned. And that can be okay."

"I don't . . . I don't know what I'm . . ." The silent tears become choking sobs. "I just feel hollowed-out."

I fetch a cloth napkin and hand it to the woman. "Sometimes the troubadours told stories of their travels instead of singing. So tell me: How long has it been since you ate a meal?"

"I had a box of Triscuits this morning. The chili pepper thin crisps."

"Hmm . . . So you like spicy?"

The woman nods.

"The kitchen is closed for the night, but I can feed you a bowl of the best chili in Southwest Texas. How does that sound?"

"But I don't have any money. And the credit card company just cancelled my account."

"Tell me your story instead. You can start with your name."

"I'm Lily," the woman says, meeting my eyes for the first time.

"Howdy, Lily. I'm May Belle Stiles. That wasn't so hard, was it? And what's his name?"

"His?"

I glance pointedly at the baby bump that's pressing against the wooden tabletop.

"Augie," Lily says and the sobs start again. "His . . . name is . . ."

"Augie? Well, that's a beginning. You still owe me a middle and an end. But let's get some food in you first." I lead Lily back to the kitchen, heat a bowl of the one-alarm chili in the microwave, butter a thick slice of sourdough bread. Then we walk back out to the corner table, and I sip coffee while Lily wolfs her meal.

"I didn't realize how hungry I was until I started eating," she says, swabbing the bottom of the bowl with the last bit of bread. "Thank you. That's the best chili I've ever had."

"I make it myself," I say, frankly pleased, as I top off our cups. "I'm more partial to the three-alarm recipe, but the one-alarm is probably better on an empty belly. Now that you've finished, I'd like to hear the rest of the story. Your name is Lily, and his name is Augie. Why don't we pick up from there?"

"Augie and I met in Fort Worth, which is where I'm from, and we fell in love. Anyway, I thought we were in love. Every minute we didn't spend at work, we spent together. Then I got pregnant. And he left."

"So you followed him?"

Lily shakes her head. "Not at first. Augie grew up in an orphanage and in foster homes—his mother gave him up—and when I told him about our baby, he said he needed to get out of town for a few days and think the whole fatherhood thing through. He texted me the next day and told me that he loved me. Then he called from Jasper, in middle-of-nowhere East Texas, and we talked. He said he was on his way back to Fort Worth, that he was ready to give family life a try." The tears start to flow again. "That was two months ago."

"He never showed up in Fort Worth?"

"No. But he's still paying his rent. The man who owns the house Augie lives in, and who introduced Augie and me, is an old friend of my family. He lives right across the street. He'd tell me if Augie came home."

I find myself studying Lily. She's young—early twenties, I guess—

and thin, naturally pretty, with pale delicate skin and a fiery intensity in her eyes despite the tears. She reminds me of myself thirty years ago. Wild. And crazy in love with Rooster. I'll never forget the way I felt when I lost him. Heartbroken. Hollowed-out.

"I was born in Jasper," I say, "and I spent my girlhood there, before my father came to Jordan for the last oil boom. The thing I remember most, besides all the pine trees, was a parrot named Pal. He belonged to a retired sea captain who lived next door, and he would perch in a chinaberry tree in the front yard every morning and curse the mailman. It was only the mailman he cursed. I never understood why."

"The captain probably had credit card bills," Lily says. "I've cursed the mailman once or twice myself." For the first time since she walked into the Second Chance Café, she smiles. "I was in Jasper last week. I found the bed and breakfast Augie stayed in. The lady who owns the place remembered him. She said he'd gone to the library to try and track down his family."

"What in the world led you here? I'm guessing you didn't come to Jordan for the oil boom."

"After Jasper, I drove to San Antonio, to the orphanage Augie grew up in. He'd been there and looked through their records. He searched through the files at the county courthouse too. Augie works in the construction business. He's a subcontractor, a framer, and I figured he'd need money. So I checked with the big home construction companies. Turns out he'd worked as a framer for Toll Brothers. A guy he crewed with said that Augie had a contract to do framework on one of the hotels they're building here in Jordan." Lily fiddles with her cell phone, then reaches it across the table. "That's Augie. He hasn't been in here, has he? This is the kind of place he likes."

I look at the photo on Lily's cell phone. The man I see is lean and dark-haired, with green eyes and a strong jaw, his skin darkly tanned from working in the Texas sun. He looks an awful lot like Rooster, and I feel a stab of pain in my chest—the same mix of longing and of loss that I felt a week and a half ago when Augie first walked into the Second Chance Café and ordered coffee and breakfast tacos, which I serve from 6–9 a.m. He's been in every morning since, except for Sunday when the restaurant is closed.

I shift my eyes carefully from the photo to the eager look on Lily's face. "Sorry," I say at last, shaking my head for emphasis. Then I look back at the phone. "Arthur has a cell phone just like that. I don't have much use for one myself."

"Arthur?"

"Arthur is my partner."

"Is he here?" There is pleading in Lily's voice now. "Could I ask him if he's seen Augie?"

"Arthur doesn't work in the restaurant. We own the building together, and he runs the antique shop next door. He's kind of a silent partner, I guess. In more ways than one." I pause, lock my eyes onto Lily's. "But before we get to the end of your story, there's a question I need you to answer: What are you hoping to get from this man who keeps running away from you?"

"Love," Lily says, glancing down into her cup. "What else?"

"How about a father for your child? A life partner. Someone you can count on not to go hopscotching across Texas the minute things get tough. What if Augie can't give you any of those things?"

"But he can! When Augie took me out on our first date, instead of dinner and a movie, he took me swimming and hiking at Cedar Hills State Park. It was early spring, and we were driving out there in Augie's old Ford truck with the windows down. All of a sudden he pulled over to the side of the road and bounded out of the truck into a field of bluebonnets." Still staring down into her decaf, Lily half-smiles, as though she can see the memory reflected on the dark surface. "He picked an armload of flowers—as many as he could hold—and stood there grinning back at the truck until I got out and walked over to him. Then he handed me this mass of bluebonnets, and as our arms linked around the flowers, he kissed me for the first time. And I knew, right there and then, that he was the one. It wasn't just the flowers and the kiss. It was the promise of that kind of life, and that kind of love, you know? Full of grand romantic gestures. I knew I'd spend the rest of my life loving Augie."

I have to press my lips tight together to keep from saying what I'm thinking. Except for the baby bump, when I look at Lily, I see myself thirty years ago. Loving Rooster. I remember the peaks and valleys of our fiery, turbulent, cut-short married life—full of grand romantic gestures—and although the peaks were incredible, I've learned enough about living to know now that the valleys were deeper. And the financial hole Rooster left me in when he died from an early heart attack took me the better part of three decades of hard work to dig out of.

"And if the love isn't still there?" I ask finally. "Or if you can't find him?"

Lily starts to take a sip of decaf, hesitates, puts the cup back on the table. "How far is it to Laredo from here?"

198

"A couple of hours, depending on how fast you drive. You're a lot closer to Piedras Negras than you are to Nuevo Laredo, if you aim to cross the Rio Grande. Why?"

"I'm thinking of disappearing. Just crossing the river and keeping on going. If Augie won't have me, I've got no place to go."

"What about your parents?"

"They won't even speak to me. And anyway, I don't want my parents. I want Augie."

I reach across the table and pat Lily's hand that feels slender and delicate, a child's hand. "Do you have a place to stay the night?"

"I was planning to sleep in my car."

"You sit right here while I put these dishes away and rinse out the coffee pots. Then you can come home with me. I have a spare room you can stay in for tonight, and maybe—just maybe—tomorrow will take care of itself. In the meantime, there's something I'd like you to see."

I shut down the restaurant and lock the front door, then we walk to our cars and I lead Lily through downtown Jordan, past the post office and the historic courthouse that hulks like a castle in the light of the full moon that is rising, and out South Prospect Street to my house on the edge of town. Arthur has left the porch light on, but the moon blazing just above the tops of the mesquites lights the low ranch-style house and the close-cropped grass and the ocotillo that is in full bloom as I lead Lily up the sidewalk—she's pulling a suitcase with wheels—and across the front porch into the living room.

I show her the guest room, and once she's dropped off her things, we walk through the kitchen and out onto the back porch. The night air is still and warm. The glow of a candle on the wrought iron table lights an open bottle of wine and two glasses, and softens the sharp angles of Arthur's profile as he startles up from one of the two chairs.

"Well, um, this is—"

I press a finger against his lips and then kiss him deeply, savoring the taste of red wine and the warmth of his hand as I reach down and squeeze it. When I step back to introduce him to Lily, I lace my fingers into his. "This is Lily. Lily, meet Arthur, my partner. Lily is in a bit of a fix, and I've invited her to spend the night in the guest room."

"Ah, hello, Lily." I make out a hint of confusion, but no hesitation, in Arthur's voice. "Welcome. Would you, um, excuse me while I fetch another chair?"

"Hello, Arthur," Lily says. "Thank you."

I sink into the seat Arthur vacated and motion for Lily to take the other. He comes back out with another chair and a wine glass, sets the chair next to mine, and pours three glasses of wine. Then he raises his glass.

"A more civilized welcome," he says, smiling at Lily. "I hope you like pinot noir."

Arthur and I sip our wine, but Lily sits with one hand on the stem of her glass and the other on her belly. "I do," she says. "But I don't think I should have any. I'm pregnant, you see."

"Oh, I should've, um, asked first," Arthur says after a too-long moment. "I'm, ah, I'm sorry, Lily."

"It's my fault," I say, feeling as awkward as Arthur sounds. "I ought to have remembered. Can we get you something else?"

"How about a cup of hot apple cider?" Arthur offers.

"That would be nice."

He takes Lily's wine glass and heads back inside.

I wait until the screen door slaps shut behind him, then turn to Lily. "Would it be okay if I shared your story with Arthur? I promise you that it couldn't be in safer or surer hands."

"Is Arthur your husband?"

"Arthur would like that. Very much. But Rooster was the only husband I'll ever have. One was enough."

"But the way you talked about your late husband back at the restaurant," Lily says, "about Rooster I mean, made it seem like—"

"Rooster was the most beautiful man I've ever seen. A hell-for-leather cowboy, and the best dancer I've ever had the pleasure of two-stepping with. We fell in love at a rodeo dance, and he made my life an adventure."

"I don't understand why you wouldn't want that again."

"I don't want love to be an adventure. Life is hard enough as it is. What I want from love is companionship, stability, trust," I raise my wine glass, "and a little romance. The rest is mostly hormones. It took the better part of a lifetime for me to realize that. And I never would've learned it without Arthur."

The screen door swings open, and Arthur bustles back out onto the porch carrying a steaming mug that he sets on the table. The scents of apple and cinnamon fill the night air, and Lily leans her face down into the steam. "It smells wonderful," she says. "Thank you."

Lily sits sipping hot apple cider while Arthur and I drink our wine, and I recount what she said about her search for Augie. "I told you earlier that Lily was in a bit of a fix," I say at last. "I guess I should've said that she's come to a crossroads."

"So you've called and you've texted and you've crisscrossed Texas," Arthur says. "What now?"

"Now I'm flat broke," Lily says, "and it won't be long before the phone company suspends my account. I'm way past due on the bill. But I'm so close to finding Augie. I know that he's working at one of the construction sites here in Jordan, and tomorrow I'll go around to them all."

"What if I offered you a cashier job at the café, and said that you could stay in the guest room until you get your first paycheck?"

"I'd rather have an old Ford truck and an armload of bluebonnets."

"Fair enough," I say. "But I've got to open up for breakfast at 6 a.m., and it's going on midnight. I told you that I had something I'd like you to see. It's time." I turn to Arthur. "I thought we'd show her the Queen of the Night."

"The queen of the what?" Lily asks.

"Queen of the Night," Arthur chuckles. "It's a cactus. Its proper name is Night-Blooming Cereus. Some people call it *deer-horn*. And for most of the year it looks like a deer horn, or a dead bush. But one night a year, usually around midsummer, it blooms. And the blossoms are the most majestic and fragrant flowers I've ever seen or smelled."

I rest a hand on Arthur's shoulder. "Do you think they've opened up yet?"

"I was out there just before you arrived. There were five or six buds that looked like they were about ready to pop. I'd be willing to bet that we've got some blossoms by now. Shall we go and see?"

The full moon lights the cactus garden in the backyard, the combination stable and hay barn on the far side of the fence, and the open land beyond that stretches away west into the pale distance. Arthur takes my hand and leads me along the stone path that snakes among the cactus beds with Lily walking just behind.

"Watch out for the thorns," Arthur says. "The cacti are beautiful, but they bite."

"Did you plant all of this, May Belle?" Lily asks.

"I'm no gardener. Arthur gave me the plants, and he's the one who tends them. But I do use the peppers that he grows for my chili."

"The Queen of the Night cactus is right over here," Arthur says. "I've trained it to grow up the fence."

In the moonlight I make out the spindly stems of the Queen of the Night that are lead-gray. Speckled like stars against the gray background, I see a half-dozen white flowers. Three of the buds are open—two fully, one partway—and the trumpet-shaped blossoms, waxy and white and many-petaled, smell unbelievably sweet.

"Oh, Arthur," I say, "it's gorgeous."

"Come on up, Lily, and have a look," Arthur says, moving aside to make room. "You can lean in close to get the full impact of the fragrance, but be careful. The stems are covered with spines."

"Okay." Lily steps up next to me, and the two of us press our faces against the open blooms.

"It takes about a half-hour for the flower to fully open once it starts," Arthur says. "It's too slow for you to see. But if you look away for a couple of minutes, and then look back, you'll be able to tell that it's moved."

"And they only last one night?" Lily asks.

"Yes. They'll close forever with the first rays of the sun."

"It seems like such a shame," Lily says, stepping back.

"The flame that burns twice as bright burns half as long." Arthur takes out his pocketknife, cuts the two fully open flowers, hands one each to Lily and me. You'll be able to see the colors better in the candlelight. You two can stay out here as long as you like, but I'm off to bed."

I brush my lips against Arthur's. "I'll be there in a little while," I whisper. Then I catch his eye and smile in a way that Lily doesn't need to see. Or maybe she does, I realize. Maybe she does at that.

"Thank you for the flower," Lily says. "And for everything."

"Good night," Arthur says, giving me back that same smile.

"Shall we go and have a look at the blossoms in the candlelight?" I ask Lily. Instead of waiting for an answer, I wind my way back through the cactus beds to the porch. Arthur has taken the wine bottle and the glasses, and the only thing left on the table is the candle, blue-flamed at the wick and flickering yellow-orange with each faint breath of the warm night air.

Lily lays her flower next to the candle. I set mine next to Lily's, and we both sit down and study the blooms. The thin creamy outer petals surround broader pure-white inner petals, which in turn surround bright yellow stamens that protrude in a delicate ring from the center of the blossom. The sweet scent of the flowers wafts up into the air, and in the candlelight I can see that Lily's eyes have filled again with tears.

"This is how I feel inside," she says, nodding down at the flowers, "when I'm with Augie."

"Oh, child," I murmur, just loud enough for my words to carry across the table. "Until a minute ago, I had no idea what to say about that

202

feeling. But hear this. There are two kinds of love that I've felt in my life, and two men I've shared that love with. What I had with Rooster was a brushfire, white-hot and fast-moving, and we lived every minute like it was the last one we'd ever get. Arthur and I were good friends before we became lovers. What we have is more like this candle flame: warm and steady, and longlasting. I'm happier with Arthur."

"And yet you won't marry him."

"He has his house, and I have my house. We spend a lot of time together, but we both have our own spaces when we need to be alone."

"But I don't want to be alone," Lily says.

"Be that as it may, I can tell you for sure that you do have options. I meant what I said earlier about the cashier job and the guest room. Love is more than wildflowers and grand romantic gestures. And your whole life doesn't have to revolve around one man, although it may not seem like that now."

"It doesn't."

"Then I'll tell you one more thing before I turn in," I say. "I have seen Augie. He comes into the Second Chance Café every morning at six for coffee and breakfast tacos." I stand up and take the flower Arthur gave me off the table. "I'll be heading in at 5 a.m. to open up. You're welcome to come with me. What happens after that is up to you."

"What would you do, May Belle?"

I pause at the screen door and look back at Lily as she presses her own cactus flower against her cheekbone. I see the lifepath she'll start down tomorrow blaze out ahead of her: the fiery peaks and the valleys of ashes, the pleasure and the pain, the heartbreak. And nothing that I've said or done tonight will change it.

"I'm going to bed," I say. "Goodnight."

"I'll see you in the morning," she says, and the creamy outer petals of the blossom and the paleness of her cheek seem to blend into a single skin.

Lament for a Larcenist
in which Cecil says goodbye
(2013)

"Mr. Jubak," the pilot says, tapping the fuel gauge in front of him, "it's time."

I take a long last look inside the cremation urn that lies heavy on my lap, then tip the black plastic box into the open air outside the cockpit. The downwash of whooshing rotors churns the thick gray remains. And for a timeless moment, as his ashes swirl and eddy in the blastfurnace breeze, my uncle is the only cloud in the Southwest Texas summer sky. He billows and folds past the skids, spiraling gracefully to rest in the mesquite and cactus and drought-cracked ground that used to be the Jubak ranch—it's a part of the Mulebach spread now—and the place L.B. called home until the day I watched my father beat him bloody.

Most folks say my uncle had it coming.

L.B. was no role model. The years he didn't squander on prison or parole, he spent in perpetual motion. I could count the days we had together on the fingers of his beautiful pianist's hands. But the only instrument he ever played upon was human nature.

By all accounts, he was a virtuoso.

The one and only real job L.B. ever deigned to hold was roughnecking in the Texas oilpatch. He got fired for stealing pipe, a development that resulted in his first stretch in the penitentiary. L.B., though, upon his early release—for good behavior—was the polar opposite of penitent. "If the clutch hadn't gone out on my buddy's pickup," he said, "we'd have got away clean."

L.B. called himself a *sportsman*, and he always swaddled a fat roll of cash in the pocket of his gray silk sport jacket. On the rare occasions when I saw him in the flesh, at my grandmother's house in town, he'd flash his sportsman's smile and cross my palm with a crisp twenty peeled slow and sweet off the money roll that was the color of a khaki-clad country boy's dreams. "Cecil," he'd say, "whatever else you may do, don't tell your Pop."

I'd heard enough of my father's lectures about the wages of sin to know better.

But on my sixteenth birthday, I got careless. When I jumped back from the yearling calf I'd been holding down so Pop could brand it, he spied the hundred-dollar bill L.B. had given me peeking from the pocket of my khaki workshirt. Pop snatched the banknote with a callused hand and tossed it into the fire with the branding irons. L.B.'s birthday gift burned to ashes before my eyes.

I expected another sermon about death being the wages of sin. But instead, Pop told me to look at my shirt. It was covered with dirt and sweat, the wages of a birthday afternoon spent branding calves in the corral out back of the ranch house that L.B. and my father both grew up in. Then Pop asked me to look at his shirt, which looked the same as mine. "Son," my father said, staring into the fire where the business ends of the 06 branding irons glowed red in the coals, "this ain't something I'm proud to tell you. But the time has come for you to hear it. L.B. was a sickly child. Your granddaddy never made him step foot into this corral, or ride through the brush after outlaw cattle. I had to do the work for both of us, and L.B. was given everything I busted my tail to earn. When your granddaddy died, I went down to the bank and borrowed the money to buy this land from your grandma, though I didn't have to. The mortgage note, that I've been working to pay off ever since, built her house in town where your uncle stays free of charge when he's broke or on parole. L.B.'s gray silk suits look mighty smart. But without the dirt and sweat on these khaki shirts, he'd have nothing. A dollar earned is worth more than a hundred stolen or tricked from the man who had to earn those dollars to begin with. L.B. is a petty larcenist, nothing more."

The next time I saw my uncle, I told him what Pop had said. L.B. belly-laughed and peeled me off another hundred. "Sucker born every minute," he said. "He couldn't even bring himself to call me a *thief*." Then, to my amazement, L.B.'s eyes glistened. "I may be a larcenist, but what I do is the polar opposite of petty. I live by my wits. Your Pop is a slave. A slave to that piece of dirt he grubs with his hands, and a slave to the banker that really owns it. If you never remember another word I say, treasure this up in that memory of yours: just because you're born a slave, it doesn't mean you have to die one. Learn to live free."

My wife, Juno, who is better educated than I am, once told me that the Roman philosopher Cicero called memory "the treasury and guardian of all things."

She was talking about raising our daughters, who my uncle never met. So I don't think family had much to do with what L.B. meant. But looking back across the tug-of-war life I've led—pulled back and forth across Texas between my uncle's wits and my father's hands—memories of family are the most precious things I've carried along the way. I remember best the morning L.B. and I soared above my father's ranch, surrounded only by clear blue sky and a Plexiglas cockpit. The pilot, hired to flush outlaw cattle out of brush too thick to ride through, hadn't wanted to take a five-year-old up. L.B. smiled, peeled a pair of twenties off his bankroll, and we ascended into blue.

Although I've learned a bit about living since then, I've never again felt so free. The world seemed to me at that moment an infinite possibility, bright blue and cloudless. But when we descended in a whirl of dust, my father was waiting—Pop was terrified of flying—and I watched my father pound L.B.'s sportsman's smile into a mask of blood. Until the day we buried Pop, neither brother ever laid eyes on the other again.

Forty-three years to the day after that distant morning when L.B. and I ascended into the cloudless summer sky, I watch the last of his ashes swirl earthward to join my father's bones on the land that another family now owns. I nod at the pilot. He banks the helicopter, and we peel away into blue. I think about wits and hands, about bones and ashes, about the way life has of pitting brother against brother. And I hope the sportsman and the sucker will finally be reconciled in the dry Southwest Texas soil.

Adventures with Seamus Heaney and My Mother-in-Law
in which Joe comes home to stay
(2013)

Spoiler alert: this has a happy ending.

It is not a mother-in-law story, not really. It's a story about a dog, a little girl, and a modern-day American family that's a lot more like the Brady Bunch than Ozzie and Harriet. So I guess it could be about anyone, or maybe everyone, in these crazy new days. But my mother-in-law does figure prominently in the working-out of the plot.

The dog's name is Seamus Heaney, after my second favorite poet. And he is my dog, I guess, if it can truly be said that a dog belongs to anyone. It's probably more accurate to say that I am his person. Seamus Heaney didn't start out to be my dog, but we'll get to that part of the story later on.

The little girl's name is Ariel. Ariel is my step-daughter, pale-skinned and lovely. Except for her dark hair, she is a miniature version of her mother Sara.

Sara is the love of my life.

Jacob and Ben are the other members of our modern-day Brady Bunch. Jacob is my son, and Ben is Sara's and my son together. The children are a tangled mix of half-brothers and stepbrothers, half-sisters and stepsisters—it's enough to boggle the mind, especially during holidays and summer visitations—but they all love Seamus Heaney in the rough-and-tumble way that kids love dogs.

As for my mother-in-law . . .

Well, Belinda is the reason Seamus Heaney (the dog, not his Nobel-winning namesake) made the 160-mile trek from the Texas Hill Country to the Southwest Texas cattle ranch that I grew up on—the place that Sara and I now call home, and that the two of us work together when I'm not busy teaching. Despite Sara's and my adamant refusal (I actually used the words *over my dead body*), my mother-in-law was absolutely determined that her granddaughter have a dog.

I should probably pause to explain why an Assistant Professor of Latin chose to name a Welsh Border Collie after an Irish poet. Our orange tabby housecat, Virgil (named after my favorite poet of all time), might well answer: *Cur non?* But there are several reasons why that I think are pretty good, not the least of which is my Anglo-Irish heritage. My late father came from a family of no-nonsense English landowners, while my mother is descended from a brood of wild-eyed Irish ne'er-do-wells. Even more important is the fact that—like his Irish poet namesake—one of Seamus the dog's best things is "Digging." This is particularly the case when Seamus the dog feels that he hasn't been played fetch with enough by me (obviously still breathing despite losing the dog battle with Belinda) or rough-and-tumbled with enough by Ariel and Jacob and Ben. And like all great poets, Welsh Border Collies are wicked smart when it comes to language. There is a recorded case of a collie who knows, and responds to, more than 1000 words of the Queen's English. Seamus the dog's favorite words include *fetch*, *ball*, *squeaky* (a beloved chew-toy that makes a high-pitched squeal when bitten), *outside*, *peanut butter*, *bone*, *wrestle*, and *go*. His least favorite word is *no*, although he freezes instantly when he hears it.

Surprisingly, the word *fetch* has also become a favorite of mine. It turns out that there is no better therapy, when the stress level of twenty-first century family life rises to a fever pitch, than throwing a slobbery tennis ball to a black-and-white-and-brown streak of a dog whose eyes are afire with the pure joy of running.

While the word *no* works wonders with Seamus the dog, it has turned out to be less effective when it comes to my mother-in-law. But before I can continue, I see that another explanation has become necessary. Belinda is not really my mother-in-law, although I refer to her in that capacity. She is actually the mother of Sara's first husband, Ariel's father David, who died driving drunk before Sara and I met. So Belinda is Ariel's true-blood grandmother (my own mother being her step- grandmother). And Belinda has been more of a mother to Sara than Sara's own mother-by-blood, with whom Sara has not spoken in over a decade. Crazy new days indeed.

As I said earlier, Belinda is nothing if not determined. A regionally prominent practitioner of the art of fortune-telling—I swear to God—who used to be Sara's business partner at a combination coffee and tarot-reading shop on the San Antonio River Walk called the Mystic Café, my mother-in-law has achieved excellence in her métier through the combination of talent and single-minded intensity that all great artists (including Irish poets laureate) share. After she bought out Sara's majority stake in the Mystic Café, and the business thrived, Belinda invested in a combination plant nursery and registered Welsh Border Collie farm in the Texas Hill Country. It was there that Belinda introduced Ariel to the black-and-white-and-brown puppy who would eventually be named Seamus Heaney.

As an aside, Sara and I used the buy-out money from the café to build the new house where our family now lives, easy walking distance from the ranch house I grew up in and where my own mother-by-blood frequently hosts sleepovers for the kids. But back to the story.

Over the course of one summer's visitation, between tarot-reading sessions at the Mystic Café, Belinda took Ariel out to the Welsh Border Collie farm where she became acquainted with a certain tiny, fuzzy, black-and-white-and-brown puppy who had not been born with his brothers' and sisters' perfect markings. Make no mistake: Seamus is the scion of not one, but two, noble (and hence shockingly high-dollar) lines of show dogs. If not for the accident of his imperfect coloration, he would have been far beyond the modest means of a university professor and part-time rancher. This fact, relayed through the (then) eight-year-old Ariel—despite the fact that we were all on speaker-phone—played a key role in my mother-in-law's strategy.

"Mama," little Ariel said, "can I have a dog? One of the puppies here at Grandma's Border Collie farm has fallen in love with me."

"Oh, honey," Sara said, "we could never afford one of those puppies. And besides, what would Virgil say?"

"*Super mortuum meum corpus*," I said.

"What was that?" Belinda asked.

"Over my dead body," I said again, in English—a translation I would come to regret.

"Shh!" Sara said.

"We could afford this one," Ariel continued, as though I'd spoken not a word in either Latin or English. "Grandma says that he's not perfect like the other puppies, so he only costs a hundred dollars."

"Ariel," Sara said, "would you please take your grandmother's cell off speaker-phone, and hand it to her?"

The ensuing long-distance difference of opinion featured several less-than-pleasant moments that I'll not recount here. Relevant details include: undeniably ungenerous comments from a ranch-raised husband (with the exception of Virgil, at the Jasmine ranch on the arid Southwest Texas plains, the only animals that eat are those that work); assorted objections from a practical wife (who foresaw the difficulties a dog would add to already-complicated holiday travel arrangements); and the single-minded persistence of a grandmother (whose sole concern was the fact that her granddaughter had fallen in love with a certain black-and-white-and-brown Welsh Border Collie puppy). The tear-choked promises of that same dog-besotted granddaughter to feed said dog, wash said dog, and play with said dog every day figured prominently in each conversational pause.

Has a pair of practical and well-meaning, but heart-crushingly loving, parents ever won an argument like this one?

I contend that the answer is yes (although Belinda, who is a purist, argues otherwise). Admittedly, Seamus the dog came to live—and to eat without working—on the Jasmine ranch. And of course, Ariel's tear-choked promises about dog care were fulfilled only for about the usual term of such desperate and emotion-fueled oaths. The duties of daily dog maintenance devolved upon Sara and me. Sara took over the dog-washing chore; the feeding, watering, and playing-with responsibilities are now mostly mine. But in my humble opinion, having taken a couple of years now to consider the question, these details are beside the point.

In his Nobel Lecture, Seamus Heaney (the Irish poet) said that as "writers and readers, as sinners and citizens, our realism and our aesthetic sense make us wary of crediting the positive note." With all due deference to the late great poet and Nobel laureate, this has not been the case with Seamus the dog and me. Over the course of my newfound dog duties, I have become—to my great surprise—even more besotted with a certain black-and-white-and-brown Welsh Border Collie than Ariel ever thought about being. And I'm pleased to report that my love has been returned a thousandfold (literally). Sometimes happy endings do happen.

For both Seamus the dog and myself, the most positive note in our relationship has been our daily game of fetch. Every afternoon when I get home from my job at the university in San Antonio, I walk in the front door and set down my briefcase; Seamus bounds to the back door, where he proceeds to bounce up and down; and I follow, pausing only to take a tennis ball from the dog pantry before we head into the backyard. Then I throw, and he fetches, over and over and over again. He has trained me well. His favorite thing is for me to throw the ball up high, so that it ricochets off the close-cut carpet grass and he leaps after it, snatching the yellow missile out of the air. The slobbery testament of his affection coats my fingers and palms like a glove as the stresses of full-time tenure-track university professorship, part-time ranching, and holiday travel arrangements fade into throwing and leaping and catching *ad infinitum*.

If saying that Seamus Heaney has become an integral part of our modern-day Brady Bunch family means admitting that my mother-in-law was right, so be it. But in the broadest and most positive sense, aren't we all winners here: Belinda and Ariel, Jacob and Ben, Sara and myself, and of course Seamus the dog?

If you wanted to press the point, I guess you could say that there actually is one loser: our orange tabby housecat, Virgil, who has not exactly grown to love our family's newest addition. But then again, to paraphrase the (Irish) poet, happy endings don't work for everyone.

Andrew Geyer's latest book is the hybrid story cycle *Dancing on Barbed Wire*, co-authored with Jerry Craven and Terry Dalrymple, and edited by Tom Mack. Geyer is also the co-author of *Parallel Hours*, an alternative history/sci-fi novel; and *Texas 5X5*, another hybrid story cycle from which one of his stories won the Spur Award for short fiction from the Western Writers of America. He co-edited the composite anthology *A Shared Voice*, also with Tom Mack. Geyer's individually authored books are *Dixie Fish*, a novel; *Siren Songs from the Heart of Austin*, a story cycle; *Meeting the Dead*, a novel; and *Whispers in Dust and Bone*, a story cycle that won the silver medal for short fiction in the *Foreword Magazine* Book of the Year Awards and a Spur Award for short fiction. A member of the Texas Institute of Letters, and recently selected for induction into the South Carolina Academy of Authors, Geyer currently serves as English Department Chair at the University of South Carolina Aiken.